DEDICATED

Rhythm of Love, Book I

NEVE WILDER

ACKNOWLEDGMENTS

Thanks to C. Decherd for reading the first two chapters and demanding more. To Leslie, my go-to for basically all the things, and to Julia and Jill for their keen eyes.

Heaps and heaps of gratitude to Sandra for her edits, suggestions, and insane timeliness. I hope one day you have time for real sleep.

Thanks to those I consulted about various things, but especially M. Jahnig, who let me ask five billion questions about the music biz, knowing all along I would take that knowledge and flout it in many instances.

And to my number one dance partner for life. Your support is an amazing gift.

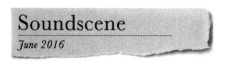

Your chemistry onstage is legendary. Is there something you attribute that to? Did it come naturally?

Evan: Is that something that can even be quantified? I think a band either has it or doesn't, and you can tell the difference between someone phoning it in and a band that's having fun when performing. We spent a long time before releasing our first album just writing and playing together, and we love what we do.

Les: It helps when the person you're onstage with is also your best friend.

Evan: Absolutely. Wait, did we just give an entirely serious, straightforward answer right out of the gate?

Les: We did. Oh God, have we slipped into an alternate universe?

Evan: A flux has occurred in the space-time continuum.

Les: Maybe I should punch you in the face real quick and fix it.

Evan: Try it and see what happens.

Les: Annnnnnd we're back. Next question.

CHAPTER 1

I'd always thought there was something poetic about moments of certainty: the way someone kept their gaze riveted to yours, the hand that lingered a little too long passing a napkin, a lighter, a beer. That moment I knew it was going to happen, that it was a sure thing. Whatever else may have come before didn't matter. The starting line moved. *This* was the new beginning.

There were lyrics in that, maybe a whole song, but I was too busy riding a nice buzz and capitalizing on one of those very moments to chase after the words—which I realized was ironic considering I was a lyricist with no fewer than eight number one ballads to my name. I should work on that, probably, but right then I was taking advantage of the nice smile the guy next to me kept feeding me like loose change into a slot machine.

He wanted it.

I wanted it, too.

We'd spent the last two hours in the cramped hotel bar trading small talk back and forth like playing cards, dealing out hometown stories, anteing up with dumb escapades, raising the stakes with a few bedroom scorchers until we were both primed and ready to cash in the chips elsewhere.

I'd always been slightly pickier with men than women, and earlier I'd had my eye on a curvy redhead down the bar who still had her attention trained on us. But there was something about this guy, Jamie, when he walked in that hit me in just the right spot. He'd draped over the bar like his jacket was made of long days and disappointment, yet when he'd smiled at me it was so ineffably bright and resilient that I kept looking back. He wasn't searching for love, and neither was I. I'd planted that seed before, and it still lived in me somewhere I guess—hibernating, rotting, or maybe frozen in some state of suspended animation.

Jamie was taking off tomorrow for Pennsylvania on the last leg of some business-related trip with details too boring for me to bother remembering, while Evan and I were set to play another show at a smaller venue in Cleveland. *Intimate*, our manager Byron had said. *Let's get you guys off the pedestals and back to your roots.* Which I thought was a diplomatic way of saying, *You assholes aren't booking the big gigs anymore. Fix it.*

We had a couple of shows left on the tour before a much-needed four-day break, and then we'd reconvene at the East Tennessee cabin where we'd written all our albums. So I was planning on getting while the getting was good. And Jamie, with his quirky charm and sexy smile, definitely fit the bill.

"Nightcap upstairs?" I asked him.

He grinned and tipped his head back to finish off his beer. "Sure thing."

We flung money at the bartender and headed for the elevators. There would be no nightcap upstairs; we both knew that.

Jamie wasn't a starstruck groupie like some others. He'd played it regular-guy cool all night, and I liked that. But the way his steps hastened the closer we got to the elevators was telling. It was gonna be a good night.

As soon as the elevator doors shut, I hooked him by a belt loop and pulled him toward me, running my hands over the T-shirt beneath his jacket for a tactile preview of his rib cage and abs, imagining the way they'd look when that shirt was on my floor and he was on my bed beneath me. The vision was a promising one.

Jamie planted a palm against my shoulder and shoved me backward against the brushed-metal wall, his mouth dropping to sweep a kiss over the hollow of my throat, tongue caressing a slow burn that radiated in a wave toward my groin.

By the tenth floor, I was as hard as a fucking rock. We were in safe territory, though: four short floors left and not many people went up on the elevator. At least at this time of night.

Right as I was thinking that, with the backs of my knuckles skimming over his strained fly, the fucking elevator dinged and stopped. Jamie took a breathless half step aside, and I wrapped my arm loosely around his waist. *Nothing to see here besides the bulges in our pants.*

I just wished it wasn't Evan standing there to witness our flustered rearranging. Because there he was when the doors slid open, the heel of his hand smoothing over the bridge of his nose in a way I knew meant he was frustrated or tired. My bandmate, my friend. My ultimate secret crush. It was one of the few times I wished the body next to me was a woman's. Or better yet, not there at all. That dormant little seed inside of me, the traitor, rattled around in my chest.

Fuck.

CHAPTER 2

Evan

I was tired. I was thinking of my place in Nashville where I'd missed the spring—my favorite season—rising up from the ground in green shoots that made the Midwest tundra we'd been cycling through feel that much colder. I was thinking of the call time tomorrow, the set list, the balls of fast-food wrappers piling up on the bus, how I felt like I was wearing a second skin of road dust and smog. Whether this tour had been successful or not. Sleeping in my own bed—a novel concept since I couldn't even remember what color my sheets were at this point. And also, about a couple of weeks from now when Les and I would seal ourselves in a cabin and try to recreate the success of our second album after our utter bomb of a third.

But mostly I was thinking about crashing hard in my hotel room as I came down the hall from drinking a few beers with some of our roadies. Leigh, my girlfriend, was up there waiting to curl around me. Or should be. And I knew she'd smell good. Like home. Like coffee and Southern sunshine.

So I was caught off guard when the elevator opened and there stood Les, his dark hair mussed, a heated flush across his neck, his arm wound loosely around a dirty blond who faintly resembled me. Maybe it was ridiculous. Maybe I was just being a jerk. But it got to me a little, and I could feel it in my expression, in the way I had to fight the automatic downturn of my mouth.

"Leigh here yet?" Les asked as I stepped into the elevator. It reeked of booze, and his tone struck me as self-conscious. But when I looked up from the columns of buttons, he had a half-cocked smirk on his face like he was already high on the post-fuck endorphins of the sure thing beside him—who I was trying to pretend didn't exist.

"Should be. She said some time around midnight."

And then it got quiet. I eyed his blond prize up and down and waited for Les to fill in the gap with an introduction. *Something.* But he didn't. There was just more of that thick, heavy silence. The kind you could dent with the poke of a finger. After another couple of seconds, I couldn't take it any longer. "The guys want IHOP tomorrow. You in?"

"Fat stack of pancakes and endless coffee? You know you don't even have to ask."

My gaze flicked up to meet Les's. Brilliant green set within olivine skin, that leonine-lazy curl of his mouth so damn confident and desire-flushed. I knew that look. I wished I didn't.

I blinked away and focused on the display above the doors that flickered as we rose, but in my periphery I could still see Les's thumb moving in slow sweeps low on the other guy's hip, pushing up his T-shirt just an inch to expose his skin.

I couldn't get off that elevator fast enough. When the doors opened, I launched forward down the hall, calling over my shoulder, "See you at eight." Then, before I could stop myself, I tacked on, "Be safe."

Stupid. I was irritated with myself all the way down the damn hall.

I SLID MY ROOM KEY FROM MY BACK POCKET AND PAUSED OUTSIDE the door, hearing the elevator doors snick shut behind me. I should've been more excited to see Leigh than I was. We'd known each other for years. She shot our first show, but it was only in the last five months that we started dating. She had her own career, traveling the country as a photographer, and lately our schedules aligned less and less. And for some reason I wasn't bothered by that, but I suspected I should be.

The green light blinked on the door, and I pushed it open, forcing my mouth into a smile even as I wondered if Les and that guy had made it to his room yet. Or if they even would. Les was capricious. His give-a-fuck was a nuclear wasteland where nothing grew. For all I knew, the second the doors slid shut again, Les had pulled the guy's pants to his knees and fucked him right there in the elevator.

I hated the way the thought soured in my stomach.

"Ev?" Leigh's voice was soft like a comb of honey warmed in the sunshine. Feminine and familiar. She pushed her laptop aside and slid from the edge of the bed as I came around the corner, her lips curving up in a shy grin. The distance between our visits always made the first five minutes awkward, like we needed some time to resituate ourselves in the relationship.

"How was the show?" she asked as I pulled her into a hug and buried my nose in the scent of her shampoo, trying to drag my mind out of that elevator.

"It was good. I think? I don't know. I kept seeing the empty seats and the gaps between people."

She chuckled and stood up on her tiptoes to brush a kiss over my cheek. "I think you've been spoiled. I caught a live feed and the crowd looked decent to me."

"The label's on our ass constantly. It's all I can see now. Song downloads, tickets bought." I exhaled a long breath that ruffled the fine blonde hairs on the crown of her head and then released her so I could flop backward onto the bed

Leigh sprawled next to me, rolling onto her side and running her fingers through my hair. Her touch was light and calming, and as soon as I closed my eyes, exhaustion crashed over me.

"Is Les behaving?"

I nodded without opening my eyes. "You know Les. Caught him on the elevator up with his hands stuffed down some dude's pants. But Mars hasn't had to cold shower him in three days."

She was quiet for a moment, making a face probably. "Typical."

Leigh knew how Les was. He'd tried to get in her pants the first show she shot for us, and she'd shut him down so soundly he'd spent the next three days soothing his bruised ego with a revolving door of women and men.

Leigh's lips brushed over mine, her mouth yielding and warm, and I reached for her blindly, eyes still closed as I pulled her on top of me. Maybe I could just bury myself in her for a while. Forget about the show, the road, the last shitty album. She spread her thighs, grinding her hips against me, a quiet hum of pleasure escaping her mouth as I arched into her. Her hands roamed my chest, pushed under my T-shirt, then slid behind my waistband and stopped.

I knew why. My eyes snapped open.

She broke the kiss and straightened, her golden hair falling in a curtain on either side of my face. The tips dusted over my shoulders as her gaze searched mine. She was beautiful: the slight pout of her lips, the big blue eyes. I should be aching to sink inside her and I barely had an erection. Releasing my grip on her thigh, I smeared my hand down my face and shook my head in frustration. Another failure to rise to the occasion. Except it wasn't funny. "Fuck, I'm sorry."

Leigh put her hands on my chest and then rolled off me onto her back, frowning up at the ceiling while I studied her profile.

"It's not you." It felt like such an ineffective and lame thing to say, but it was true. Had to be. There was nothing wrong with Leigh. Leigh was great.

"I keep telling myself that. That it's the tour or the album or stress. But shit, Evan, it's not like this is the first time. And I'm trying to be understanding, but it's like you can't relax or can't let go. With me, at least."

I drew in a deep breath. "I know. It's going to get better. Once we get that next album down. I can feel it."

I didn't sound very convincing, and she gave me a doubtful look as I leaned over and kissed her again, then pushed the hem of her dress up to expose the tops of her thighs and the lacy band of her panties. I brushed my mouth over her inner thigh. "In the meantime, other parts of me are fully functional."

"HAVE YOU EVER CONSIDERED JUST GOING OUT ON YOUR OWN again? After this next album, I mean?" Leigh asked later, once we were curled in the bed together. I stroked her hair, playing with the ends. It was nice to have someone to lie next to; that part hadn't changed for me.

The question made me edgy, though. "I don't know. Somehow it doesn't feel right."

"Do you think Les has ever considered it?"

I hated that question, too, because it immediately made me bristle and panic at the same time. Les had never intimated anything of the kind, but then he wouldn't. Les was a force you'd never see coming or going, and the way this tour was going, it seemed like a possibility.

"Probably, but he hasn't said anything, and we still owe MGD another album." I flipped off the light and nestled against Leigh in the darkness, resting a hand on her hip. "Guess I'm just waiting to see how it goes when we sit down to actually write it."

Leigh found my hand and gave it a light squeeze, making a humming sound as she settled. "I just wish you wouldn't stress over every little thing."

She didn't know the half of it.

Four years ago, Les and I had come out of nowhere with an album that went somewhere fast, riding the comet-tail success of the rock-folk supernova all the way to platinum. Except it wasn't really out of nowhere, not for us. There were two years of our blood and guts in those twelve tracks that made us. A year of self-initiated touring across college campuses as Porter & Graves, playing to a crowd that could have been us if Les hadn't dropped out to pursue music and if I'd had the money to go in the first place. It was a scary fucking risk. For me, at least. Les was happy flying by the seat of his pants, but I'd always been the level head, the calculator, the staying hand. The seat belt that kept him from flying too far out of control. It was part of why we worked so well together. Or used to.

We'd met on the circuit in Nashville. I was playing solo gigs, and he'd just dropped out of a band, where he'd been their drummer. In his downtime he'd been learning guitar, and I happened to catch his first solo gig. He was mostly playing covers, but I liked the way he twisted the sound of his guitar with a percussive rhythm. It was different. Magnetic. At the end of his gig he'd tacked on a couple of songs he'd written. The music seemed a little generic and basic, but the lyrics were stellar. I'd felt that familiar itching in my palms and stomach, that desire to tinker and fix. His voice was solid, and as he sang the words, I tuned out the guitar and laid my own melody below it and I knew we could be a good fit. I wasn't much of a lyricist, but I was a hell of a guitar player and vocalist—that wasn't bravado. *Rolling Stone* agreed. And *Rolling Stone* also agreed that our last album sucked despite that fact.

We'd introduced ourselves. He was a sophomore studying communication. I was a bartender trying to crawl out of the backwater mud puddle I'd been born in. I didn't think I'd even asked what he was studying when we met, though, because a part of me knew it didn't matter—that once we started playing, something phenomenal was going to come together. And I'd been right. People packed in to hear us play. Cover songs gave way to originals. It was a business arrangement first. Our friendship came secondary and slowly, but once we got there, it was good, too. He jerked my chain about my serial monogamy and barefoot Southern roots, and I jerked his about treating groupies like his personal smorgasbord and his penchant for black... everything. But when we got together to write and play music, there was something transcendent about it. A language all our own, instinctive and expressive. Music flowed between us as easily as conversation. Sometimes easier.

How we got to the place we were now, with a shit album behind us and a friendship that felt like it was hanging on by its bloody roots, still blew my mind. At the same time, I was pretty sure it was my fault. And I still wasn't sure how to fix it.

How about post-show on tour? Do you guys go out a lot? Mingle with your fans. See the sights?

Evan: [laughing] …mingle with your fans…

Les: He's laughing at me.

Evan: Yep.

Evan: Let's just say Les excels at "mingling."

Les: I'm really a very friendly guy.

CHAPTER 3

"Things always that awkward between you two? Seems completely different when you're onstage," Jamie said, sotto voce as Evan hightailed it down the hall.

"Sometimes. Well, no." I'd gotten distracted watching Evan slip his key card in the door and disappear inside his room. More specifically, I'd gotten distracted by his ass in those butter-soft jeans he'd had since I'd known him. "It's been a long tour. Months and months on the road. He's got a girlfriend he hardly sees. Our last album..." I trailed off with my explanation as we reached the next floor and stepped off the elevator. My attention swerved back to Jamie's patient expression as I fit the card in the lock and opened the hotel room door. Jamie was right, though: Evan and I were different onstage, cutting up and bantering back and forth. It used to be natural. Lately it felt like we were working off the memory of tours before. The script still functioned, I knew all my lines and hit my marks, but it'd probably run out of steam soon. People weren't stupid. At the rate we were going, we were probably one tour away from going down bloody like Oasis.

"Your last album was good." Jamie's fingertips dusted across my wrist in passing as he walked into the room. A year ago, my penthouse would have been a suite with a foyer and a fucking view. This was a single. A very nice, single penthouse room, but a status reminder all the same.

I laughed, and it wasn't completely bitter because Jamie seemed sincere, but the judgment had been passed on our last album both in sales and critical reviews. "It was a disaster, but that's okay." It wasn't. "In a month we'll be at it again. A lot of bands blow their load on the first album and enter a sophomore slump. We had two ringers. I'll take a dismal third. We were due for some humbling." I said it confidently and ignored the way the admission burned in my lungs.

Jamie took off his coat, tossing it over the back of the chair. Underneath he had on an old metal band T-shirt that stretched tight across his pecs and shoulders. It looked good. *He* looked good. So why was I having second thoughts?

"So you're saying you've got plenty of loads left in you, huh?" He said it with a cocky grin that didn't quite match his posture, and I knew right then that I wasn't going to be bending him over the bed and fucking him into the mattress. Maybe it had something to do with seeing Evan on the elevator, and maybe it didn't.

But I wasn't necessarily giving up entirely.

"I've got at least one load in store for you," I murmured. It was a terrible line. I'd found, though, that people didn't really care. They saw the musician: the messy-haired, soulful-eyed, off-kilter lyricist —not my description; that was from an article in *People*. At a certain point, the men and women I brought up to my room or onto the back of our tour bus weren't really listening to me anymore. They transposed my lyrics over my words or maybe some article they'd read about me, and that became all they saw, just the projection of me from someone else's point of view. I'd tested the theory more than a few times. I'd once told a girl I couldn't wait to cram my meat stick in her face hole and she didn't bat a lash. I told a guy the same thing and he'd given me a funny look, then shrugged and got on his knees.

Jamie didn't even wince. I found that same belt loop I'd hooked in the elevator and yanked him closer still so I could push the hem of his T-shirt up. My dick was making a comeback. That was both a pro and a con of a dick. Or at least mine. It was usually ready and willing even if my thoughts were scattered all over the map.

"God." He exhaled a breathy sigh as I fanned my fingers over the smooth skin of his stomach. He brought his mouth toward mine, lips parting, and I skirted it without thinking, giving him my jaw instead. His lips brushed my stubble, tongue running the ridge of my jaw lightly in a tease. Why the fuck wasn't I kissing him?

I knew why I wasn't kissing him. So I turned my chin and fucking kissed him, made myself do it, like it was some great feat or horrible task I had to pump myself up for. It wasn't. His lips were warm and soft, his tongue beer tainted and slippery across the slide of mine. I sucked it, dragged my teeth across the taste of him, then lower to his throat.

"Take your shirt off," I said, and he did so immediately. He flicked at my nipples, sending needling bursts of pleasure through me while I bowed my head to his pecs, lapping at one flat circle and then the other until the rise and fall of his chest quickened and his nipples stood up in hard points that I could close my teeth around.

"I want to suck your cock," he rasped while working the top button of my jeans open.

"I want to pummel the back of your throat. I'm glad we agree," I teased back, then hauled him toward the full-length mirror positioned just outside the bathroom door. I had plans. And Evan said I didn't. Wait, why the fuck was I thinking about him again?

"I want to watch you while you suck me off." Wanted to watch the muscles of his back ripple, the curve of his spine. Whatever momentary failure of testosterone happened back there in the elevator had been fixed: my balls were already aching for a good, hard suck. I needed this release. Evan could fuck right off.

JAMIE SAT BACK ON HIS HANDS PANTING WHILE I SLUMPED DOWN against the wall, slick hand resting limply across my thigh. His eyes were lust hazed and satisfied. A glance in the mirror showed mine were the same.

"You do this a lot, I guess. Or as much as you want to, huh?" Jamie sounded almost wistful. We were in that postorgasmic, oxytocin-fueled intimate zone. The one that loosened lips. It was my favorite time to write, and I knew in a few minutes I'd rush Jamie out of the room in favor of picking up my notebook like I usually did. Maybe this time I'd actually write something that didn't deserve to be tossed screaming into a pit of fire, unlike the hundred nights that had come before. Optimistic. That was me.

"Not as much as you'd think. Not as much as I used to," I confessed. I was bored and restless, and Jamie was the first person I'd brought up to my room in a while. Sitting there with him right then, already wishing he'd leave, made me think of a conversation I'd had with Evan two months ago in Chicago. We'd been at the hotel bar, post-show. He was drinking a PBR, Nashville roots on full display, his blond hair slicked back. I could smell the dried sweat on him courtesy of the blazing stage lights we played under and underneath that, generic hotel soap. I'd studied his profile while pretending to eye the bottles—the straight slope of his nose, how his lower lip sealed against the rim of his can. Completely pathetic in how much I wanted him even then. I was grateful for my poker face. Being around Evan constantly had helped me hone it.

"Don't you get tired of it?" he'd asked. My gaze had skipped down the bar, landing first on a buxom blonde, then on a waifish brunette. I didn't have a type, I didn't think. I just liked what I liked. Male, female, whatever.

"Tired of what?" I'd replied, feigning bored unawareness, even though I knew exactly what he'd been asking. Was I tired of the endless parade of meaningless hookups? My sex life: an increasingly crowded kaleidoscope I couldn't stop adding color to. I obsessed over it. But I enjoyed it, too. The world was big, and life was short. And the only person who could possibly tempt me to settle down had been treating me like an infection for weeks.

"Sticking your dick in everything like you're on a personal mission to..." Evan was more blunt than I'd expected him to be, and he'd waved his hand instead of finishing his sentence. He actually laughed at whatever expression I made back, which must have included some surprise in spite of my best attempts to hide it. *"There's no diplomatic way to say what you're doing. It's not romantic. It's like you're out to prove a point or on a vendetta. And if it's me you're trying to prove it to, you can stop worrying. I already got it, all right? I got it in the first month after we left the cabin."*

His Adam's apple bobbed as his throat worked down the rest of his beer in a long draught. I'd had that skin between my teeth before. Right then it'd felt like mine was between his. How transparent I must have been. I was certain of it, but he'd looked nonchalant. Resigned. He was right. There was no romancing the way I tried to plug the little holes that'd sprung inside me by plugging everything else externally. It didn't work as well as it used to, but it was still some kind of solution, right?

JAMIE TILTED HIS HEAD TO ONE SIDE, WATCHING ME IN A WAY THAT made me realize I'd checked out for a second. I swam out of the undertow of my thoughts and pushed myself up off the floor. He took the cue perfectly, God bless him.

"I should get going. Early flight and all." Jamie stood and pulled his pants back over his hips, doing up his zipper and belt. I was grateful as fuck that he was cool, not trying to cling on or stay over and make some night of this. He knew as well as I did that we were done. Was it fucked-up that that made me like him a little more? Or at least appreciate him. Two weeks from now, his face would be a blur to me, his name forgotten, and our entire conversation boiled down to a few random key words that would make no difference in the grand scheme of things.

"'Blue,'" he said as he opened the door. "That's my favorite of your catalog."

Okay, maybe I wouldn't forget him after all.

Fucking "Blue." Despite it being the single bright spot on our third album, I was really starting to regret writing that goddamned song.

CHAPTER 4

Evan

SIX MONTHS AGO

"Let's take a break."

I knew what that meant. Les took jerk breaks like some people took smoke breaks, and he got cranky if he didn't get his fix.

"Jesus, man, you jerk off more than anyone I know." We were in the cabin's basement, the walls layered with egg-crate foam that kept sound cupped between us and protected from the world outside. When we wanted echoes and reverb, we crammed into one of the tiled bathrooms upstairs.

Les bounced his guitar atop his knee in a quick, restless tempo. A glance at the wall clock showed we'd been at it for hours. Felt like minutes to me.

"How do you know? You have a pie chart in your head keeping track? Shit, you probably do, obsessive bastard." Les laughed, the sound lazy, muffled by the walls.

I played along, trying not to smile. "Not just one chart. Many. Jerk breaks, how many seconds pass before you check your phone —average is every 1.5 seconds, by the way; f bombs dropped in live interviews—too many to count; number of times you've tried to convince me or Byron to let you go onstage in a robe or Snuggie— at least fifteen."

"Please, I haven't looked at my phone in at least a half hour."

I noticed he didn't address any of the other things, probably because I was right. Or very close.

"What about Travis? He's got to be a close second for jerk breaks."

Travis had been the bass player on our last tour, when we'd taken a backing band with us, and now that Les mentioned it, I recalled him being a big fan of breaks, too. Me, I liked to hammer through stuff while in the zone, didn't like my focus pulled away. Any more than a piss break threw me off when a new song had its hooks sunk deep into me. Not so for Les.

"Distant second, maybe." But I set my guitar on the stand beside me, a sure signal I was giving in to his request. "Your hand's going to fall off, one day. You don't run out of mental fodder?" We'd been in the cabin for two weeks, making only a few trips out on occasion, sequestering ourselves like the solitude would cast some magical spell on the construction process—which was a really accurate description of how we created an album. I'd been skeptical until it appeared to have worked pretty damn well on our first two albums. This time around we were churning out music and lyrics as efficiently as a mill, and they seemed on point. Not all of them, but enough that I felt certain by the end of the month we'd have a third album at least as good as our second. If not better. But while I was usually happy with little social interaction, Les was an extrovert with a notable, and widely publicized, appetite for... everything.

"My hand's in great shape, thanks, and there's always my laptop for inspiration, too." He narrowed his eyes to catlike slits as his lips twisted in a smirk. "Of course, if I'm doing it in your room, I'm thinking about how much it's gonna piss you off when you figure it out. I really knock one out fast, then." A wicked grin split his lips that cracked wider still when I flicked my pick at him. "Shit, did I say that out loud? Oops."

The pick popped him square in the forehead, and he laughed all the harder for it. He had a nice laugh, though, as uninhibited as the rest of him, like no one had ever shushed him in his life.

Of course I didn't believe him, so I didn't really know why I asked, "Where?"

"Where what?" His brows knit in confusion, his quick mind having already jumped to the next thing, apparently.

"Where in my bedroom?"

Les gave me a funny look that I read as disconcerted, then picked up and continued as easily as he did one of the riffs I tossed his way. "Pillow. Definitely. I lean down and sniff it first. The scent of control issues gets me hard as a damn rock. I come to the thought of my dried jizz in your neatly combed do." He could hardly finish before the solemnity in his expression broke around amusement, but I lagged behind a few mental paces, stuck on the idea of Les coming on my sheets and pillow. He wouldn't actually do that, would he? No, he definitely would.

The idea of it didn't turn me off like I expected it to. Les had a weird effect on me; we'd been playing together for so long now that it seemed impossible for him to shock me the way he enjoyed doing to others. The last prank he'd pulled off involved his nuts, an actual bag of nuts, a judiciously placed hole, and our noob-at-the-time roadie, Ed.

"I've got the heart of a child," he'd said, beaming brightly at Ed as Ed shook out his hand like it'd been doused in acid.

"No, you're just a child."

"Anytime you wanna be my Daddy, just let me know, Porter. I've got a Mr. Rogers fetish, though, so we'll need Mars to supply you with some cardigans."

"Fucking nut job," I muttered and waved him out of the room. The door clicked shut behind him, sealing off his laughter, and I was left alone in the graveyard quiet.

Les had left his guitar faceup on his chair, and I plucked at a few of the strings, seeing the ghost of his fingers moving over them. He favored taps and slides, hammer-ons, plenty of percussion. I loved watching him play, and I sat there trying to figure out whether or not the fact that I was possibly mildly turned on by the idea of him jerking off bothered me. Did I want to get with Les? My dick apparently had an ambivalent opinion a few minutes ago. Maybe it was just a reflex. Or maybe we'd just been closed up too long. Judging by the population around me—which, granted, currently only consisted of Les—my libido didn't seem on par. That wasn't to say I didn't have a sex drive, because I knew I did, but when it came to actual humans, it was safe to say my dick was highly selective.

"No way that was long enough for a jerk break," I said when Les returned a few minutes later.

"My pump's always primed and ready to go." He shot me a smirk and took his seat, balancing his guitar over his lap again.

"It's a miracle you ever get anything done." I watched him fiddle with his strings, long fingers nimbly making adjustments.

"No, it's a weird superstition, actually." Les sobered and leaned nearer to me like he was letting me in on a secret. "I work better when my dick's on E. Swear. All my best lyrics? They come *after* I blow my load." He gave me a sly look for his own pun and picked up his notebook, which resembled a chalkboard scene torn from *A Beautiful Mind*: tight black, illegible scrawl all over the pages, angled in every direction.

"So in a way, my pillow is a sacrifice to a greater cause?" I mused.

"Exactly." Les's gaze flicked up to meet mine as he turned a page. "You should consider yourself honored."

I ran out of quip steam and changed direction, picking up my guitar up again and running through the riff we were working on before.

"Not that one," Les said abruptly. "Let's switch over to that sound we were playing with yesterday."

"The one in drop D?"

He nodded, so I set about adjusting my tuning.

"I don't have lyrics for it yet, but they'll come. I can feel it."

I liked to work linearly, but Les jumped all over the place. I conceded because it was evident in the way his eyes narrowed to just slivers of bottle green that his mind was working over something that might be worth the detour. It was a habit of his I'd picked up on. One of those looks that could be called penetrating. He'd aimed it in my direction on more than a few occasions. Sometimes in frustration and sometimes with something else that was inscrutable, an undercurrent I couldn't quite grasp the meaning of. The second I thought it was desire, I slapped the thought away.

Shifting on my chair, I nodded, ready to see where he was taking us, then added on a whim, "We should get out of here tonight. Go to some dive and get blitzed." I could handle a lot of alone time, especially after our last endless tour, but we'd been sequestered so long working on this new album that even I was ready for a scenery change.

Les glanced at me, surprise showing in his expression, then muting as he looked back down at his fingers drifting over his guitar strings. "Sure. That's a great idea."

I'd had no clue that my stupid idea to go out and get hammered was going to change everything.

Guitar Times

March 2017

Favorite breakfast food?

Evan: Les doesn't actually know what a breakfast food is. He's never been awake for it.

CHAPTER 5

Les

A half hour after I shut the door behind Jamie and cleaned myself up, I sat on the floor at the end of the bed, squaring off against a blank sheet of notebook paper. I was on the losing end, as predicted. In that half hour I'd been sitting there, I'd made a single mark on the page—a black ballpoint slash. I used to just set the pen to the paper and bleed out. That's what it'd felt like, like everything running around in my head consolidated and flowed onto the page and all I had to do was sit there and transcribe it. I'd fill up an entire notebook, then go back later and shuffle, rearrange, mark out, rewrite. Sometimes a song would come to me all at once, and sometimes I'd have to pick it out from a bunch of gibberish. But at least there'd been something to work with.

White space was pressure I felt in my chest like the squeeze of a fist. A year ago, if someone had told me I'd be sitting here like this, I'd have laughed. I'd felt invincible and infinite back then. I'd told *People* magazine I dreamed in lyrics. It was true at the time. Lately, I just fell asleep and then woke up. There was nothing in between.

It was one thirty in the morning, but I knew Evan wasn't asleep.

One thing we had in common was that while on tour, he was nocturnal like me. He might've been fucking Leigh. He was *probably* fucking Leigh. *I'd* be fucking Leigh. Still, I picked up my phone and called him anyway.

"What's up?" His voice was alert. Not asleep, not fucking. I felt more relieved than I should have, and then anxious because I didn't call with a plan. I just did it.

"You said eight, yeah? Tomorrow?"

"Yeah." He paused. "If you'll still be *busy*, don't worry about it."

"Nah. I'm done."

His laughter came out hushed, but I thought a little derisive. "You writing something, then?" he asked, knowing how I usually worked.

"Nope. I'm about done with that, too."

"Bet one was more satisfying than the other."

"Yeah, at least there was something I could see. I've been having a showdown with this fucking notebook for the last hour. It wasn't impressed with my opening fire." I wrinkled my nose at the page and squinted, like I could will that black mark into becoming something I could work with.

"You get even a word out?" Evan wasn't one to pressure me, but we both also knew that I was on the line with the next album. We needed some fucking words to sing, and I was the supposed wizard.

"A black line. I think I made it accidentally when I looked over at the clock." My laugh was self-deprecating. Evan laughed, too, and that time it was a little warmer with sympathy. He was having a similar problem, but at least he could still sit down with his guitar, let his fingers wander over the strings, and eventually a riff came together. He needed something to sing, though, and I wasn't providing. And he may not have known, but I did: he didn't actually need me. Our label had kindly reminded me of that a week ago when Evan was out of earshot.

"It'll come back."

"Maybe." I'd started having serious doubts, which was gonna be a problem if there was any credibility to them, because I'd dropped out of college to make music with Evan, and I was hardly qualified to do anything else.

"It will. Maybe after a good jerk session at the cabin," he said, and I could tell he was trying to lighten the atmosphere, but the silence on the line between us after he'd spoken was palpable. I grabbed for a different subject.

"Leigh good?" I didn't care if Leigh was good. Leigh could kiss my ass. I had no idea why Evan was with her. Sure, they'd been friends for a while, but before they'd gotten together he'd never given any indication whatsoever that he was into her.

"Yeah, she's good. Asleep." More silence. Less palpable but still awkward, and it was like I could hear the strain for connection on both our ends. Well, maybe more from my end than Evan's. He could be laconic and hard to read. Especially over the phone.

"Do you think this idea of returning to the cabin is an effort in futility?" That wasn't what I'd wanted to ask at all. What I'd wanted to ask was *"Are we going to be okay? Can we fix the thing hanging over our heads?"*

"I don't know. But I don't have a better idea anyway." He might well have answered my unasked questions without knowing it. I heard him shift and imagined him sitting against the wall in the hall, his spine hunched, his T-shirt stretched across his broad shoulders. Or maybe he was shirtless.

I didn't mean my exhale to be so audible. But it was. It was definitely a sigh. "I'm gonna try to sleep."

"Yeah, me too." And then he added, "Free association. Try it. Don't throw up any mental roadblocks, just put the pen on the paper and let it go. Basically the same thing I do when I pick up a guitar and try to find the tune. I rummage through a bunch of notes until some of them start to get warm on my fingers."

Of course I knew what free association was. But usually what I ended up with was a random assortment of words and lyrics that somehow related to Evan. Things used to just come to me. Some move a girl would make. Or guy. The look in their eyes, how they moved, or how they made me feel. For the last year and a half, I'd had a hard time seeing anything other than Evan. The last thing I'd written that flowed onto the page like I'd bled it from deep within my consciousness was "Blue." And it had been for Evan.

Our biggest fucking hit was a love song I wrote for my band-mate. And he had no idea.

If he did, it would probably ruin us.

CHAPTER 6

Evan

By 9:00 a.m., it was evident Les wasn't coming. The other roadies stood beside the tour bus, smoking and shifting their weight, growing restless while my jaw wound tighter. I'd texted him five times, called three. No reply, no answer. Wordlessly, I extended my hand, palm up, to Mars, our tour manager, and he slapped the hotel key in it.

We'd started giving him an extra key to Les's room after our first tour when pretty much every other day required one of us going up to drag him out of his room because he was always late. It didn't happen as much on our second tour, but it'd picked up again this tour, and it was still annoying. It'd been more forgivable when we had a hit record to prop him up. Back then, the world waited for us. Not so much these days. Now he was just wasting everyone's time.

Striding back into the hotel, I mentally ran through all of the options that might lie in wait for me behind his door: Les passed out, Les in bed with a couple of chicks, Les in bed with a couple of dudes. Les in bed with a couple of chicks and a couple of dudes. That'd been Vegas. It wasn't a pretty aftermath, but Les had smiled for three days afterward like he'd uncovered the secret of the universe.

"God, you should have been there, Porter. It was magic."

"I don't even want to think about the mechanics involved to pull that off."

"It's easier than you might think."

He was always trying to invite me in, to share, but I didn't want any part of it. It threatened a level of intimacy I didn't think should exist between us. Spending twelve hours a day in close quarters with Les for six to eight months out of the year was enough. My sex life was just fine separate.

That didn't mean we hadn't crossed paths that way occasionally. And unintentionally. A month after the release of our first album, the hotel screwed up and we'd had to share a room in Tucson. I'd walked in on him fucking some girl he'd picked up after the show. Pretty and slender. A brunette. Her hands gripped the headboard like she was hanging on for dear life, and she was up on her knees as Les fucked the ever-living shit out of her from behind. I was surprised they hadn't been reported for noise. I'd stood in the doorway, trying to decide what to do, when he tipped his head back over his shoulder and said, with a salacious grin, "Want to get in on this?" Just like that, like it was no big deal.

I was tired and hungry and irritable, so instead of leaving like I might have another time, I'd just flipped him off, plopped down on my own bed, and turned the TV on. I thought maybe he'd take the hint, but he didn't. He'd chuckled and gone back to banging the girl. It was one of the more awkward stalemates in my life, but I was hell-bent on sticking it out, even though I got uncomfortably hard because they were noisy as hell. And, well, peripheral vision. I quickly learned Les was a talker with a filthy fucking mouth, and try as I might to train my attention on the TV, hearing him murmur about how wet she was, how good she felt, asking her how much she liked his cock inside her in that low, sexy voice he used on stage made it impossible. All the while, the slick skin-on-skin smack of his balls against her provided an undercurrent soundtrack that overwhelmed the sitcom laugh track on the TV screen. He looked over at me once and said, "Feel free to jerk one out, altar boy, no one's going to tell. You've gotta be dying over there." And I was, but I also wasn't going to give in.

Once they'd finished and collapsed and I was sure they were asleep, I'd gone into the bathroom, taken my cock in hand, and blown a load in about a second flat.

There were other times, more than I could even remember, and then there was the one that I always tried to forget. That was the fucked-up irony of memories; it was always the ones you really wanted to forget that got stuck on repeat like a shitty B-side track.

So I wasn't sure what I was going to find when I stuck my key card in the door. It could've been a menagerie of zoo animals for all I knew. I'd thought he was alone last night when he called me, but I could've easily be wrong, considering the guy I'd seen him with on the elevator.

The door clicked open and cool air poured into the hallway. The smell of booze hit me immediately. The blinds were pulled tight, the room dark as Halloween. I left the door open when I stepped deeper inside, and from that angle spotted his bare foot hanging off the bed.

The sight stoked another fear I had revolving around Les—maybe irrationally, but not without some merit—that one day I would walk in and find him dead, having overdosed on something. Because Les was reckless with everything. He might have laid off the hard drugs, but he was unpredictable that way. I broke out in a cold sweat as I stepped around the corner.

But he was just passed out. I took stock of the nightstand—the empty beer cans, a half bottle of Jack—and inwardly rolled my eyes at the cliché. That there was no one else with him in the bed was a little surprising. He was stretched out, the covers bunched up in one corner of the mattress. I exhaled relief I didn't know I was waiting for. Naked, he was all olive-toned curves and dips: ankles, calves, the backs of his thighs, the deep valley where his lower back gave rise to the tight, round cheeks of his ass. His face was buried deep in the pillow, dark, unruly hair spread out over the pillowcase. It was a view I'd seen on many occasions. His exploits were legion, splashed all over the internet in online groupie forums, and he loved nothing more than to share the tales that accompanied photos of him snapped in various states of undress and/or wakefulness by his hookups. He'd been deemed one of the more "generous" celebrity fucks, and when I'd asked what the hell that even meant, he'd given me a wicked grin as he said, *"It means I make sure everyone's satisfied."*

I bent over the bed, placing my hand on Les's warm shoulder and giving him a rough shake. He groaned and rolled onto his back, cracking a bleary eye at me. One hand flew reflexively to his hard dick, stroking up its length as I tried to ignore the salute. "Fuck."

"Five minutes, asshole, or you'll be taking a cab to Cleveland." I tossed one of the pillows at his dick, and he curled up with an *oof* as it landed.

"Jerk," he muttered and rolled over.

I turned and walked out. At the elevator bank, I stabbed at the button repeatedly the same way I wished I could push the sight of his dick out of my mind. That loose stroke of his hand upward, those long, strong fingers wrapped around his shaft.

The trouble was, my mind still recalled the feeling of them on me.

BACK AT THE TOUR BUS, I HANDED THE KEY OVER TO MARS, WHO eyed me speculatively, then said, "Cold shower?"

I nodded, glancing at the time on my phone display. "Give him five more minutes, then douse him and drag his ass out."

Mars returned fifteen minutes later, laughing as Les pounded on his back with his fists. Les wasn't small; he was six feet and wiry, not weak, but Mars was the size of a Titan. Les was soaked, naked from the waist up, goose pimples spread all over his back and dimpling the ink of his tattoos. His dark hair dripped on the pavement, and his jeans were pulled only halfway up his ass. I was sure the hotel staff loved having that paraded across their lobby for all the guests taking advantage of their free continental breakfast to see.

Mars dragged Les's suitcase behind him, and Les shot a bird to the roadies who were hanging out beside the bus and cracking up.

We both got along with our roadies. They were our family away from home, and they loved fucking with Les because he'd fuck with them back.

Not this morning, though. He snarled as Jimmy, our driver, catcalled at him. I watched it all unfold from the silence of our tour bus while I drank coffee. That there was no pap around to catch the drama was either lucky or a bad sign. Lately, I thought it was more the latter.

The door swung open and Mars deposited Les on the steps in a heap. Les wobbled to a stand and yanked his pants the rest of the way up. "I'll fire you one day," he threatened, sticking his finger in Mars's face.

"You wouldn't dare. I'm your goddamn fairy godmother." Mars nipped at the end of Les's finger, then smiled sweetly back at him before slamming the door so hard Les had to leap backward to avoid a crack to the nose.

Les kicked his suitcase up the stairs and finally registered me sitting there on the couch. "What's up, Mr. Goody Two-shoes?"

I pointed at the table across the aisle impassively, used to his alcohol-fueled declarations. "Made you some coffee."

I caught it, just barely: surprise darted through his eyes a second before they darkened with suspicion. "Aren't you a sweetheart." His voice was a tool like a Swiss Army knife, and he'd long ago figured out how to twist it just so into my side for maximum effect.

"Anything for you, darling." I kept my tone light as I set my coffee down and strummed a few chords on my guitar, looking for an appropriate song to capture the moment. I settled on The Replacements' drunkard's lament, "Here Comes A Regular."

He snorted as I played, kicked his suitcase again, then stumbled past it to reach for the coffee I'd made him. As I watched, he brought the mug almost gingerly to his lips, giving me a big fake smile and taking the tiniest of sips before he turned and dumped the rest into the sink, then dropped the mug in after, letting it clatter noisily as Jimmy started up the bus. He lurched backward and disappeared behind the curtains to the bunks as the roadies piled through the door.

To say Les could be a real asshole when he was drunk was putting it mildly.

I set my guitar aside and sighed as I got up to clear his suitcase out of the aisle.

No one would be the wiser tonight, though. The house lights would go down, and we'd come out onstage together. Les would give me that wild grin, the one that could suck a person in like a vortex, that pulled at everything you were and made you want to give anything to him. And that was just his warm-up, because when he turned to the crowd, they'd get the full wattage like a switch flicked on, and they'd eat it up. They'd surge forward for it. The girls would take their shirts off for it, and the guys would line up backstage for it after the show. For just a second more of its warmth directed personally at them, people would do a fucking lot. I'd seen it countless times, and I'd fallen for it once.

And that was where our label was wrong, no matter what they tried to tell me when he wasn't listening. Les was the secret ingredient, the X factor, and I needed him because I wasn't ever going back to slinging suds in dive bars, scraping together tips for rent, and busking on street corners.

So I had to fucking make this work.

After spending so much time together on tour, do you guys hang out during downtime back in Nashville?

Evan: I had to file a restraining order last week just to stop Les from hanging out in the tree next to my house, peering through my windows.

Les: I was looking for evidence that you're not actually an android. Still haven't found any.

Evan: We don't really get much downtime, honestly.

CHAPTER 7

Les

I came to nine hours later, mummified by the sheet on my bunk and drenched in sweat. After unsticking my phone from where it had gotten wedged against the side of my ribs, I held it in front of my eyes until the blur in them cleared and the numbers swam into focus. Two hours until showtime. *Shit.*

My head pounded like an out-of-control kick drum, and my stomach was a sour, empty wasteland. I'd missed the fat stack of pancakes. Hell, I'd missed the day. When I pulled back the curtain on the bunk, twilight greeted me, along with a view of the empty parking lot outside the bus. Familiar scenery. It used to be more exciting. It used to be a prelude, like an appetizer to the night. I'd get pumped up imagining the lot as it filled up with cars crowded with fans who'd paid money—good money—to listen to the words that came from my head. Today I looked out the window and just saw an empty parking lot I didn't remember arriving at.

I shot a text to Blink, our front-of-house engineer, telling him to get his ass to the bus. He arrived ten minutes later, slipping inside soundlessly. He was a compact force of nature and could fix any sound glitch in the blink of an eye. Hence, Blink.

"Fuck, dude," he said when I slid out of the bunk and pooled in the center aisle of the bus at his feet. "You may be beyond my capabilities."

"That's bush league, Blink. Gimme something that'll make opening my eyes less like medieval torture." I gazed up at him with my best rendition of puppy dog eyes.

"Could whip out my cock," he suggested.

I managed some raspy, dry-throated laughter that hurt. "I need a pick-me-up, not something that makes we want to gouge my eyes out."

"Harsh, dude." And he sounded like he meant it. "What're you thinking? I wouldn't go hard." He fidgeted and searched through his pockets while I considered.

"Probably just the Never Better."

Blink nodded, his fingers darted through the pockets of his jacket and cargo shorts, plucking out pills. The guy had a tool or a combination for everything. And he named all of them. The Never Better was his best hangover cure that wouldn't leave a person with another harsh comedown: a combination of a joint and B vitamins followed half an hour later with a thin rail of Adderall. All were acceptably within the limits of the no-hard-drugs rule.

He fired up the joint immediately and passed it over to me. My stomach unclenched after the first deep inhale, like it knew relief was on the way. Then, he assembled the B vitamins, dumping them in my left hand. He turned to the counter, popping the Adderall into a tiny baggie and crushing it with the side of a coffee mug. "Remember, half an—"

"Hour, I know. I'll be right as rain."

"That one's definitely not for you today."

We chuckled. The last time I'd asked him for a 'Right as Rain,' I'd ended up at a twenty-four-hour rave in the Arizona desert dancing until the sun came up before crashing for two days straight.

"How about an Act Together," a low voice said over Blink's shoulder. "Can you get one of those?"

Blink shot a look over his shoulder at Evan, letting out some tentative laughter. They didn't get along as well as they used to. Evan thought

Blink enabled me. Which… was not entirely untrue. But he was also one of the best sound guys out there, and he'd been with us from the start. And besides, in a week's time, I'd be cut off in the cabin with plenty of time to detox my body and get my act together. So why rush it?

"Fresh out of those, dude," Blink said.

"No shit." Evan thumbed at the door. "They need you out there. Something's off with the amps."

Blink frowned and tossed the baggie to me as he jetted. Then it was just me, Evan, and the whole big awkward world of unsaid dangling between us. I hated that it was like this more often than not lately. I hated knowing it was probably my fault. And I hated the fact that I couldn't seem to fix it, mostly because I wasn't sure what exactly needed fixing.

I waited for a lecture or some serious side eye, but Evan only uncapped the water bottle he was carrying and took a few backward steps to drop onto the couch while I pinched out the joint and tucked it in my pocket for later.

I must have looked pretty pitiful, because with a sigh and another long look, he handed me his bottle of water. I tossed the vitamins into the back of my throat and washed them down before handing the water back.

He studied the set list for the night, then set it aside and rubbed at the fine blond stubble on the side of his face. "You ever come up with anything last night? That bit you had the other afternoon was good, about the canyons."

"Yeah?" It was pathetic how even the smallest praise from him streamed through my body like sunlight.

He nodded, but I couldn't read much more from his expression aside from a general wariness. "Seemed worth expanding on." He was talking about a verse I'd come up with the other day. One I should've worked on last night. Hell, maybe I had. I couldn't remember what I'd written last night. I couldn't remember getting on the damn bus.

I must have said that aloud because Evan pulled a face at me.

"You didn't get on the bus. Mars dumped you inside. Then you basically told me to fuck off and threw the coffee I made you in the sink. Mug and all."

I'd become mostly immune to shame, though I knew if ever there was a moment I should feel it, it was then. I was too hungover to muster it, though. "Sorry," I said lamely. It was an empty apology, and he knew it.

There was a flash of something moving across his features, and I couldn't tell if it was concern or pain, or closer to disappointment, but it landed on me like a weight and settled heavily in my stomach, undoing the calming effects of the weed.

"Les," he said, that same expression taking hold and etching deep into his face. It was earnest and so raw it hurt to look at. For a second, I thought I'd finally done it: he was going to give me the big fuck off and leave me behind. He could do it. He was the more talented of us, the more ambitious, the more versatile. The more everything, really. The things he could do with a guitar and his voice didn't just make people dance. It was breath and movement. His music was alive in a way that endlessly fascinated me, like he'd peeled the notes from his soul or the collective consciousness, somewhere deep and primal where everything resonated in harmony together behind the cloud of iPhones and universal disconnect and self-created loneliness. He didn't think his lyrics were as good as mine, but he was wrong. And besides, music without lyrics was still music, but lyrics without music were just words.

The way he'd said my name right then, it sounded like some kind of confession he didn't want to make. I braced myself. *Rip the fucking Band-Aid off, already*, I thought. My jaw tightened as he studied my face. Then, he exhaled loudly through his nose and passed the set list over to me. "You think this looks all right?"

I studied him a beat longer, until he blinked and looked away and it was evident he wasn't going to say anything else, then I glanced at the song order he'd written down. It was one we'd done before, but this was Cleveland, and Cleveland loved some of our B-sides and bonus tracks from the first album. I touched the tip of my tongue to the point of my canine, thinking. "We should skip 'Blunder,' 'Siren,' and 'You Expect,' and do 'Disorder,' 'You Were Mine' and ummm…"

"'Chanteuse'?"

"Yeah." I nodded, warming to the idea and relieved to have moved on to a language we rarely had trouble conversing in. "Good call."

"I think so. End with 'I'm Leaving You,' still, and encore with 'Blue'?"

My stomach clenched up again, the way it did every time someone mentioned that damn song, but especially when it was Evan. "We kind of have to," I mumbled. "Remind people that at least one thing they like came out of that last album. Keep them from giving up on us."

"They're not going to give up on us," Evan said, but even he didn't sound convinced.

BY THE TIME THE HOUSE LIGHTS WENT DOWN THAT NIGHT, MY hands were steady again. The buzz of the crowd settled into an anticipatory lull that lasted a span of seconds, and then burst with applause that swelled and surrounded us. The venue was new to us and smaller, maybe five hundred people at most, but I could tell just from the applause ricocheting off the walls that the acoustics were stellar.

"You good?" Evan had to speak up to be heard over the rowdy crowd. He had his guitar slung across his back and raked a hand through his hair one last time to make sure it was settled. I licked my parched lips, nodded, and grinned. "Never better."

He wanted to frown—I could see a line trying to etch itself between his brows—but, like me, he still got high off a crowd, and he ended up quirking a quick smile back. "Good. Let's do it."

Jared, our instrument tech, handed me my guitar, and we walked onstage. Cheers and catcalls rushed us like a wave breaking against the shoreline, engulfing us in a cocoon of wild energy. It had amplitude and emotion and was as addictive as anything I'd ever put into my body. It was energy exchange back and forth, an intimate conversation on another level between my soul and the hundreds in the crowd before us. I loved the feeling of connection, and I didn't think I'd ever get tired of this moment. And I'd never get tired of sharing it with the man beside me. I hoped Evan was right about the fans not giving up on us. But more than that, I hoped Evan didn't give up on me.

CHAPTER 8

SIX MONTHS AGO

I was drunk. Not outright hammered, not glaze-eyed blitzed, but definitely drunk. A few tequila shots and a lot of beer cartwheeled through my veins. Also known as a recipe for a class B hangover. Better than class A, which would have me out for a day. A class B just made for a shitty morning. Unless I slept through it. I didn't care, though. Evan was drunk, too, and after being holed up in the cabin for so long, I enjoyed watching him cut loose. He wasn't out of control or like a different person or anything. He was still Evan Porter—a guy born with his skin wrapping him just a little too tightly, an ounce more tension in his spine than most people had. He relaxed when he was playing or on stage. And also when he drank—which he didn't do to excess often.

I liked seeing him cut loose in any way, shape, or form. How the corners of his mouth went a little lax, and when he smiled there'd be a crooked wobble in it that drove me crazy. I wasn't the only one. Any time a pap captured it, our fan page went crazy posting about it. It was something of a rarity. If I saw it between the pages of one of the tabloids, I always tried to guess what it was that caused it. There were times I knew it was me. A pic of him coming out of Ralph's with his cell to his ear—I was on the other end of that call telling him about the jackhead roadie who'd clogged up the tour bus toilet. Evan had thought it was hilarious that I was so worked up because I was usually pretty laid-back about everything. But getting hit by a wall cloud of someone else's shit stench when I opened the door of the bus, knowing we were about to settle in for a ten-hour haul, pissed me off. So I was ranting in the phone about Rick's traitor asshole and how he was banned not only from Taco Bell, but from stepping more than five feet into our bus until he'd detoxed his colon.

AFTER SPENDING HALF THE NIGHT BARHOPPING, WE ENDED UP taking two waitresses back to the cabin. Evan didn't seem as interested in Mandy as I was in Ella, but he'd been a good sport about it. We hung out on the back porch for a while playing drinking games and doing a dumb version of karaoke, even though my fingers were getting numb to the point where they slipped over the strings and had trouble holding a note. When we needed another round, I dragged Ella inside with me into the kitchen where I pushed her up against the fridge and kissed her. I'd been stuck in a cabin for days, and she was cute and horny and we'd been flirting all night, so making good on it was overdue.

At some point, I registered a faucet running, which was weird because we hadn't moved from in front of the fridge. I had my hand in Ella's panties, and she was moaning with her eyes screwed shut when I turned my head to the side and caught Evan at the sink, filling a water glass as he stared out the kitchen window. I guess he'd gotten used to ignoring me.

"What happened to Mandy?"

Ella cracked her eyelids open as I spoke, registering Evan's presence with a sharp intake of breath.

Evan shrugged. "She had to work early tomorrow."

"So? Since when does that preclude slipping a chick the D?"

"Maybe I didn't want to slip her the D." He tipped the glass up to his lips, swallowing the water all in one go, then refilled it.

"Why the fuck not?" She'd clearly been into Evan.

Evan paused with his glass midway through its arc to his mouth. "If you're going to keep interrogating me, you think you could take your hand out of her drawers?"

"Drawers," Ella echoed with a snicker, as if she didn't have the same Southern twang. "That's so cute."

But I complied, sliding my hand free and wiggling my fingers at him.

He rolled his eyes and shook his head with something close to exasperation, then addressed Ella. "This guy's a barbarian. You like that?"

"I don't hate it," she purred, one shoulder rising and falling. She had on some kind of slouchy knit dress that exposed her shoulder and bladelike collarbones with the motion. It was careless and sexy and part of her whole allure, but I found my attention riveted to Evan again as his gaze swept her figure and then swerved toward me. After her reply, he seemed uncertain of what to say next. Guess he'd been expecting her to say something different.

"Do a shot with us," she said, and extended her hand to him.

Warmth began to spread through my stomach, because it was quickly apparent to me exactly what Ella was aiming for. And holy shit was I into it. Evan's mysterious sex life was like the lost gospels to my promiscuous Bible. You couldn't turn a page in the tabloids without running into one of my sexual exploits. Evan, on the other hand, was hardly ever mentioned. He had girlfriends off and on, but I had no idea what went on behind closed doors. He kept a low profile and didn't talk about it, not even with me.

So I didn't know how he was going to handle this incredibly obvious overture, but I expected an immediate shutdown and prompt retreat.

Imagine the jolt of sheer, electrifying surprise that zipped through me when he reached out, took her hand, and let her reel him into our little enclave by the fridge.

"One shot."

Tease

May 2017

Name one thing you can't stand.

Evan: Losing a sock. It drives me crazy.

Les: Really? That's it? Out of the multitude of options of shitty occurrences, a lost sock is the first thing you thought of?

Evan: What can I say? Why do you think I'm wearing flip-flops right now? It's on my mind.

Les: I know where that sock is.

Evan: No… No you fucking didn't. I shouldn't even be surprised by that. You know what? You can keep it. I'll even give you the other so you'll have a matched set. That's so wrong.

CHAPTER 9

PRESENT DAY

I f I had to give props to Blink for his mad-scientist chemistry, so be it, because the show was amazing. Les was tuned into the audience, feeling their energy, which in turn rubbed off on me. We had a reciprocal relationship onstage, a constant psychic feedback loop between us. I could hear it in his voice and in the way he was playing. Lately I'd been worried it was gone, and was so relieved to feel the connection again, that when he broke with our reordered set list during the last quarter of our show, I went with it without question, my faith in him restored. At least where music was concerned. We spent eight months out of the year with each other, almost twenty-four seven. Trust had always been de facto. Lately it'd felt like a spotty internet connection, but at least tonight proved it still existed.

I picked up my bottle of water and took a swig on a song break, checking out the set list at my feet. We always set the stage with two stools next to each other and two mics in front, but we usually ended up wandering all over the place.

Les stood at the edge of stage left playing to the crowd, teasing them. Leave it to Les to successfully flirt with five hundred people at once. He glanced over his shoulder at me and grinned as I recapped my water bottle.

The audience loved this part. I parked my ass on the edge of my stool, then stretched my legs out and waited with my hands dangling over the top of my guitar.

Les roamed back to the mic stands, hitching his jeans and letting his guitar droop to one side as he paused to grab a drink of water before prowling back to the edge of the stage, where he paced.

"We've got a set list back there," he said, hiking his thumb over his shoulder in my direction, "but I'm kinda curious what y'all want to hear."

His back was to me, but I knew exactly what he was doing: his eyes were narrowing to a laser intensity of green as he skimmed faces in the crowd. He'd be catching his lip in his teeth, squinting one eye slightly, like the decision was a tough one and then, *boom*, he'd single someone out.

He pointed to someone about three rows back. Heads turned to look as he nodded at what appeared to be a petite redhead bobbing up and down excitedly. She quickly glanced behind her, then to either side, then pointed to herself to make sure, her lips poised in a little "o" of delighted surprise.

"Yeah, I'm talking to you." Les let out a low, velvety chuckle. "What do you want to hear, sweetheart? Doesn't even have to be one of our songs. Name it and we'll do it."

This bit of interaction always made me nervous. I liked things planned out well in advance, and Les's favorite crowd-pleaser had bitten us in the ass a few times.

Les stood at the edge of the stage now, leaning over, one hand cupped to his ear as she shouted, then aimed a rakish grin over his shoulder at me. His eyes smoldered with mischief. "Did you hear that, Porter? She says I'm smoking hot." The audience whooped and catcalled.

"Stop encouraging him," I said drily. "We share a bus, and his ego already takes up all the cargo space."

"Are you sure that's not his dick?" someone in the front row shouted. Les's grin broadened, his eyes gleaming.

I smirked, sliding fully on the stool, idly twisting the tuning knobs on my guitar. "Nah, his dick would fit in the ashtray."

The audience roared, and Les twisted around to flip me off. I gave him a syrupy smile.

"Evan's just jealous. It's all hearsay, but I believe in hard proof. Y'all want to see some hard proof?"

He turned his back to me again, but I could tell by the bend of his elbow that he was thumbing at the button of his jeans. He'd do it, too, I had no doubt. Les would flash his dick to a pigeon if he thought he'd get a reaction.

Screams of encouragement replaced good-natured laughter. The front row especially was working itself up into a hot lather, and I could only assume by the fresh wave of cheers that followed that he'd unbuttoned the top of his pants. I had no desire to bail him out of jail for public indecency.

"Rein it in, Morrison," I told him, leaning in so it came clear through the microphone. "No one needs to ride that storm right now. We've still got a concert to finish."

A mixture of cheers and boos followed. Our fans tended to love our back-and-forth, and our bickering, my good-guy schtick to his bad-boy swagger. We were like the Gallagher brothers except… less hateful. And also not blood related. Thank God.

Les cackled madly, then put up his hands in surrender, but not before saying, "I'm happy to give private showings after we finish." He clapped his hands once. "Right, now where were we?"

The girl he'd originally pointed out cupped her hands over her mouth and called out after the applause had died down, "'Crash Course'!"

"Ohhh, interesting." Les took a couple of steps back from the edge of the stage with a slow nod, angling toward me as he tapped the tip of his finger against his lower lip a couple of times in consideration. "I don't think anyone's ever requested that one before, which is kind of a shame, because it's a good one and"—he paused for another look over at me, that same sly glint lighting up in his eyes like coals in a fire—"Evan should tell the story that goes along with it."

"Crash Course" wasn't a love song, per se, but it did have a story behind it. One that came mostly at my expense, which was why Les was grinning wickedly at me.

"I think you should tell it."

"Not a fucking chance," he said, dropping back onto the stool and folding his arms over the top of his guitar. He gave me an expectant tilt of his head, like he was settling in for story hour at a public library, and when I met that stare levelly, he started chuckling.

I sighed and told the tale that involved a bottle of caffeine pills, a long overseas plane flight, Les's stupid idea that we should drive our own car in Italy for an immersive experience, and the mess with the Italian *polizia* that followed.

"He didn't take kindly to you just pulling over to the side of the roundabout and hopping out of the fucking car, either," Les finished for me.

I'd been in a near panic and thought I was about to have a heart attack from the stupid pills. But hey, the audience didn't need to know that. Or how pissed I'd been at Les for passing out in the back seat in the first place. It had been his idea to call our liaison, though, because by that time he'd gotten out of the car and was trying to calm both me and the policeman down. I couldn't even think straight. Once the liaison spoke to the policeman, he'd settled down and pulled the car onto a side street for us, and we took a cab the rest of the way to the TV station where we were supposed to be doing an interview—which Les had to carry because I was so out of it. Ironically enough, that interview was one of our most watched on YouTube. Les said it was because no one ever saw me cracked out of my skull and him being the sensible one. Which was probably true.

Les continued. "How a song comes out of that, I don't even fucking know, but the next morning in our hotel, I just got up and wrote it, thinking about how the unexpected can lead to some of the best experiences."

He glanced over at me then, something darting through his expression that I couldn't quite get a read on. Something like hope and amusement and cynicism all at once, and only Les could manage all three; even his emotions were promiscuous.

He plucked a few strings on the guitar and then turned back to face the audience. I jumped in right behind him, picking up the song.

POST-SHOW MEET AND GREETS WERE MY LEAST FAVORITE PART OF touring. I liked the audience to be the audience. Once they separated out into individuals, I didn't know what to do with all the small talk and fanfare. I guzzled a liter of water and tried to stay attentive, but I was thinking about that night in Italy and how different it was from where we were now.

We'd known our first album was good, but there wasn't a lot of pressure behind it. Now it felt like a cement block on my feet. That night when we'd gotten to the hotel, we'd hung out in Les's room until four in the morning, partly because I couldn't possibly go to sleep, but mostly because we were talking. We'd ordered rounds and rounds of room service and stuffed ourselves stupid while lying on the bed, talking about what we hoped would happen with our album, what we wanted to do on the next one, what we loved about music. Everything. I think it was the first time I realized that we'd become more than just bandmates and business partners and were actually friends. Our whole first tour was full of nights just like that.

Now, we went our separate ways as soon as we walked offstage. I missed it, and the feeling hit me as sharp and sudden as an elbow to the rib cage.

I glanced over at Les where he leaned up against the wall with a Sharpie in his hand, cutting up with a group of girls and waving the marker threateningly at them. When I finished rattling off a distracted spiel on how I'd chosen my latest Gibson to a rapt guy with a tight ponytail and horn-rimmed glasses who scribbled every technical detail in a little spiral notebook, I excused myself.

The girls looked me up and down as I approached, beaming me smiles bright as the spotlights we'd just left behind while Les seesawed the marker between his fingers, eyeing me. "They're asking me if there's a body part I haven't signed before."

"Doubtful. If it's humanly accessible in any way, shape, or form, he's probably signed it or put his mouth on it."

One brow hiked up as if Les had taken my sarcasm as a personal challenge.

The blonde standing to his left puckered her pouty lips, then smiled. "Well, if I can't be original, how about..." She hitched her foot up on the arm of a couch next to Les, sweeping her dress up to her waist casually and exposing a lean thigh. "Here?" She pointed to her inner thigh, just in front of her black satin panties.

Les looked up at her, tongue darting out over his lower lip as his hand closed over the top of her thigh and his thumb swept softly along the inside. I could see the goose bumps rise on her skin as he touched her. "Here?"

She gave a breathy murmur of assent accompanied by a nod, and when their gazes locked as Les's marker descended, I almost rolled my eyes.

"There are other places you could write your name, but I wouldn't want you to use a marker," she said, biting her lower lip coquettishly. Her friends giggled, and I snorted. Then she turned a narrow look aside to me and added, "You too."

I didn't know if I blushed, but my blood instantly started to simmer. It had nothing to do with the girl and everything to do with being slingshotted back into that night six months before at the cabin. A mixture of remorse and the memory of desire flooded my throat and drowned any chance I had at firing back some smartass comment.

"He's not into shit like that," Les murmured dismissively, eyes darting up to me, then flickering back to the girl's thigh just as quickly. I caught the darkness in the look, though.

I fit the stereotype of a musician in probably every way except one, but that one thing had been endless fodder for our roadies and Les: I didn't sleep around. I wasn't interested in it. It wasn't some issue of moral high ground—as much as Les enjoyed teasing me about being a prude. It was that the whole idea seemed pointless. It wasn't like I judged anyone who felt differently—except Les because he slept around too much, in my opinion. I just liked relationships. I liked knowing a person and feeling a connection.

Unfortunately, relationships and being on the road for months at a time hadn't worked out very well for me. Even with Leigh the other night, I got the distinct impression that we were starting to peter out. Her job as a photographer had her hopping around just as much, and at first I thought that would be a good thing, but we were just growing further apart. And honestly? I wasn't even that upset by it. Probably not a good sign.

Les studied me, fiddling with the marker as the girls wandered away to the craft service table.

"You didn't give any of them your number. Color me impressed." I watched the girls as they grabbed some plates and piled fruit on them.

He shrugged lightly, stuffing the marker in his back jeans pocket. "Meh."

"We should hang out tonight," I said. "Like we used to. We could send Mars out for food."

His mouth curled in a smile, and I could see him warming to the idea. Maybe having this show under our belts and some solid hangout time would get us out of our rut. I'd definitely rather go into our songwriting retreat on friendlier terms than what we'd been like lately.

"Yeah, that'd be good. Wings?"

"Garlic, teriyaki, honey-glazed?"

He slitted his eyes at me like I'd asked a trick question. "Just straight up hot wings, no need to get fancy."

I grinned. "Agreed."

Speaking of the devil, Mars lumbered in and beelined for us, snatching up a bottle of water on his way that looked like a test tube in his huge hand. Another group of fans lingering nearby divided in half to get out of his way. He had a fierce frown painted on his face, but he usually did.

"That reporter's here, waiting. He's an arrogant little shit."

I blinked at Les, and he gave me a wide-eyed *no clue* look in return.

"What reporter?"

"Dunno," Mars said unhelpfully. "Says he cleared it with Levi. Asked who was going first."

I frowned. Les and I usually did interviews together, but separately wasn't unheard of. I pulled my phone from my pocket and thumbed through my texts until I discovered one from our publicist, Levi, that had come through while we were onstage: *Last minute, sorry. Adam Slade is in town. Wants to do interview for String and Strum. Do it. Profile piece on each of you. Should be good pub.*

"We doing it?" Les eyed me skeptically as he cracked a beer.

"Guess so. I can go first. Good behavior," I warned Les, who grinned like a maniac, instilling absolutely no confidence in me.

"No worries. I'll dazzle him."

I should've known better than to trust that grin. Les was really good at charming people when he wanted to. Phenomenal, actually. A five-minute conversation with him and he could have people eating out of his palm. And it wasn't like he was pretending or being fake. If he was talking to you, ninety percent of the time he was interested and was giving you untempered, charming Les, because the rest of the time he wouldn't even bother, and that was the problem; he was fickle. We once did a disaster of an interview with a guitar magazine that I had to limp us both through. Les was hungover, firstly, but the biggest issue was that he decided he didn't like the writer. *"He's a closet homophobe. I've read his articles,"* he'd grumbled. I'd read his articles, too. I always did before we did an interview and I didn't see it. But Les just shut down. It was right after we'd cut what was to be our slump album, and it certainly didn't help things that he sat through the entire interview giving one-word answers and looking sulkily out the window the entire time. I think he'd even oinked at one point when the reporter asked him a question.

CHAPTER 10

Evan

An hour and a half later, after I'd finished my interview, Mars and I returned so weighted down with sacks of wings, we could've opened our own buffet. Mars split off for the venue, where the roadies were breaking down our equipment. I headed for the tour bus. We'd be driving straight to Indianapolis so we could do a publicity gig pre-show early tomorrow.

The interior was quiet as I elbowed the door open and stepped inside. I'd gotten way too used to our bus. Every time we finished a tour and I returned to my own home, I inevitably walked through it in wonder at having so much space after sleeping in a bunk or hotel room for so many months. I still had rooms that had nothing in them.

I shut the door behind me and could tell by the tinge in the air that Les was there. I didn't know if it was aftershave, actual cologne, hair product, or deodorant, and I'd never asked, but Les had a distinctive scent that reminded me of a forest at night: dark and green, a little spice, a little wood, a little earth. I figured he was in the back of the bus in the lounge, the one area capable of being fully closed off besides the bathroom. We had a few gaming consoles, a couple of guitars, and God knew what else in there. Mars always made sure it was stocked for us. I couldn't even remember what we'd put in the original rider, except that Les got denied fresh cut tulips every day—which he didn't even want; he was just seeing how far he could push it. But he did get his stupid request for a constantly replenished cornucopia of green and purple Skittles. *"Best flavor combo ever, man,"* he'd said. Les's extravagance had risen in direct proportion to the number of albums we sold, but he was still nothing like some other bands we knew, and it was one of the things I really liked about him. He was hedonistic to a fault, but also delighted by the smallest things. Like the perfect Skittles combo and high-end hotel soap.

A groan filtered out from under the door leading into the lounge as I set the bags down on the built-in dining table. Plastic crackled, Styrofoam squeaked, and like a bassline underneath came another groan, louder this time. Les. No doubt about it. I'd spent enough time with him to distinguish even the incoherent sounds.

This wasn't Les's miserable ate-too-much, fucked-too-much, drank-too-much, took-too-much groan. Heat trickled upward over my neck, spreading across my cheeks. He couldn't forgo a lay for one fucking night. I shook my head in disbelief, finished setting out the boxes of wings, and strolled to the back of the bus, sliding my hands in my pockets.

When I nudged the door with the toe of my boot, it whisked open with a sound like a sigh.

Adam Slade had sat across from me in this room earlier, all smiles and polite laughter, acting the consummate professional as he asked me his questions. Now he was on his knees, the back of his gray T-shirt rucked up over his hips, the waistband of his jeans loose and sagging to reveal the shadowed furrow of his ass as his head bobbed up and down in Les's lap. Les's head was thrown back in slack-jawed ecstasy, his fingers rippling rhythmically through strands of Adam's hair. He was shirtless, bare chest rising and falling in panted breaths, pecs coated with thin shafts of light that slipped through the blinds on the windows and illuminated the tattoos inked there.

They were both in their own world of arousal and pleasure, and part of me was in awe, wondering how Les had pulled this off. The other part of me was boiling over. It took a minute, maybe the shift of my shadow against the backs of Les's eyelids alerting him enough to register me. Adam stopped and twisted around to gape at me, his mouth slick and swollen. The same mouth that asked me earlier if I found temptation on the road to be a threat to my relationship. I hadn't answered. I never answered those kinds of questions.

I felt this strange disconnect at seeing him down on his knees in front of my bandmate. Les tilted his head, a dreamy distance in the gaze he fixed on me. "'Sup, Porter?" I didn't know if he was slurring from lust or from alcohol, but it didn't matter. His hand kept on riffling through Adam's hair, lazily affectionate. Almost possessive.

I tried to logically dissect the sensation roiling inside me and twisting around in my gut, sending hot tendrils snaking up my spine and unfurling over my shoulders. It was anger and it wasn't. It was disappointment and it wasn't. It was jealousy and it wasn't. For every thing I thought it might be, it was also the opposite. And only Les was capable of making me feel that kind of paradox.

"We're heading out in fifteen minutes." I backed out of the doorway and shut the door behind me, leaving the wings on the table and not caring whether they got cold or not. Then I slammed out of the bus and headed back into the venue with Mars and the roadies.

Later, when I climbed into my bunk and closed my eyes, I laid the scene out in my mind like a specimen on a slide, trying to examine and pinpoint my feelings exactly. Once, my reaction would have been different, less weighed down by emotion, more amusement that Les could get a seasoned reporter like Adam Slade on his knees. Never mind what it said about the guy's ethics. His morals weren't my business and Les's shouldn't have been, either, but it was different now, and it'd been that way for the entirety of this tour. And as much as I didn't want to admit it, as much as I'd tried to put it out of my head, things had changed after the cabin and I was still struggling to figure it out. And what to do about it.

The memory of Les's expression in that lounge wound sinuously over the backs of my eyelids, that half-lidded, deep green, arousal-heavy stare, the parted lips, plump and lush and wet. Once, I was the cause of it, and that was what was really fucking with me.

What inspires your lyrics, Les?

Les: Everything. My mind's a crowded place. I walk down a street and there's potential everywhere. I don't really know how to explain the mechanics of it. People, places, random shit I see and get kinda hung up on.

Evan: He has frequent run-ins with telephone poles.

Les: That was one time.

Evan: At least twice. Remember Melbourne? And then there was the time I had to yank you back from stumbling in front of a bus in Rome.

Les: Oh yeah. Shit, well, that's what you're there for.

Evan: Loyal guide dog, yes.

Les: We need to get you one of those special guide dog vests so you can start coming inside at restaurants.

CHAPTER 11

SIX MONTHS AGO

There was a heavy current in the air, like the metallic tinge just before a storm, foreshadowing in the way Ella glanced between us after I'd scrambled to pour three shots, and we lifted our glasses and clinked them together. We huddled in a little cluster, and we all tossed back our shots at the same time, all swallowed at the same time, all lowered our glasses at the same time, then shoved them back on the counter and laughed.

A pregnant silence followed, a knowing silence glued together between the three of us by Ella's hand on Evan's forearm and the finger she'd hooked through my belt loop. I wasn't sure what kind of line we were walking, but I was afraid to even speak and accidentally nudge it in the wrong direction.

Luckily, Ella stepped in by leaning to brush a kiss over my mouth, her hand still on Evan's arm. It was brief, but I was shocked as hell to find Evan still standing there when it ended, this intensely focused gaze on me that softened when, in one smooth swivel, Ella's lips were within a hair's breadth of his.

"Please?" she whispered. I could see resistance in the way his hands hung slack at his sides. His shoulders twitched once, like he'd been about to take a step backward and stopped himself. He glanced away from Ella's pretty mouth and back at me again, his eyes hard, almost challenging. Then he put his hand on her cheek and kissed her gently. Tenderly, as if he was making some kind of counter to what Ella had said earlier about liking my brand of roughness.

Ella reached for me, pulling me closer until I was anchored at Evan's side. My hand collided with his as I wrapped her waist. I knew what she wanted, and I definitely knew what I wanted. And I could only assume that since Evan was still there, he was okay with it, too.

Triple kisses were one of those *great in theory* things, but the spatial configuration proved tricky. Ella tipped her head a little when I joined in, making room, and the space between the three of us became a breathless microcosm of tongues and lips lashing out sloppily. There wasn't a lot of finesse to it, and mostly it was hot *because* it was so dirty and disorganized.

I caught a swipe of Evan's tongue, a darker, masculine flavor and heat compared to the light pink dart of Ella's. She shifted her focus between us. One second I was lapping at the sides of their mouths as she kissed Evan, the next my tongue was flicking smoothly over the length of hers and I felt the background scrape of Evan's teeth at the corner of my mouth.

Someone groaned. Me. And I realized I had a hand on each of them and my fingers were sneaking drowsily behind the hem of Evan's T-shirt to spread across his lower back. A handful of minutes passed in this strange tango of lips, and somehow we seemed to get closer together until we were all squashed against each other and I wasn't sure who was touching me where. I thought Evan's hand was near my shoulder and Ella's around my waist. She sucked at Evan's lower lip, and I dropped my mouth to her throat, pulling a moan from her when I nipped at the tight cords of tendons there.

All I was thinking about was how insanely fucking hot this whole situation was and how damn awkward it was going to be if one of us stopped. I didn't want that. I'd have done anything to keep us from getting stuck in an awkward, foot shuffling silence.

I was into Ella, I really was, but the second Evan got involved, it was over for me. I'd been rocking a low-key hard-on for him for months. Maybe even since shortly after we'd formed the band. There was something about him. Some presence that drew me to him that I couldn't explain. I was sure some of it had to do with our music and how on the level and connected we were when writing and performing together, but there was something else less definable there, too, a longing in me that went beyond the songs we composed. I wondered about him all the time, and though I spent weeks and months on end with him, watching him with Ella was like having the curtain ripped back on this side of him he'd kept from me. A side I found very fucking intriguing indeed.

The moment she reached into his pants and stroked him, his eyes went hot with desire. His lips parted on a soft, surprised exhale, and I was a goner. My low-key crush exploded into full-on cosmic-sized lust. I wanted a hit of him the way I wanted my next breath, and even though I already knew that whatever I got tonight wasn't going to be enough by a long shot, I was still bound and determined to get it.

CHAPTER 12

Les

PRESENT DAY

I wasn't even sure how what happened with Adam Slade happened. He did the interview, asked the questions, and sometime around the end, I became aware that he'd been giving me that look, the hungry I-want-you look that I was more used to receiving from fans than reporters. And when I flicked up my eyes and caught him doing it again, he'd jerked his gaze away, swallowing hard. I suppose you could say I instigated it by stretching my arms out over the back of the couch and letting my legs sprawl wide. When he looked back at me again, I tilted my head to the side, watching his expression and reading everything I needed to know in how it shifted. He was on his knees for me less than a minute later.

It wasn't until I closed the door behind him as he tripped down the steps of the bus that I registered the scent of wings and remembered Evan and I were supposed to hang out. Probably the reason he'd been so gruff when he opened the door. Or maybe he was just pissed at the reporter for crossing a line of integrity, but shit, that happened all the time and, if nothing else, I figured I'd just guaranteed us a raving write-up. Evan could thank me later.

Or so I told myself, because I still felt guilty. I poked through the bag of food as the bus started up. The roadies trundled through the door, with Evan bringing up the rear and heading directly for his bunk. I cut up with the crew for a while, then went back to the bunks to see if I could make nice with Evan. But when I peeled back the curtain, he had his back to me, and even a poke only roused him enough to mutter a curt, "Exhausted." Then he fumbled behind him and yanked the curtain back into place.

I gave up and returned to the lounge to stare at my notebook for a while. Nothing came. I felt words distantly, but I couldn't coax them out onto the page. I was braintied. Was that even a thing?

Giving up, I climbed into my bunk, plugging my earbuds in and listening to a playlist Blink made for me. He was good at finding new music he knew I'd like. The bus swayed gently beneath me, a three-ton rocking cradle. I'd gotten used to how the vibration of the pavement below hummed in my bones for hours after we stopped anywhere. Some days I felt more highway than human. More parts moving with purpose than skin and bone. I had trouble slowing down. I had trouble just being still. Maybe it had something to do with moving around a lot growing up, the wandering and very fluid nature of my parents' relationship and being their sole offspring. I'd always been aware of everything. And I'd always felt this freeform sense of... loneliness, I guess. A sense of not being fully grounded, and yet anytime in the past when a lover tried to tie me down, I'd be the first to flee.

I hadn't had a girlfriend or boyfriend in years. Not since I'd started on this crazy journey with Evan. In a fucked-up kind of way, he was my primary partner, even if we weren't in a sexual relationship. I had no idea whether or not he felt the same. But it was powerful in a way I'd never experienced with anyone else; the times when we were onstage and I looked over at Evan only to find him already looking back at me, how we navigated intuitively around each other, how I knew the song he wanted to play just by watching how his fingers stretched toward his strings. I wanted to touch him constantly, touch him like I had that night with Ella. My fingers permanently ached with the need, and they ached then as I lay there, knowing he was three feet across the aisle from me, his stocky body folded up in the bunk, and still somehow a world apart. But he'd made it clear that that would never ever happen again. He didn't want it.

WHEN I WOKE UP THE NEXT MORNING, WE WERE IN INDIANAPOLIS, parked on a side street near the venue—some old theater that'd recently been revamped. Jimmy lay sprawled on the couch, catching a nap, and I dug through the minifridge, contemplating leftover wings for breakfast when the door swung wide and Mars poked his head in.

"Pancakes?"

"Fuck yes." I tossed a T-shirt over my shoulder and clattered down the narrow staircase. Just outside, Evan was bent over stretching his hamstrings. He was drenched in sweat, an empty water bottle tucked in his waistband and another one in his hand. His running shorts were plastered to his ass, and he looked like a *Men's Health* magazine come to life. He emptied the rest of his water bottle, then set it down to peel off his shirt and wring it out while I tried not to stare.

"Your healthy habits are an insult to musicians everywhere," I told him.

He sent a dismissive gaze over me, and I tugged at the hem of my T-shirt self-consciously. He was literally the only person in the world who could make me self-conscious, and I fucking hated it with a passion. "You should try a few sometime."

"Nah. I'm good. I'm now a lifetime member of Fitness Underachievers Anonymous. About to go make some more shitty food choices so I can level up. My stomach's screaming for pancakes and bacon with a side of aspartame."

"Are you sure that scream isn't an SOS for something green?" His brow ticked up as he swiped a bead of sweat from his forehead with the corner of his shirt.

"Pretty sure it's a mercy plea for excess sodium, yep." I hesitated, trying to read his expression, but he had his hand shading his eyes from the sun, and all I could see were planes of shadow on his sharp features. "Sorry about last night, by the way. I forgot."

"I noticed." He dropped his hand to his side, pulling his lips in, like he was debating saying something else, then shook his head. "It's fine."

"Yeah?"

"Yeah."

"You coming for pancakes?"

"Shower first, then I'll be over." He mopped his shirt across his bare chest, and I gave myself an allowance of a measly two seconds to admire the hard lines of his torso coated in a healthy sheen of perspiration—which wasn't enough. His body deserved at least a handful of minutes. Preferably a whole night. Then I forced my gaze away and headed down the street to the IHOP.

We took up three booths in the restaurant. I packed in next to Blink and Reg, a ball cap pulled low over my eyes. The other patrons didn't recognize me, but I could tell by the gaggle of servers clustered around the hostess stand darting looks back and forth at us that they did. Mars, sitting across from me and next to Terry, speared a pancake and ate the entire thing in two bites. I was two deep into a stack of four and already getting full.

Blink relayed a story about some dimwit sound guy at the last venue, then turned a scathing eye on Mars, who was licking syrup from his fingertips. "You need a trough."

"I'd eat from a trough. No problem. Would save me the trouble of forks and knives," Mars said, like silverware was a huge inconvenience. I snickered and passed over the rest of my pancakes to him and then turned a look aside as Blink muttered a "whoa" under his breath.

When I glanced up to find the source that earned such a reverent sound, Evan was walking toward us. Evan was... Evan could come across as really intimidating unless he was smiling, because he was hard all over. Not just his body, but all of the angles of him, too. Super structured cheekbones, a steel-edged jaw, insanely attractive in that kind of fierce, untouchable, reserved way that made you want to get inside him and figure out what made him tick. He was lines and edges and definition, not a soft spot on him, except maybe his lips, and now was definitely not the time to be thinking about those. He had a fierce resting bitch face, which was why Blink was muttering. I didn't even know it was possible, but Evan's RBC had achieved new heights. His brows were tightly knit, and Oscar the Grouch had nothing on the scowl he sported as he stalked toward us.

"Did someone replace his hair gel with lube or what?" I asked, half-serious. Mars laughed and shook his head, but we all got quiet as Evan reached the table. He dropped onto the bench across from me, next to Mars without a peep, then picked up the menu and glared at it before he looked up and actually snapped his fucking fingers for attention. When the waiter ran over, he barked out a terse order, then slumped down on the bench. He did all of this as we watched in silence because his behavior was so unusual that none of us were sure how to approach it. Evan got mad on occasion, sure, but it was always this kind of inwardly directed thing. He could be complaining to a sound guy, but the second the guy's face fell, he'd go soft and backtrack.

Mars and Blink both stared at me, which meant I'd been silently elected to figure out what the fuck was wrong with him. That was a bad idea.

"Your G-string sitting too deep in your crack or what, Porter?" And that was why it was a bad idea. When I got nervous or flustered, I inevitably resorted to what was probably the worst thing to say. And people always ended up even angrier. Always.

Evan didn't bat a lash at first, didn't even look at me. Then he blinked slowly and leveled a gaze on me that could've frosted the Devil's ass cheeks. "Sorry, not sure I heard you right. Thought I'd check and see if you had a cock crammed down your throat. Looks like you don't, though—at least not right now—so I guess that means you were just spewing your usual meaningless horseshit."

Every jaw at the table dropped because Evan and I antagonized each other back and forth, but even when it was bitchy, it was never overtly aggressive the way it was now.

"Uhh... I'm gonna go check the equipment," Blink said, and bailed, sliding from the booth so fast the plastic seat squeaked. Mars followed with an excuse so lame I didn't even register it. The other guys trickled after them, trying to act natural, but very evidently wanting to leave us alone.

The waiter delivered Evan's order, and he plowed into it in surly silence. I kicked my feet up onto the bench across from me, leaving Evan plenty of room, and folded my arms over my chest as I watched him. He kept eating as if I wasn't there.

"I can't tell if you're waiting for me to ask what the fuck is wrong with you or if you're just hoping I'll ignore it."

"The last one," he said around a mouthful of hash browns.

"Well. You're kinda making that impossible. You're putting out a vibe that's got people running like an elevator fart."

"So get off the elevator and let me finish eating in peace. Funny you should mention elevators by the way."

He was still focused solely on the wobbling yellow cluster of scrambled eggs that he jabbed at and poked into his mouth.

"This about last night, still?"

He gave me a sharp glare, one he probably hoped would morph into acid and melt the skin from my face. Then he straightened, swiping the back of his hand over his mouth, and damn, I swear it felt like he could see straight through to the part of me that ached with how much I wanted him, even right then when he was being an obstinate, insulting ass. I liked dick, but I didn't typically enjoy a guy acting like one, so I was annoyed that the intensity of his expression sent a flinch of heat rocketing through my groin even as I wanted to shrivel away from it.

"Why is it impossible for you to go a night without someone on your cock?"

"I've gone strings of days without screwing someone. I told you I was sorry. I tried to hang out with you after. You wanted nothing to do with me." I shrugged.

He rubbed the knuckle of his thumb between his brows, then closed his eyes and exhaled a long sigh.

"Leigh broke up with me."

"Blameshifting much?"

He grunted something that sounded like *maybe*, but I didn't respond immediately because I was chewing over this news. Even though they'd been together a while, Evan never really seemed all that into Leigh. I mean, he seemed like he liked her well enough, but not to the degree that her breaking up with him should turn him into the troll he was currently. I'd never heard him talk about a future with her. I added, "I'm sorry, though. That sucks. I guess?" I honestly couldn't tell if he was angry at me, Leigh, or both of us.

"Fuck." Evan blew out a harsh breath, raking a hand through his hair until it stuck out at odd angles in an annoyingly sexy tousle of blond. His shoulders curled inward a little as he pushed his plate away and started unfolding bills from his pocket, counting out a dozen twenties—much more than was needed—and laying them under the check the waiter had dropped off minutes before so stealthily Evan didn't notice him. Which had probably been the point. I didn't blame the guy. "You remember the first time we went to the cabin?"

I tipped my chin in a short nod when he glanced up for confirmation.

"It was just about making music. About making something good. No label on our backs, no personas to live up to, or unspoken quotas to meet. The crazy thing is, though, I knew that all of this was what I wanted. The success, the money. Like, I was actively working toward that, and now it's here and I'm stuck on this hamster wheel of wanting it to be the way it was, but wanting the financial stability, too. And I can't have it both ways. I get that. They're interconnected." He wet his lips and stared at me, and behind the brightness of blue was the shadow of an ache I recognized. Loneliness. Exhaustion. "But it gets to me sometimes. All this shit around us is so meaningless and empty. The photo shoots and interviews, all the free shit we're given just because of our name. It's not real. And I feel like an ass complaining about it. It's not really a complaint even, but I need... I need something to ground me. *Someone* to ground me. I thought someone removed from all this bullshit would make me feel that way. And it worked, kinda. When I was with Leigh, I was still just me. She knew the me before the person I am now. Being with her was like being home again."

A melancholy note plinked in my chest and harmonized with jealousy. So he *was* really upset about Leigh. "Why'd she break up with you?"

"She said there wasn't a spark. We were more friends than anything. And she's right. " He put his forehead to his palm and shook his head from side to side, seeming dejected as he continued. "The last time she was here, the sex was just... mechanical. We might as well have laid next to each other and masturbated. I screwed it up."

I tried to focus on what Evan was saying and stop imagining him lying on a hotel bed jerking off. He'd rarely ever even used the word sex and himself in the same sentence, but boy it was having an effect on me. Shit, he was right. I couldn't go two seconds without my mind free-falling into the gutter. I sucked in a breath and attempted to muster up a more convincing expression of sympathy. He was hurting, and I didn't want him to hurt, after all.

"I'll hang out tonight, dude, I promise. You, me, wings, and some Call of Duty. Mars got the new one. I saw it last night."

BUT WE DIDN'T DO ANY OF THOSE THINGS. BECAUSE AFTER WE GOT offstage that night—our last show on the tour—he out-of-the-damn-blue hopped a red eye and flew back to Nashville by himself.

Nashville Times

May 2017

Black Dove **hasn't done as well as your previous two albums.**
Les: It's a flop, you can say it. It's the truth.

Anything you'd attribute that to? Any changes in how you guys approached the writing and recording.
Les: I think it's just one of those things that—
Evan: No. Next question.

CHAPTER 13

Evan

I was the first to arrive in Gatlinburg, which came as absolutely no surprise. I'd texted Les earlier that morning and had gotten no response. I'd heard from him once in the four days we'd been off, which was probably fair turnabout since I'd jetted without warning after our last show. I knew he thought it was either his fault or because I was upset about Leigh, and it was a little of both, but not in the ways he'd probably thought it was.

As I pulled onto the downtown strip to pick up the keys to the cabin, my phone buzzed with a message from our manager, Byron, saying Les was on a flight from Vegas and Blink would drop him off at the cabin that afternoon. I wondered how much money he'd lost, how much alcohol he'd funneled into his system, how many people he'd fucked. Les never did anything half-assed, and to be honest, I was a little surprised to hear he'd actually made it onto his flight in the first place.

Evan: *What kind of state is he in? Do you know?*

Byron: *You should probably pick up some Pedialyte.*

So my next stop after picking up the keys was a Walgreens, where I roamed the aisles until I found the Pedialyte. I stood in front of the colorful display next to diapers and baby food, debating the different flavors and which one he might like until I stopped, wondering what the fuck I was even doing. I left without buying anything because maybe he could do with a little suffering. I was tired of cleaning up his messes, tired of picking him up, dragging him out of hotels, being responsible for him. All the peace I'd found over the past few days being back in Nashville in my own place, with my own sheets and plenty of room to roam around, started to disintegrate and my stomach knotted up all over again.

It eased up once I arrived at the cabin, got out of the rental car, and stood in the gravel drive, looking at the little placard hanging next to the door that read "Tune Out." Memories poked holes in my foul mood like sunlight through clouds: the first time we came here, our gear jammed in my beat-up SUV, Les wedged in the front seat. The cabin was set into a downward slope, its rustic face framed in logs, a couple of tidy flower boxes beneath the windows crowded with a few plants I recognized as geraniums. It was homey and inviting and looked like it would smell clean and lemony inside.

"So quaint," Les had said, unfolding from the car and stretching his long legs. His T-shirt had risen up over his stomach, revealing the tattoos that banded his torso. *"You think it has a heart-shaped tub?"* He'd waggled his brows at me playfully.

"If it does, you're free to start a lonely-hearts club in it." I'd smirked at him, and he cracked up. We used to do that more. Banter back and forth like we did onstage minus the bitter edge that seemed inherent in our conversations nowadays.

A dull pang rattled around my chest, and I took a deep breath, then went to the back of the car and started hauling my gear inside.

The inside of the cabin smelled as it had the last three times we'd come, and like I'd predicted it would that first time. Clean and lemony, faintly of bleach and pine. It reminded me of growing up, and though this cabin was pretty small, my childhood homes — because there'd been a few — had been even smaller. Still, there was something comforting and cozy about it. Peaceful, and I was glad the wildfires that had devastated the area a while back had spared it.

Two bedrooms and a bathroom off the short hallway opened into the living room kitchen combo. Down a steep flight of stairs, a basement opened onto the wooded slope outside. The music room was down there, too, so I dropped my guitars there first, then jogged back upstairs and claimed the same bedroom I always claimed, with a view of the forest— currently a thick canopy of green. There was a TV with local channels we rarely used, and Wi-Fi, so I set up my laptop in the kitchen and checked our numbers. Still unimpressive. Byron sent me the SoundScans to look at every few days at my request, even though he'd promised me time and time again he was keeping a close eye on it. It drove Les crazy that I fixated on them.

When I turned to grab a bottle of water from the fridge, Les's voice coiled and curled seductively around my ear so acutely I almost looked over my shoulder to see if he was there. *Make him feel good, sweetheart.* The echo of his words that night rolled through me, and my heart hammered in my chest, blood rushing to my cock so fast I should've been light-headed. I gripped the edge of the counter, but that was no good either because I immediately thought of how my nails dug into the underside the last time we were here.

Fuck, maybe this had been a bad idea.

It was a quarter past nine when Blink hammered on the front door and the two of them stumbled inside. I looked up from where I was flipping through an old copy of *Rolling Stone* on the couch at Les dragging his suitcase behind him. Blink saluted me, then turned and hurried back out.

My gaze lingered on Les, assessing him, and he knew it. A stare down ensued. I took in the four-day scruff along his jaw, the circles under his eyes, and the dry crack in one corner of his mouth. Les was universally attractive in a way that a human of any orientation would agree. He had an enigmatic allure, like he carried around his own atmosphere with him, and the closer you got, the more he'd absorb you into his world. I'd been trying to pinpoint it for years—whether it was the deep set of his eyes, the thick black lashes over muddy green, the dark brows and carved cheekbones over a sensuous mouth—which more than a few magazines had rhapsodized over. He was both masculine and feminine at once.

But I'd only seen him look like ransacked garbage on one occasion, when we'd both gotten hit with food poisoning in Germany.

This was the second time.

It wasn't just that he physically appeared hungover or strung out or exhausted. It was something else, something less tangible, like a soul-deep tiredness that dimmed his eyes as they flickered over me blankly. He looked like he was tired of his own skin. Or maybe I was just projecting my own irritation at feeling like his constant custodian. My desire to find some common ground with him again butted up against extreme annoyance. He'd clearly partied hard in Vegas.

"It's good to see you," he said. The greeting surprised me so much I didn't know how to respond back. I was expecting animosity, or snark, but he sounded like he meant it.

One side of his mouth twitched up in a tentative smile, then he pulled a small black plastic bag from his pocket and tossed it toward me. "I'm gonna go crash."

I caught the bag, lifting a brow in a silent question that he didn't answer as he snatched the handle of his suitcase up again and tugged it down the hall after him. The door to his bedroom clicked shut behind him.

Blink returned, bobbling a couple of guitar cases and bags, which he set beside the door. Then he stood there, looking around and rubbing his hands together briskly as he gave me a tight smile and seemed uncertain of what to say.

"How was Vegas?"

He seemed surprised by the question and shrugged, wandering deeper inside the cabin to drop heavily into the chair across from me.

"It was Vegas, I guess. You know, a place where nothing changes yet is constantly changing."

I'd never understood the draw. Vegas was just noise to me. Noise and overexposure on every front. "That's why he likes it."

Blink considered, running a finger over his upper lip. "I don't know if it goes that deep for him. I think it's more like an exciting distraction. Shinies everywhere." He wiggled his fingers, and I cracked a small smile. He was right about that, too. There was a lot about Les that was almost fae; he loved everything bright and scintillating.

"Looks like y'all had a good time."

Blink's mouth screwed up in a wince. "We went hard, yeah." He paused, and I could tell he was debating saying more or just leaving it alone. "He's stressed. He knows he's on the line, Ev."

"We both are," I said impassively.

"Yeah, but you do well under pressure. Les just sort of... collapses."

I flipped the magazine shut and tossed it aside where it skittered over the couch cushions and landed on the floor. "Then it's time for him to figure his shit out. I'm tired of doing it for him."

"Not gonna lie, even I'm having a hard time keeping up with him, lately." His hands were fidgeting all over the place, with threads on his shorts, the hem of his shirt. Part of that was just Blink; he was full of energy, always restless, but I felt like I was making him nervous somehow. I guess I could understand. He didn't want to be caught in the middle.

"It's not your job to keep up with him," I pointed out. "It's not anyone's job."

He narrowed his eyes slightly. "I'm his friend, too, and hey, it used to be fun."

"Things change." I shrugged. "He get into too much trouble out there?" It was Les, so I didn't really need to ask. He'd ride the Whore of Babylon, then ask who was next.

Blink rolled one shoulder, looking back over to the door, probably itching to leave. "Nah. Nothing out of the ordinary." By which I deduced plenty of drinking and plenty of sex. I got an unwelcome sinking feeling in the pit of my stomach.

"Actually, for him it was pretty tame. Anyway—" Blink stood. "Guess I'll head out."

"You can crash if you want. Take the couch. I'm fixin' to go to bed."

"Nah." He waved off the offer as he started for the door. "I'm picking up a few gigs in Nashville, so I need to get back."

"You sure you're good for the road?" I had no idea how long he'd been up, but it was entirely possible he'd only slept a few hours over the past few days.

"Oh yeah. I pounded a couple of Red Bulls." He cut me a confident grin and opened the door as I trailed along after him.

"That shit'll kill you eventually."

"Everything will. At least I'll be awake."

We exchanged a loose, mostly insincere hug, and I lingered in the doorway as he walked out to the rental car.

"Take it easy, write some hits, all the good shit," he called over his shoulder. He stopped after he opened the car door, glancing up at me like he had something else to add. I suspected it would be about Les, so I was glad when he changed his mind with a quick shake of his head and ducked into the car.

Back inside the cabin, I picked the magazine up from the floor and threw it on the coffee table among its other out-of-date brethren. The black plastic bag Les had tossed me was still on the couch, tempting me. I snatched it up and turned it over to find a small plastic case with a clear top and a sticker that read "Lundgren Hand Made." Six wooden picks of varying thicknesses and wood types were slotted into a gray foam bed. Popping the case open, I ran my thumb over the smooth edges. I'd been interested in playing around with wood picks for a while because of their reputed warm tones, but I'd never gotten around to actually getting any. These were exquisite, probably not cheap, and I examined each of them individually before selecting one indicated as being made of rosewood. I grabbed one of Les's guitar cases from by the door, too lazy to go down to the basement, and set up on the couch, running quietly through some scales, getting a feel for the way wood changed the level of attack on the strings.

It was a thoughtful gift. Les was good with stuff like that. So often he seemed absorbed in his own world, and then *bam*, out of nowhere he'd say or do something that let you know he'd been paying attention to everything all along.

It also seemed like an apology in a way, but maybe I was reading too much into it. Regardless, it kept him on my mind, and twice that night I almost walked into his room. But I didn't know what I wanted to say, besides *thanks*, and he needed the sleep anyway, so I abandoned the idea and went to bed.

CHAPTER 14

Evan

L evi started blowing up my phone at eight the next morning.

"You hooked up to Wifi yet?" he asked right off the bat when I answered. I was puttering around the kitchen, dumping coffee grounds into a filter, but the urgency in his voice gave me pause.

"Yep. Need me to look at something?"

"That'd be good. Go over to TMZ. Les around?"

"Sleeping it off. What do you think?" I hit the button on the machine to start the coffee and poked through the fridge before closing it, empty-handed.

"Get him, take a look, and call me back."

"You're making me nervous," I said, already on my way to the kitchen table where I reached into my messenger bag to pull out my laptop.

"It's not a huge ordeal really, but I know how you are about privacy."

I figured the news about my breakup with Leigh had finally gotten out, though why that would be newsworthy, I had no idea. I'd done such a good job of keeping my shit locked down that my love life was rarely mentioned these days, and it wasn't like Leigh was some high-profile celeb, anyway. I got my laptop fired up, then navigated over to TMZ.

I recognized her instantly, even at thumbnail size. *Ella*. I couldn't think of her name without a hundred images flashing on the backs of my eyelids. My hand in her hair, Ella on her knees, the dart of her tongue along Les's cock.

My eyes glommed onto the headline next, a sour mash of feeling erupting in my gut. "Porter & Graves Share More Than Music; Gatlinburg native spills all the details of her steamy tryst with the dynamic duo."

The next photo was grainy, as if she'd zoomed in from a distance on her phone while standing in the doorway of Les's bedroom in the cabin, but it was unmistakably me and Les in that bed. Unmistakably Les's dark hair slicing at an angle over his cheekbone, unmistakably the small tattoo on my bicep visible where my arm wrapped around a pillow, and unmistakably Les's arm draped low over my back. I didn't remember that. At all. Granted, we'd been sleeping, and with Ella between us, but when I'd woken up, Les and I had migrated to opposite sides of the bed.

"I think they're secretly together" was called out in a big block quote and given plenty of real estate next to the blown up shot of us in bed. My heart thudded in my chest as I read in mute, horrified silence. A lot of cruel words for Ella ran through my head before I got ahold of myself, tried to remind myself that she wasn't at fault and technically hadn't done anything wrong besides selling us out. But I couldn't quell the sense of panic at having my privacy violated like that. I might have lived in the spotlight, but there was a part of me that would always resist my personal life being dragged out as fodder for gossip sites. After my last breakup, rumors had circled for weeks that I'd cheated on the girl with the singer for Flow. And that wasn't the case. So, I was careful to make my love life seem as boring and ordinary as possible, and now that appeared to have backfired in the worst possible way and made them eager to pick up this story. I wondered how much they'd paid Ella. And I wondered why the hell she'd done it in the first place. She hadn't seemed the type.

Without Ella to be mad at, that left Les, who was currently still in his self-induced coma coming down off his probable booze and sex orgy in Vegas—which only pissed me off more. I yanked the laptop from its power cord, then carried it with me down the hall to Les's room and kicked the door wide.

The blackout curtains were drawn tight, and he stirred briefly with a groan when I entered, fumbled for a pillow, and pulled it over his head.

I flicked the overhead light on, crossed the room to drag the curtains back, then stalked toward the bed. Once at the edge, I reached down and tore the covers from him with more force than was needed. He shriveled back into the mattress like an unearthed bug, goose bumps erupting over his bare skin.

"What the fuck, Porter?" His grousing was muffled by the pillow that I promptly yanked from his face before opening the laptop on the mattress in front of him.

"This. Open your fucking eyes and look."

Les made an exasperated noise but finally rolled over in my direction to squint at the screen. His eyes were bleary and shot with thin red threads. He needed more sleep, and he probably could have used about two gallons of water.

He rubbed a hand along his forehead, pinching the skin between his brows, then blinked at the photograph. "Shit. When did she take that?"

"Obviously while we were sleeping."

Shockingly, Les grinned then. "We look very cozy."

I stared at him, slack-jawed and uncomprehending of his complete lack of alarm. "You need to read it."

"I am." He reached out, lazily swiping the touchpad to scroll down, and flopped on his back as he pulled the laptop onto his bare chest to read the article. I continued to stare, feeling the heat behind my gaze magnified as I waited for the proper reaction, which was definitely not casual perusal.

"So?" He wet his lips and glanced over to the nightstand next to me, before ticking his chin to indicate the bottle of water sitting there. Unbelievable. I ignored him, my eyes widening with incredulity.

"So? So it's not true. The blind items are annoying enough, but this is a straight-up lie. She's saying that we're a fucking couple."

"Technically it's not a lie, it's supposition. She's relating her experience as it happened and which, as far as I can read, is a perfect recounting, except she's got it mixed up a little. I was the one—" He paused to check the screen before quoting, "—giving her 'the greatest head of her life.' Not you. Maybe I should call and ask them to correct that part. I deserve credit for that." He huffed and leaned around me, grabbing the bottled water, then twisting the cap off and guzzling half of it.

My fists tightened at my sides, and I felt close to punching him. It wasn't the first time. It was just like Les to blow this off. Something in my expression must have tipped him off to the hellfire blazing through me, because he sobered, capping the water, then rolling onto his side and pushing away the laptop. His gaze bored into me, patient if exhausted.

"Porter, this isn't that big of a deal. Really. We just don't do anything and it'll die down. Anyone who knows us knows it isn't true, trust me. And the fans... they know what a slut I am. They'll never believe I'm in a relationship." He let out a chuckle as if the mere concept was ridiculous.

"It's not even about that. Bullshit like this overshadows the music. It's why I don't snort lines of coke off a girl's tits or fuck a groupie with a mud shark, because I'm not in it for that. I'm in it to make good fucking music. Music that matters, not to be some flash-in-the-pan band more remembered for the stupid shit they do offstage than what they actually play."

"Led Zeppelin is hardly flash-in-the-pan. And their music is legendary." Les pushed up on his elbow, grinding the heel of his hand against one eye before raking dark strands of hair from his forehead and scrutinizing me. "I think you're overreacting."

"It's calling attention to us for all the wrong reasons."

"But it *is* calling attention to us. All publicity is good publicity and all that bullshit. And this isn't even bad publicity. She says a lot of nice things about you, too."

I gave up, dropping heavily to the edge of the bed and staring at the far wall, my heart racing as I tried to figure out what kind of impact this story might have on our fans and beyond that, our sales. It was clear Les and I weren't going to see eye to eye on this, so the best I could do was hope it blew over quickly.

Les reached around me again for his phone on the bedside table. When he thumbed the screen to life, he grimaced. "God, I'm getting blown up. There's, like, fifty unread messages here."

"See?" I folded my arms over my chest, vindicated.

He grunted and began scrolling through the messages, which reminded me I was supposed to call Levi back.

"Levi wants to talk." I told him and sprawled on my back in the bed as I pulled up Levi's contact info and hit Send. Les adjusted his legs to make more room for me while his fingers flew over his phone's keypad.

"You've both seen it?" Levi answered. "Les with you?"

"Yes and yes. Can you fucking call them and tell them to take the article down or something?"

Levi laughed. "You know as well as I do they're not going to do that. And besides, it's already gone viral. Is it true?"

I actually pulled the phone away from my ear and stared at it in disbelief for a second before replying, "Are you fucking kidding me? No, it's not true. I mean the threesome happened, but Les and I aren't together for fuck's sake."

Les shot me a dark glare. "Watch it, asshole. It's not like I'm the Antichrist."

"That's not a slight aimed at you. Jesus." Between the two of them, I was on the verge of losing it. This trip was supposed to be about composing a brilliant album, something good enough to pull us out of the slump from our last one. Now I was fielding questions about a relationship that didn't exist and trying not to mortally insult my hungover bandmate.

"Whatever, it doesn't matter," Levi continued on quickly. He sounded almost... excited? "But can you make it *look* true?"

"What? What the hell are you even talking about?" My blood pressure shot up quicker than mercury in July. I considered just hanging up, but Les leaned to pry the phone from my hand and put it on speaker as Levi continued: "...It's not that hard, just play into it."

Do you have a spirit animal?

Evan: What's a spirit animal? Like a mascot or something?

Les: Porter's spirit animal is Gollum. That's all you need to know.

CHAPTER 15

"N o." The single word grated out of Evan's mouth like it'd been wrenched with force from the infinitesimal spaces between his clenched teeth.

Silence followed. Painful, thick silence. If Evan's anger was animated, it'd be something like a gryphon, a wide-jawed beast ready to swoop from its perch and attack me. A vein bulged threateningly in his forehead, and I was becoming seriously concerned for his health. If he stroked out, the nearest hospital was miles and miles away. "It's bullshit for one, and it takes away from the music."

More silence, and on the other end of the line, I imagined Levi was recalibrating, trying to figure out how to attack from a different angle.

After another beat, Levi spoke again. "Do you have your laptop nearby?"

"Yes," I chimed in, sitting up in the bed. My head felt like a dam about to crack, but I pulled the computer back to me since Evan didn't look like he was moving unless it was to reach through the phone and punch our publicist. And maybe me.

"Good, go log in to the back end of your website."

I did as he asked, though Evan had to remind me of the password, which he grumbled, still seething. My hands trembled a little as I typed, something that didn't go unnoticed by Evan. His gaze flickered up to me, not exactly condescending, but enough resignation in it that I felt about a foot tall. I needed hydration and food desperately. Vegas had sucked me dry. Or maybe it was the other way around. I probably looked like death.

"Look at your downloads and the hits."

I wasn't as savvy at web stuff and tracking as Evan was, but I found the graphs and went slack-jawed, turning the screen so Evan could see it. The frown stuck on his face like it'd been cemented there lessened by a couple of degrees as he looked over the data.

"I'm going to assume by the silence that you're seeing the numbers like I am," Levi said. "Guess what? It's happening everywhere. On Spotify and iTunes, too. Everywhere."

The download hits started spiking a half hour after the time stamp on the TMZ article and were steadily rising. It was similar to what happened on release days for us. In between albums, the hits would dwindle down and slow but shoot up again whenever we did an interview, posted a live show, or got picked up by the tabloids or something. But it was never anything like this.

I glanced over at Evan, trying to gauge his expression. Was he even a little impressed? It didn't look like it. He bit the corner of his thumbnail and shook his head, looking like he wanted nothing more than to set the room on fire. I'd heard human combustion was possible but had always been a skeptic. Now I thought there might be something to it.

"It's just a blip. It'll pass and then come back again the next time we do an interview."

"That's the thing, Evan," Levi said. "I'm looking at the spikes from all publicity over the last year and they're declining."

"But that's also not unusual. Our fan base is still solid."

"For now," he agreed, although there was an ominous tinge to his voice. Then again, he was a publicist; exposure was his life.

"And once we put out the next album—"

"There's no guarantee. If it's like the last album, those numbers are going to drop further. And with it, possibly MGD's interest in supporting you guys."

Evan cocked his head. "That... is that a fucking threat?"

Levi exhaled a sigh. "No, it's not a threat, it's reality. I work for you, remember. So I'm telling it to you straight. Your numbers are going down. Your interviews are spacing further and further apart because there's nothing to talk about. The last album is a dead horse, and no one's even interested in picking up the stick anymore. You two have been profiled out the fucking wazoo, and there's nothing else to say right now. But this? This is something to talk about. You're not denying it happened, which means it's not an outright lie, even if the part about the two of you being together is. But the response overall has been amazing in terms of sales. And overwhelmingly positive on other fronts, too. Look at your fan group on Facebook. Most of the response I've seen so far leads me to believe a majority *love* the idea that you're together."

While he paused for a breath, I opened a new tab on the browser bar and clicked onto our Facebook fan page, blinking at the buzz of activity happening there. Someone had posted the story into the group and people were going crazy. Levi was right: most of it was positive. Lots of excited squeeing and heart emojis. There were a few naysayers, though.

"Look," Levi started up again, "I'm not saying you have to go live and *talk* about it. I'm suggesting you just coast on it. Do nothing to discourage the rumors, maybe a few things to support it for a while. It's not forever."

Evan didn't look at all convinced. He looked, if anything, dejected. Dejected and pissed off. The overarching theme was definitely still pissed off. He drummed his fingers in a silent, desperate tempo over the tops of his thighs, restless with energy and anxiety the way he sometimes got before a show when he was all twisted up in his head and just waiting for the outlet of his guitar and microphone to unleash into.

"We're not the Kardashians," he snapped.

"You're right. They'd milk this shit all the way to the bank and premiere their next show to even higher ratings," I pointed out.

Levi wisely stayed silent.

Evan pushed off the bed, sweeping the laptop up with him. "It's a fucking farce, and my answer is still no." He stormed from the room, leaving me holding his phone.

"You still there, Les?"

"Yeah." I mashed the button and took it off speaker, then flopped back onto the bed and tugged at the ends of my greasy hair. God, I needed a shower and caffeine at minimum. I'd have killed for one of Blink's upper cocktails right about then.

"Good. You're going to have to be the sensible one here."

I chuckled, and it was a little bitter because I found his comment slightly insulting. I might fuck around some. Okay, a lot, but I'd put as much heart and soul into this band as Evan had. My methods were just different.

"The label is on board with this."

I was on alert in an instant. "Did they say that?"

"It was implied."

"Of course." I rolled my eyes.

"I didn't want to tell Evan because he seems to have taken that last album more personally than you, but you guys are on thinner ice than you might think, and a sales boost is going to go a long way to keeping doors open once you guys have met the terms of the original contract."

"Yeah, if I tell Evan that right now, he'll probably threaten to bail—"

"And I don't need to remind you that you guys are under contract for another album. You can reassess after this next one, but it's going to be a much smoother path, whichever way you choose to go, if it ends on an amicable note."

Okay, so it wasn't a threat, but a strongly worded reminder that the industry still had major pull with the media that helped send us soaring. I knew more than a couple of musicians who'd burned bridges and flamed out into nothing. I didn't want that. And I knew Evan didn't, either.

"I'm down with the idea, okay? And I think I can get Evan on board if you give me a little time." A tranquilizer dart might've helped, too.

"Days or hours?"

"Hours. Maybe a day. Jesus, is it that critical?"

"Rina's working on a press release right now. Timing, you know. It's everything. We're not going to confirm or deny anything, just fuel speculation with a general 'no comment' statement."

I took a deep breath and tried to squash the fluttering in my stomach. Suddenly this felt much bigger than it had initially. Music itself was manipulation. It was playing with resonance, tapping into brain waves and the primacy of a heartbeat to provoke feeling. I didn't write my songs and sing them in a vacuum. I did it for the love of expression, because I wanted to share. I got high off knowing that we had a good fan base, one that seemed to believe in and trust in our music and our ability to create songs that moved them. So, I agreed with Evan that it shouldn't matter who we were with, but people wanted narratives and stories, too. I got that. It added depth to the musical experience. And really, was faking a relationship with Evan even pure manipulation if, deep down, it was something I'd dreamed of? Because regardless of what else was true, I one hundred percent wanted Evan, and one hundred percent would be with him in a heartbeat. Music was the only thing tying Evan to me. If the music disappeared, so would Evan. And I couldn't let that happen.

The enormity of what I was about to try and convince Evan to do washed over me and made me dizzy. I closed my eyes and sucked in a breath.

"I'll keep you posted," I told Levi.

"Do that." I was about to end the call when he started up again. "You know what was funny, though? Her timing. Why'd she wait so long?"

"Who fucking knows?" I ended the call, then dragged myself out of bed and headed for the shower so at least I wouldn't smell like a back alley after last call while trying to convince my angry bandmate he should fake a relationship with me.

CHAPTER 16

Evan

I needed something to do with my hands so I wouldn't throttle Les, so after I rushed out of his room, I went straight to the basement. It was my favorite place in the cabin for obvious musical reasons, but there was a cozy comfort to it, too, a cocoon from the outside world. The couple we rented the place from used to be in the business. They were retired and closing in on their late seventies now. We'd met them once, the first time I set up the rental. She was a writer and singer, he a producer, and they called this cabin their love shack. What studio equipment they had was woefully out of date, but both Les and I liked an organic process anyway. It satisfied our basic needs, and that was just fine. We brought our own guitars, obviously, but there was an old drum kit in one corner and a slew of other random instruments, including a glockenspiel, of all things. There was the cowbell Les had tormented me with last time until I'd threatened to secure it to his throat with a zip tie and choke him with it. The foam on the walls was deteriorating, and we always found bits of it on the floor. In another corner was a turntable that was probably the height of chic in the eighties and next to it, six stacked plastic crates of records.

I sat on one of the stools and fiddled around with my guitar for a while, but the strings weren't gliding under my fingers like they usually did. They were biting. All the notes came out cluttered with noise and my frustration, so after a couple of minutes, I gave up.

I opened the laptop back up and read the article again, though I didn't need to. Ella's account was pretty accurate, and my mind filled in the discrepancies, visuals running through me like a movie at high speed. One I'd stuffed into the corner and vowed not to look at ever again the day after it had happened.

"They had this really intense connection. The same I've seen in the YouTube clips of their live shows, but different, more intimate. It was really strange. Not bad strange. Beautiful. It was all very natural and fluid, and to be honest, there were times when I felt like the third wheel, but it was so hot while it was happening. Les is very loose and fun, joking around, laughing a lot. Evan was more reserved, but he was into it. I mean, at least I think he was. And God, the way he looked at Les—"

I stopped right there. What the hell did that mean—the way I'd looked at Les? I reeled back my memory but found nothing too strange there. I'd been watching what was happening, sure, but who wouldn't if they'd been in the middle of it? It'd been a surreal experience in the first place. It wasn't like there was some protocol of where I should be looking at which moment for me to follow.

When Les came in, I was standing in front of the stacks of records, my back to him as I flipped through the old cardboard sleeves. I'd been through them so many times I could probably name half the albums and artists by heart. All the greats were represented, from Ella Fitzgerald to the Eagles, and a bunch of less-popular gems, too.

The scent of soap wafted from Les's skin, and his damp hair spiked in twenty different directions when he heaved his arms over the edge of the crate next to me. "Who're you in the mood for?"

"I don't know. Is there a way to cross Slipknot and Nina Simone?"

"I think you're talking about Evanescence. Or, how they used to be, at least." He curled over, resting his cheek on his forearm and studying me as I pulled out Led Zeppelin's *III* and held it up to him.

"The good ol' days before all these bullshit publicity stunts." I slid the record from the sleeve, holding it between my fingers. I loved old records. There was something so austere about them—the pressed plastic, this physical emblem of music. Hell, I even missed the CDs I grew up on. What we did now? It was like shaping air, trying to mold sound into an invisible cage, and a lot of days it felt that ephemeral. A record had a timelessness and permanency unparalleled by digital downloads. I'd tried to convince our label to do a pressing of our first album, but they wouldn't go for it, so I had someone else do it at my expense. It'd been a nostalgic act, I guess.

"Please," Les said, taking the record from my hands after I dumped it from the sleeve. "Rex Richards and Emily Day were a total fabrication. And that was 1958."

"No shit? Really?"

"Mm." He nodded and set the record on the turntable, lowering the needle. "Immigrant Song" raced out from the speakers and filled the air with its throbbing, manic tempo. "That's the song you wanted, wasn't it? I knew it," he said when I nodded. "And then there's the White Sound. Everyone thought they were married. Tori Lee breaks up with someone every time she's about to drop a new album. It's not that uncommon, and the White Sound and Tori Lee have fans who would rip their own arms off to get a foot closer to the stage. It's all narrative like anything else."

I grumbled a nonresponse, because I still thought it was a bad idea. Abandoning the records, I returned to the couch and picked up my guitar again, funneling my agitation through the Zeppelin classic I knew by heart as Les trailed after me.

"I know you think you're more invested in all of this than me, and you hate some of the bullshit that I don't really mind. Some of it I even like. But I am invested. Deeply. As much if not more than you, though you'll never believe it." Les propped his chin on his hand, watching me from one of the armchairs he'd sprawled in. He was shirtless and barefooted, wearing loose cotton pants. Dark circles still ringed his eyes, but some of the color had returned to his skin and he at least looked alive.

I cocked my head at him. *Do tell*, said the lift of my eyebrows. He gave me a corkscrew smile, straightening to examine the records he'd carried to the chair with him while I tried to ignore a very different, much more undressed image of him trying to insert itself in the present.

"My reasons are different, and maybe they're not as noble. I'll freely admit that a lot of it's shallow as hell. I crave the acknowledgment, and I crave the appreciation and adoration. And the money is pretty nice, too." His fingers riffled through cardboard sleeves absently. "And part of all of this is playing the game. The rules change fast, but if we play along well enough, eventually we put ourselves in the position to make the rules."

It was easy for me to sometimes forget that beneath the partying and sex, Les was fucking smart. Better educated, more knowledgeable about music history and probably any other topic than I'd ever be. He'd gone to some swanky private school growing up, and he'd had a full ride to Vandy that he let go to join up with me. I think that was part of what drove me so crazy. Sometimes it seemed like he was completely careless with his future.

"We should already be in that position."

"I think we will be soon, if we do this fake couple thing and fulfill our contract. Then, we make the rules."

"It's such a fucking sham, though." A shadow of hurt flitted through Les's eyes, and I wasn't sure what it meant, if he thought I was talking about him or his music.

"I think we should let it ride," he countered. "We can put an expiration date on it. We don't have to make a big deal out of it. Go through with it, then couple of weeks before we drop the album, just a quiet press release suggesting we're not a couple anymore. Come on, man, think about it? It's not that big of a deal. No one's dying here. It's just a gimmick, and everyone fucking uses gimmicks. Audiences are used to that, but ours will be none the wiser anyway because we'll sell the hell out of it, both ways. We're good at putting on a show. Don't forget that."

"I don't want to put on a show. I just want to make music and get paid for it." I was being petulant. I knew what I'd signed up for, otherwise I'd still be busking on street corners like I used to, writing songs on my own, and playing to whoever would listen, hoping just one person would hear me, really *hear* me the way Les had. The way our fans did.

"Do this with me and I promise I'll let you make the decision what happens next. Whatever you say, I'll back you up one hundred percent. You want to go indie, that's fine. I'm there with you." Les fixed me with a stare that burned with sincerity, with promise, and maybe even a bit of a plea, and I knew right then I was going to do it, even as I tried to hedge.

None of this felt good, but maybe he was right. If we stuck with the plan, the whole thing would be done by the time we got the next album out. I was determined to make it a success, and if it was good enough, what the hell we'd been doing in our personal lives wouldn't matter. Hopefully.

I sighed. "Fuck. Okay."

WE SPENT THE REST OF THE DAY GETTING SET UP, ORGANIZING Les's disastrous notebook scribbles into a semblance of coherency and playing through old songs to get into the feel of things so we'd be ready to crack hard on some new stuff the next day. It went surprisingly well, considering the shitshow that morning. Maybe Les was as eager to dive into a distraction as I was. Then Levi called Les back late that afternoon with a schedule so ridiculous I almost went back on my agreement to play along.

He'd effectively mapped out our "relationship" for the next few weeks while we were in Gatlinburg and had set up locations, times, and dates where we were to show up and act all cozy so a photographer could get some of the action. We were buffered enough from the cities that random paparazzi shouldn't be a problem. It still felt like a covert operation with drop points, except the shit we were unloading was bogus. I had to leave the room and let Les finish the conversation because I'd started to get angry over the whole scenario again.

That was only part of the problem, though. The major key, if you will, because there was still the minor to contend with, and it might actually have been the more important thing.

That night, lying in my bed, unable to sleep, memories of our time with Ella splashed across the backs of my eyelids. I'd kept the box closed so tight for months that the minute I cracked the seal, it came pouring out like a technicolor tsunami and dragged me under.

CHAPTER 17

Evan

SIX MONTHS AGO

The three of us ended up in the bedroom. I couldn't remember how, I just remembered sitting on the edge of the bed, increasingly aroused as I watched Les with Ella. They stood in front of me, Les behind her, his hands tracing over her body slowly, reverently. She made these kittenish little sounds and writhed under his touch, but Les stole my attention, kept me riveted on his mouth when he bent low to her ear and started speaking softly. It wasn't anything special, but it was insanely hot, these whispered encouragements and compliments as he kissed and sucked the side of her neck, and she reacted like his voice was just as palpable as his touch. His hands seemed perfectly calibrated to her body, anticipating every twist and arch as he caressed her. It was the same dedication he gave on stage, this sort of transcendent awareness of what the audience craved commingled with his intuitive ability to satisfy them.

There was no doubt in my mind that Les was an exhibitionist, and the more he touched her, the more I got the crazy idea that he was putting on a show for me, playing to *me*, and Ella's body was the instrument he was serenading me with. I was completely transfixed.

I stood, fumbling my pants open in front of Ella, absorbing the two of them and saturating myself in their pleasure. Voyeurism gave way to intense desire. It was the same thing that happened to me with music. I could listen up to a certain point, and then the itch to be the one creating it overwhelmed me. This was just a different kind of song. One made of bodies and soft moans and hot, heavy breaths. Or so I told myself. We'd been busting our asses for weeks, and maybe Les was right—I needed to cut loose and go with the flow.

Without warning, he reached out and fisted my cock, making me gasp. It was part shock, part relief, part *what-the-fuck*. Tightening my hand on Ella's shoulder, I swayed a step backward, gaze darting to Les's in bewilderment. He stilled his hand, then loosened his grip reactively, but the look in his eyes didn't match up to the retreat, because when they fixed on me, they were dark and hungry with challenge. He dipped his head to lick the join of Ella's shoulder and neck, then released me and slid his hand back between her legs. I could feel the faintest brush of his knuckles against me as he explored her. My own neck warmed as if it were mine he was kissing, and my dick throbbed, pulsing at the absence of touch and aching in ways I'd never felt before.

Ella moaned and bucked at the air.

"You all right, Porter?" His gaze hadn't wavered from me, but a quicksilver flash of concern passed through the depths of green.

"Yeah." Maybe I was drunker than I thought, because I was way too into this and a little disturbed by how much Les was turning me on.

Sure, I'd seen him fucking or fooling around on plenty of occasions. But never up close like this. Never where I could feel his breath on my skin and feel his movements translated by another body into mine.

He gave me a sublime nod and kissed Ella's shoulder as I swallowed hard and said, "Your hand—jerk me."

To Les's credit, he didn't miss a beat; he just took me in his fist again, and the flood of pleasure and relief at having the friction I craved sent my head falling back and my throat swelling with a moan.

Les urged us backward until my calves hit the bed. I wrenched off my clothes, Ella shed her bra. God knew how long Les had been naked. When I sat on the bed again, Ella climbed into my lap. I slid on the condom Les handed me, and it was crazy how naturally all of it happened, as if choreographed. There was no awkwardness, no random jarring moments where we didn't know what to do. It just... flowed. Ella and I both groaned as she sank down on top me, and Les didn't stop—he kept talking in that seductive whiskey drawl while he ran his fingers through her hair and plucked at her nipples as she rode me. I fell onto my back and dragged her with me, grabbing for her hips so I could plunge deeper. Les's gaze was pinned on me, and fuck, it was hard to explain what it did to me, but it felt less like I was fucking Ella and more like she was a conduit between Les and me. I grabbed a fistful of her ass and quickened my rhythm, and the next thing I knew, Les's hand was on top of mine, spreading her cheeks. He slid his finger in alongside my cock, and another thrill rocketed through me.

When he asked her if she wanted him to fuck her in the ass, she moaned out a *yes*.

Les put on a condom and eased into her slowly, liberally dousing all three of us in lube and murmuring to her softly when she clenched up at the invasion.

Then I couldn't fucking move. Because once he was inside her and thrusting, the pressure of him against me, the seemingly negligible separation between our bodies, had me seeing stars. It was intimate and filthy and so fucking hot. I thought maybe this was what Les had meant about the magic of orgies. But it wasn't Ella getting me hot. It was Les's presence.

Ella dropped her head to my shoulder, fisting the covers as Les pounded into her and we became a tangle of limbs—her legs straddling my waist, Les between my thighs, one hand propped on the bed beside him, the other closed over mine on her hips. But his gaze was all mine, searing me as he thrust into her, and I couldn't fucking look away. Couldn't stop watching how pleasure twisted his face up, how much joy he was getting out of this. It was like a drug, and I lost myself in the flex of muscles running along his arms, his abs contracting with movement, and the tendons straining at his neck.

"You like this, sweetheart?" he growled, and the way his eyes were still locked on mine, almost felt like he was asking me, but it was Ella who answered in a groaned *yes*, and then *please*.

"Fuck," he ground out, then lost it, hips whipping against her before he pulled out and snapped the condom off. He jerked himself roughly against her ass, the tip of his cock brushing over the back of my hand where I gripped her, and exploded with a cry, hot liquid jetting all over my knuckles and her ass and sending me tailspinning into my own orgasm. Les seized the top of my thigh with one hand and wrapped the other around the base of my cock as I arched into Ella and fell apart while she spasmed against me. To say my orgasm was intense would be doing it a disservice. It was so otherworldly, it left me quivering for minutes afterward.

We collapsed in a heap, then straggled up to the head of the bed and passed out.

AND THAT WAS THE SECOND HALF OF THE PROBLEM. I HADN'T minded Les's hands on me that night. In fact, I'd enjoyed every second of it, and ever since then, I'd been so fucking twisted up on the subject of my bandmate, I didn't have a clue where to pull the string that might unravel all of it into some kind of sense.

Tell All Weekly

September 2016

Evan, you've been spotted frequently in the company of Jessica Nash. Are the two of you serious?

Evan: No comment. Next question.

Les: Seriously, you'd have better luck asking the White House for the nuclear codes.

CHAPTER 18

PRESENT DAY

Evan stared at the cereal display like he was a judge on one of those competitions on TV and he was trying to decide which one got to move to the next round. He had his fist under his chin, eyes darting back and forth between Cheerios and Cocoa Krispies, his mouth set in a tight line of scrutiny. This was pretty much how shopping with him had gone since we'd stepped foot inside the deep freeze also known as Food City. I was halfway to hypothermia in a T-shirt and jeans, my skin pebbled with goose bumps, my nipples diamond hard, and I just wanted to get through it so I could get back outside and thaw, but Evan applied the same kind of consideration to grocery shopping that he did to music. The cold seemed to have zero effect on him. He appeared perfectly comfortable in his shorts.

"Just get both," I huffed, growing exasperated. The cart in front of us was full of stuff I'd basically just thrown in Supermarket Sweep style. That's how damn cold it was inside, and plus, it was just groceries. Admittedly, I hadn't done my own grocery shopping for a while. I had a service that did most of my errands when I was at home in Nashville—which was rare in the first place—but I was pretty sure nothing had changed in the supermarket world that it required a doctorate to shop now.

"I don't *need* both." He gave me a cool blink of his eyes and went back to his internal quandary.

"But you want them both. So just get them both and let's move on before you have to debate over which ice pick is best to chip me from the block of ice I'm about to become."

He glanced over me again, his eyes narrowing thoughtfully, and I could tell he was considering making a point out of the fucking cereal somehow. "Just because you want—" And there it was, so I cut him off at the pass.

"This is grocery shopping, not couch time with Freud."

What he wanted to tell me was that just because you wanted something didn't mean you needed it, and I knew that perfectly well, but I also knew what we'd each earned over the last few years, and debating over an extra box of cereal was like worrying about stealing a glass of water from the ocean. I knew he couldn't help it to some degree; it was just how he was made. That and growing up with so little to his name that he held tightly to everything he got. His whole childhood was want versus need. On a photoshoot once, the wardrobe assistant had a bunch of shoes lined up for us to choose from, and Evan had just stood there, frozen by the choice, going back and forth as if it really mattered which shoes we wore until the woman finally picked for him. As he'd sat down to pull off his ratty Vans, she'd said he could keep all the shoes if he wanted, but he'd just shaken his head.

"Why the fuck not?" I'd asked. I'd had a bag in the corner already loaded with more dress shirts and hipster pants than I had closet space for. *"What's the point if you won't even let yourself enjoy some of the perks?"*

He'd given me a disconcerted look, like I'd insulted the very core of his being or something. *"I'm not doing this for perks and these"*—he toed at his Vans where a piece of rubber was peeling back from the side of the fabric—*"keep my head in the right place."*

I REACHED PAST EVAN TOWARD THE CEREAL SHELF, MY SHOULDER brushing his. The contact was light and innocent, but I felt him stiffen. I got it. We were both hyperaware of each other now that we were supposed to be portraying a couple. It was freaking me out, too, how conscious I was of his proximity, his every look. It was different than before, when I could just sit back and ache for him from a safe distance. Now, we were trying to navigate building this grand illusion that was a farce to him, but more like my wish come true. Minus the part where he was completely not into it.

The second we'd gotten out of the car in the parking lot, I could tell he was starting to overthink and doubt things. He'd scanned the parking lot repeatedly as we walked toward the double doors searching, no doubt, for the photographer who was supposed to show up at some point. When I'd slung my arm around him casually, like I'd done a thousand times before, he'd withered inside my grip like water put to a straw wrapper. *"Relax,"* I'd said, leaning into his peppery aftershave. *"It's just a different kind of stage."*

"You're getting both." I flipped my hand so the boxes of cereal careened over the ledge of the shelf and toppled into the cart. "And if you don't eat them, I will. In fact, I want them. I want them *both*. And now they're in the buggy, which is great, so let's move on because what I do *need* is to stop freezing." I reached for the handle of the cart, and Evan edged me out of the way.

"Par for the course," he muttered and started to push the cart down the aisle.

I snapped my foot out to the basket underneath and halted it. "What's that mean?"

"It means that's just your whole MO. You want something, you take it, because why shouldn't you have it if it's there? Why shouldn't you have anything you desire?"

"Yeah, and so? Why shouldn't you?"

"That's not real life."

I chuckled. "None of this is real life, sweetheart." His eyes flashed when I drawled the word. He hated it. "That doesn't mean you shouldn't enjoy something. There's not some kind of enforcer up in the sky waiting to snatch all of this away from you the second you let yourself relax, Porter."

He pressed his lips together, then forced the cart back into motion, one wobbly wheel squeaking as he continued down the aisle. I trailed close behind, rubbing my arms briskly.

"That's not it, but whatever," he said. "Let's just finish."

But I couldn't let it go. "It's almost this reverse snobbery thing with you. You're too hung up on your roots. Too afraid if you let yourself reap the rewards of all our work that… what? You'll be just another run-of-the-mill celebrity? We can't have that, can we?"

I could tell I'd hit a nerve because the squeaky wheel stuttered again as he slowed and pinned me with a hard stare. "The last time I fucking relaxed, we bombed an album."

Had it been anyone else, a look with that much sharp edge might have drawn blood, but with Evan, I knew it came from the fear of failure that'd been in the driver's seat his entire life and maybe always would be. "That's not just on you, though—don't be that fucking arrogant. It's on us both, and it has nothing to do with anything we're talking about."

"Anytime I relax and think I've got a handle on shit, something goes wrong."

"Got news for you, then. You haven't relaxed in six months and shit's still going wrong."

His mouth crimped up in irritation as I reached out and sped the cart along again. "And it'd be a helluva lot worse if I wasn't busting my ass to keep things on an even keel."

I snatched a bag of potato chips from a display and tossed it in the cart with more force than was necessary. "You say that like I'm inept, like you're carrying me along and keeping everything going while I'm fucking off."

"Sometimes it feels that way."

This was dangerous territory, but I sure as hell wasn't cold anymore. Heat flared and battered at my pulse. It wasn't just anger. It was frustration, too, because I knew deep down he was right. And if I opened my mouth and unleashed what I was holding back, whoever was supposed to be waiting out in the parking lot was going to get an eyeful of the wrong kind of thing. So I took a deep breath and turned down the next aisle.

Evan smacked my hand away when I reached for a six-pack of beer. "Oh come the fuck on," I groused, but I put my hands up and backed away when he gave me a meaningful stare. "Fine. I want it, but I don't *need* it," I said. "Look at that, we've come full circle."

A glimmer of a smile threatened the corner of his mouth. He didn't want to smile, I could tell, but I latched onto it, wanting to coax it wider. "Now all that's left is you throwing a case in the cart and telling me to stuff it."

He put his hand out and shoved at the side of my face, but I caught that curve of his mouth as it widened and he said, "How about I just tell you to stuff it? Also, did you call the cart a buggy?"

I blinked at him. "Maybe?"

"Have you always done that?"

"I have no idea since I haven't devoted a great deal of time to quantifying certain aspects of my vocabulary for frequency of usage. Feel free to keep track for me from now on. We don't make a habit of shopping together," I reminded him. "Thank God."

"I've just never noticed it before. Buggy," he repeated the word to himself with a little chuckle. It was one of those idiosyncratic moments where I didn't quite understand his amusement but infinitely preferred it to irritation, so I let him have it, bless his heart.

THE CHECKOUT LINE TOOK FOREVER, AND A COUPLE OF PEOPLE GAVE us funny looks, but that might have been on account of our clothing, which was definitely more dirty hippies than Southern-boy Polo chic, though no one said anything until just before we got to the exit. I was back to freezing again, enjoying the welcome blast of heat when the doors slid open with a hydraulic hiss. And then—

"Les?" A woman's voice, and she said my name with authority like I was personal friend. But when I turned around, I had no idea who she was. She was cute. Petite. Vividly dark eyes and wild dreadlocks gathered up and spilling over a scarf wound around her head. Evan glanced over at me. I knew he was assuming she was someone I'd slept with. I was pretty sure that wasn't the case. Well, more than fifty percent sure.

I gave her a polite smile as she approached, and an easy "Heyyyyyy."

"You have no clue who I am, do you? It's okay. I can forgive you." She laughed brightly. "Bonnaroo, last year. You probably saved this gorgeous face"—she preened, angling her face from side to side. Her mocha skin was flawless, her smile gleaming and perfect—"from getting trampled. But I think you were hammered, too."

The memory came to me slowly, and she was right. I'd been hammered. It was early evening when we'd played our set, and Blink and I had been sampling liberally from the cadre of booze and weed that were in abundance on the grounds. By the time Evan and I walked onstage, the crowd had become an indistinct blur of motion, an ocean of faces rippling between the play of shadow and light. I didn't even know how I'd managed to see her. There'd been a suggestion of disturbance I caught from one corner of my eye, and when I looked in her direction, an emptiness like something had been scooped out of the landscape, then a flash of white on the ground. The crowd swayed and bounced, jostling near the stage and then began parting around her. Security retrieved her and tried to muscle their way off to the side where the medics were, but there were so many people packed in they had trouble making headway. They'd turned around, heading back toward the stage, instead, and I stopped singing and hopped down to help them pull her over the barricade. Her ankle was twisted at a grotesque angle and her face tracked with dirt and tears.

"Maize!" Her name bubbled up to the surface, and she gave me a cheerful grin and enthusiastic nod.

"You just plopped down next to me and said you'd wait with me until the medics got there. It was really sweet."

"Don't give him too much credit," Evan interrupted, folding his arms over his chest. "He probably needed to sit down, and it was that or pass out."

I shot him a bird. Evan had been furious with me for ditching out in the middle of the song, but he remained onstage, picking up a few beats after I'd left off, and the audience had fucking loved it. Loved that he soldiered on alone. Most of our music featured intricate harmonies and duets, so hearing Evan's incredible range solo and stripped bare had been something special. That was my take, at least. When I climbed back onstage later, I'd discovered he was trembling. *"It's been so damn long since I've stood up here by myself, I got nervous,"* he'd explained afterward. And then I'd felt bad, though I probably hadn't apologized.

I introduced the two of them, and Maize asked what we were doing in town, so I explained how we came here to write all of our albums.

"No shit? Well, I live a couple miles outside of town. Have a drum circle that goes every Friday night if you're interested. It's pretty low-key, and I promise no one would spaz out too hard if you guys came."

I cut a look over at Evan to suss out what he was thinking, because I was game. He was hard to read with strangers, but I thought I detected some interest in the way his eyes narrowed thoughtfully, so I nodded. "We could probably manage that."

She rolled onto the balls of her feet, aiming another blinding smile in our direction. She seemed really sweet and down-to-earth, and I wished I could remember what the hell I'd spent fifteen minutes talking to her about in the pit in front of the stage while we waited for someone to come examine her. I wouldn't put it past me to have been trying to get her number, considering how attractive she was.

She put her number in my phone, hit Send, then hung up and

handed it back to me, saying, "My girlfriend comes up from Chattanooga every weekend, too, so you'll get to meet her. Again. Have you to thank for that. She was one of the medics."

"I've always been a good Cupid." I gave her a wink as Evan grunted something under his breath, and then we pushed through the doors and into the blissful oven-like furor of hot Southern asphalt.

CHAPTER 19

"You ou know we actually have to produce while we're here, right?" Evan said as we strolled through the parking lot. I scouted for cameras over the tops of cars and vans, skimming the few other people in the parking lot, but I hadn't spotted a photographer yet.

"We will. I've got a couple of things I wrote down last night. Figured we could go over them this afternoon."

Evan grunted and searched the parking lot, too. "Where is this fucker? I'm not about to wait all afternoon."

"We won't. If he's not here, he's not, and too bad." I shrugged one shoulder, wondering when grocery delivery would reach these parts as the cart rattled noisily over the pavement.

Evan popped the hatch on his SUV and started shoving groceries in the back. I'd joined in when a prickle of awareness dusted over my shoulders and lifted the hairs on the back of my neck.

"He's here. Don't look," I said, and wedged another grocery bag inside.

"I swear to God, you'd feel a damn ant looking at you from a mile away. It's uncanny. Or maybe scary," he muttered.

"So what're we going to do? Should I put my arm around you? Should we make out?" We hadn't really planned this out in advance, and now I was flailing over the logistics. Levi had said we needed to be convincing, and considering how Evan had been recoiling from even the mere suggestion of my touch, I wasn't sure how we were going to get from that to a loving embrace. Damn, we really should have mapped this out beforehand.

Evan paused, one arm extended above him, his hand curled over the hatch door as he squinted his eyes at me scornfully. "We're not making out in the parking lot."

"Why not?"

"It's total overkill."

"Okay, how about holding hands? That's easy." I reached for his hand, and he batted me away. I cracked up at that, and at his stiff posture. I could tell he was calculating, too, trying to break this event down into logical steps. So in order to save some time, grief, and overthinking, I just went for it, leaning in against him, ready to plant one on his mouth. He did the same, tipping his head aside in time to avoid my mouth landing on his as he plastered a very chaste, very dry kiss on my cheek.

I groaned and reeled back to peer assessingly at him. Surely that didn't qualify as boyfriend-worthy steam? It hardly even registered to my dick, and I had a hair trigger as far as erections were concerned. A hot, stiff wind could perk my interest on the right day. "What the fuck was that?"

"Affection? Contractual obligation? Let's go." Evan slammed the hatch door shut. I sent my gaze out over the parking lot and found the photographer, *her* camera still aimed at us.

"That wasn't affection. That was a kiss for someone you're afraid might have a nasty infection."

Evan's arched his brows, a little smirk curling coyly up one side of his mouth. "Your point?"

"Oh fuck off. I get tested regularly."

"That's about the only thing you do regularly." He might as well have stuck his tongue out at me. "I did what I was supposed to do."

He pushed off the hatch of the trunk, like he was ready to go, but I wasn't done.

"That wasn't a kiss. It was like a zombie taking stock of fresh meat, or a grandma giving a kiss to the grandkid she secretly can't stand. A hello to the long-lost brother you never wanted. A—"

"It was a perfectly nice peck on the cheek. It got the point across, it fulfilled the mission, it was—"

"Unconvincing and boring," I countered.

"I'm not going to stick my tongue down your throat in a fucking grocery store parking lot."

"Why not?"

"Because I'm not fifteen?"

Great, now we were arguing in full view of the photographer. "Just a prude." Mostly I said that because I knew it was the quickest way to get a reaction out of him.

"I'm not a fucking prude." Evan smacked the rear window of the SUV, his brows pinching together with frustration. I could practically hear the whir of the photographer's shutter capturing this stupid moment. "You of all people should know that," he growled.

I got the reference immediately, amusement fading, replaced by hunger and ache as the memory of him exploding inside Ella and the harsh cry of sound he'd made flashed in the back of my mind.

And then, without warning, he crowded up against me, his hand planting at the center of my chest and shoving me up against the car. There was a split second where I felt my mouth drop open in shock before he smothered it with the crush of his.

The memory I had of his lips was muddied by Ella's presence, just a hint of the Fireball shot he'd taken before, and the messy tangle of tongues I couldn't really differentiate.

And nothing like what was happening now.

My lips yielded automatically beneath the pressure of his, like cracking a seal, and behind it was warmth, the spicy tinge of cinnamon gum, the silky wetness of his tongue when it slipped against mine for a slow, indulgent caress. Kissing didn't get near enough credit, and I knew Evan probably thought I was only about plugging my dick in a hole. But I fucking loved kissing, and holy shit was Evan good at it. To a degree that, in a completely nonsensical way, I felt like he'd been holding out on me. *You could have warned me you kissed like every dark devil that ever seduced, asshole.*

I felt the tension of his body transferred to the slippery heat of his lips, and the few seconds of discord where our teeth clicked together as we navigated the unfamiliar geometry of each other's mouths until we found our rhythm. And once we did, it was effortless synchronicity of give and take, the same way we were onstage.

Evan's stubble prickled along my chin, and after a few moments, I remembered I had a body, that I was more than just the lips and tongue currently dancing with his. I caressed the tips of my fingers up his spine, and his hand slid up from the center of my chest to my throat. The tendons in my neck jumped beneath his roaming touch, and my pulse rippled against his palm as he tightened his grip around me and dipped his thumb into the shallow dish below my Adam's apple. I groaned again, and he staggered back with a curse, his teeth scraping across my lower lip as we parted. His eyes were fever bright and glossy, the pupils shot wide as he stared at me. We were both breathless.

"How's that? Unconvincing? Boring?" he panted out and smirked.

I swiped my hand across the back of my mouth and smirked back. "Better."

What I really wanted to do was take hold of his shoulders, shove him into the back of the damn SUV, and pull his shorts around his ankles because holy fuck was I turned on now. That kiss was no stiff wind—it was a whole tornado, and I was dizzy with the violent intensity of it. I scanned his face desperately, trying to determine whether he felt the same. I couldn't get a good read on his expression, though.

"Your dick has a stronger opinion, I think." His gaze dropped to the bulge in my jeans.

Yeah, I was hard as a rock, and his T-shirt hung down too far over his shorts for me to determine whether or not he'd had the same reaction. Unfair.

"Don't let it go to your head," I snapped back at him.

"Touché," he said, and for some reason we both cracked up, loud laughter that felt good barreling out of my chest, a kind of substitute release for the pressure in my cock, which I didn't want to think about because, yeah...

Evan turned away, walked around to the driver's side, and got in. I waved to the reporter as I adjusted myself, then climbed in the passenger seat. For the duration of the ride home, things felt normal again, the way we were before. Back at the beginning.

When you guys are working on an album, what's your process?

Les: Besides a lot of alcohol?

Evan: Les usually has some words and some kind of gist of the melody or beat and then—

Les: And then Evan organizes it, riffs off it, and makes it about two thousand times better. "Detour" was all you, though, dude.

Evan: No it wasn't. You figured out the chorus, remember?

Les: So the answer is complex. We don't have a process, we just sit there and jack around together until it sounds right.

Evan: I'm side-eyeing your word choice there.

Les: We *collaborate* around together until it sounds right.

CHAPTER 20

Evan

Maybe Les was right. All of it was just a show, and even if he was naturally better at it, I still knew how to perform—I thought I'd proven that well enough in the parking lot. I was doing it long before I met him, though, passing out charming smiles like they were candy as I shoved drinks at strangers, spilling bits and pieces of my history in smoky bars with my guitar over my lap, singing my ass off on street corners in the hopes of one more dollar or the right ear to hear me.

So I'd say I was a good showman, but when I'd leaned in to Les, I'd had a strong expectation that my kiss would be perfectly executed and yet still feel wooden and mechanical. It hadn't. Not at all. The cadence of my pulse increased with each velvety collision of our tongues, and little pinpoints of pleasure lit up over my shoulders like stars in a cage. When I'd been pressed up against him, a rumble of sound thrummed in his chest and vibrated over his tongue, like pleasure I could taste, and it had felt as natural between us as when we traded riffs back and forth. But this was a different language, and kissing Les should have been nothing, but it wasn't. It was something else entirely.

Les didn't know the half of it. No one really did. Sometimes I didn't think *I* did. But I'd understood for a long time I was a little different. A random pair of tits didn't leave me with a slavering erection. Or for that matter, a random cock. Les's cornucopia of meaningless sex didn't just seem pointless to me, but unappealing. I took flak—mostly good-natured—left and right for turning down easy lays, but I didn't want them. I could jerk off to porn in the instances I got horny with the same effect. I wanted connection, the same thing I wanted in my music. A song was just free-floating notes until you grounded it with a story. For a long time I'd thought something was wrong with my libido. At fifteen, every guy around me was popping boners over short skirts while I was more interested in fiddling with my guitar or a keyboard. What few relationships I'd had led me to figure out there wasn't anything wrong with my libido; it just had a more restrictive admissions policy than what seemed like the other ninety-eight percent of the population. I was cool with that and managed okay, and honestly it was kind of nice to not feel some deep quaking need to be with another person or get off that seemed to make everyone around me act crazy.

And that's what was dangerous about that fucking kiss setting me on fire. Les was exactly the opposite of me. He was boundless, and nothing and no one would ever be enough for him. Certainly not me.

As I heated water on the stove for some ramen after unloading the groceries, I stood there watching the bubbles begin to rise, silently listing twenty different reasons I was going through with this farce—for the music, for continued financial security, for my mom, for myself—and trying to number them in importance. But it kept shifting around on me, and I found myself looping back to that damn kiss and Les.

LATER THAT NIGHT, WE TOOLED AROUND IN THE BASEMENT, NOT really working together, and not really talking, either. It wasn't uncomfortable between us, though there was this sense of... carefulness in the air. Maybe it was just me. Les seemed completely immune to the kind of doubt and questioning that kiss had stirred up in me, which in its own way was comforting. He was just being himself. We hadn't spoken any more about what happened in the parking lot, and I wondered if he was as shell-shocked as I was or if it was just another day at the office for him. We'd both called our parents and explained the situation so they wouldn't be surprised by whatever headlines might come out. My mom's reaction had been a measured, thoughtful silence that became a lot of questions I did my best to answer, and then tentative support. She was always supportive, even if she didn't have a lick of an inclination toward music or any interest in its inner workings.

And then there was Leigh. I glanced at the phone when it lit up on the coffee table where I'd set it and sighed when I saw her name pop up. Briefly, I considered not taking it, because I'd had about enough for one day. But Les was deeply involved with his notebook, and I figured I might as well get it over with. Even after years in the business, it still mystified me sometimes how fast gossip could become a headline. I hadn't even checked the internet, assuming we'd have a reprieve of at least a couple of days before the photos from the grocery store emerged. That was the only logical reason I could imagine for her call, though.

"Leigh," I said, waving the phone in Les's direction as I stood.

Les glanced up with the glaze-eyed look he got when he was wrapped up in something and nodded. "Good luck."

I didn't need luck. I needed a time machine that would transport me back to that night six months ago where I would have, instead of taking Ella's hand, walked off to my bedroom.

I took the phone out onto the porch where a light rain had started falling. Raindrops pinged off the railing, creating a soothing white-noise backdrop as I accepted the call.

"If this is true, it means you were cheating on me," she said after my cautious greeting.

"I've never cheated on you. You know I wouldn't do that." The tone of her voice had me wincing as I stood under the overhang of the roof, leaning against the sliding door and already regretting answering.

"So this is all just made up, then? Even the threesome thing? Like a publicity stunt?"

"The threesome is true. But—" I raised my voice when she started to interject. "It happened before you and I ever got together. And I regret the hell out of it, in case you're wondering. It was a stupid, stupid fucking idea."

A long silence followed. What I'd always liked about Leigh was that she wasn't impulsive. She was reliable and even-keeled like me. Maybe that had been the problem with us, I didn't know. We were so similar that after a while it felt like we were just... partners or something. I couldn't honestly say I knew for sure what love was supposed to feel like, but I was pretty sure what I felt for Leigh was caring, not love, and the only reason I'd been so upset about her breaking up with me was that it was just one more reminder of something I'd attempted and fucked up.

"That's so unlike you, though." Her voice was soft, and she sounded hurt, which sent an unmitigated pang of sadness through me. I'd never wanted to hurt her.

"It is. Or it *was*, which is just one of the many reasons why I told you I regretted it. But I'm telling you I wasn't screwing around on you."

"So this picture of you and Les sucking face in the parking lot this afternoon is bullshit?" I could imagine her on the other end of the line, the tremor of anger in her voice drawing her mouth down. The entire time we'd dated, we'd never even argued once.

"Yeah. Our publicist thinks it'll be a good lead in to our next album." I gritted my teeth and thumped my head back against the glass door a couple of times.

She choked out a laugh. "God, you're becoming part of the machine."

I had no defense, so I didn't say anything.

"It looks so... real." Her voice had taken on that soft, small tone again that settled in my chest like a weight and made me sigh.

"It's not." I'd never thought I was a good liar, which was why I didn't do it often. And I wasn't sure that was what I was doing now, exactly, because Les and I were faking a relationship, but the feelings that kiss stirred up inside me were too raw to ignore, and there was no way I could explain something I hadn't figured out for myself yet.

Maybe she could tell, because there was a note of doubt in her voice when she spoke next. "Are you sure? Because I wouldn't be surprised. I've sometimes wondered if Les has a thing for you."

I let out an incredulous laugh. "Les has a thing for anything that's remotely attractive and alive."

"Mm-hmm." She didn't sound convinced, but I was ready to get off this topic and wrap up the conversation before it spiraled.

"Listen, I'm sorry about everything, Leigh. I was a shitty boyfriend, and you deserve much better."

"No, you were a great boyfriend, Ev—you just weren't into me the way I was you. I don't know if you ever were."

I WENT BACK DOWNSTAIRS AND FOUND LES ON THE COUCH, LEANED back deep into the cushions that had long since lost their shape, his legs kicked up on the coffee table and his guitar slung loosely across his lap while he stared at the ceiling, strumming a few aimless chords. I carried my laptop with me and set it up on the coffee table, pushing his feet aside to make room.

"She pissed?" he asked, without looking over at me.

"She's hurt, I think, and thinks this whole stunt is dumb, but she's... fuck, she's just a nice person, and I feel like an asshole." I groaned. I'd failed to really consider how she would be affected, and now I felt like a dick for thinking she wouldn't care at all.

"You should've just told her it was my fault."

"Why? I agreed to go along with this." Once the computer had hummed to life, I googled our name and clicked on the top result that read, "Just Like Us."

"Because it is. That whole threesome. I egged you on."

I took a long breath and dropped to the edge of the couch near Les, raking my hands through my hair. "Nah. It just happened. I could've said no. And you're right. People do that shit all the time and it's not a big deal, yeah?" I sounded like I was trying to convince myself, which I absolutely was.

"But you never would've done it left to your own devices." Les grabbed the neck of his guitar and straightened, resting it against the side of the couch as he angled into the cushions so he could see me. It seemed like he was settling in for a long come-to-Jesus and I wasn't in the mood for a come-to-Jesus, or for revisiting that night with Ella. It had already happened. It was done. Now I just had to ride the wave as best I could.

I glanced back at the screen where the page displayed an array of celebrities doing ordinary things, like picking up laundry or, in our case, grocery shopping. Les turned his attention to the screen at the same time I did, swearing softly, "They didn't even show the best part. Dipshits."

It was true. That scorching kiss I'd planted on Les against the side of the car? Nowhere to be found. What was shown instead was the awkward first attempt captured at the moment where I was ducking Les's advance to plant my more chaste version on his cheek. My eyes were wide open, my lips puckered, and I looked like a squirrel who'd suddenly realized he was caught in the middle lane during rush hour. Les, meanwhile, looked great, every ounce the affectionate lover, complete with a hint of a goofy, adoring smile. Fantastic.

"Why didn't they post the other one?"

Les edged closer to the screen, squinting at it. "Maybe she couldn't see it." He pointed. "We were on the other side. Maybe she couldn't get over there before you had to pull away or risk exploding from the sheer eroticism of my kiss."

I turned to look at him, giving him a slow blink. "That's what you think happened, huh?"

He grinned and shrugged. "More or less."

"Les, your mouth is basically a Dollar Store. Lots of traffic for shit that falls apart in a week." Except I actually liked the Dollar Store because their prices on paper goods near where I lived were unbeatable. And I'd liked Les's kiss, too. A lot.

"That's so oddly specific and nonsensical, it doesn't even hurt my feelings." He smirked at me and picked up his guitar again. "That photographer missed out. Now—" He played a few bars of something that must have been new. "You want to see what you've got for this or you want to kiss me some more? I'm open to either."

I rolled my eyes and closed the laptop.

An hour later, I'd migrated to the floor and Les had taken over the whole couch. He had his guitar lying lengthwise over the top of his body and plucked idly at the strings like he was playing a harp while I rewrote some of his lyrics into legible English and jotted down the chord patterns and progressions we'd assembled so far. After he hit the C string hard for the fifth time in a row, I was just about ready to throw something at him when he said, "I've been thinking."

"Yeah? Does it hurt?"

He snorted. "Har har, Dadjoke. About us, I mean." I twisted around to look at him. His profile was to me, and I couldn't really read his expression, but he seemed awfully intent on his study of the foam-lined ceiling. "What we're doing. I know I convinced you to go along with this thing, but I don't want to do it if you're not all in."

"What's that mean?" A cold spike worked its way through my stomach as I set down my pen.

"This last tour has been hell, Porter. Everything is different between us, and I can't do another tour like that." He slid off the side of the couch and leaned his back against it, dangling his hands between his bent knees. The gaze he fixed on me was cautious, but there was something else in it, too, that I couldn't decode.

I prodded the inside of my cheek with the tip of my tongue, thinking. I didn't disagree with him at all, but I was struggling to figure out why a twinge of anger ran through me. What I wanted to tell him was to stop fucking around so much, but he was just doing the same things he'd always done. I was the one who'd changed. So was it fair to suddenly hold him to these new expectations? And now there was the additional confusion of that kiss and the impression it had left on me. I couldn't get it out of my mind.

"Me either," I agreed at last, feeling like that was a lame response. But it was the best I had at the moment.

Les wet his lips slowly, the arch of his brows telling me that, yep, he'd been dissatisfied with that succinct answer. "So we have options. We commit to this stupid scheme, sell the hell out of it, and write some good songs. Or we don't and we still write some good songs and see where we land afterward. But either way, I want to feel like we're on the same side again."

He was looking at me so intently now it sent a shiver racing through me; the words he'd spoken danced around bigger-picture implications, and we both knew it.

I nodded, trying to ignore the erratic pounding of my heart and the panic inspired by the idea of losing him as a partner. "We're already committed. I'm in. But I need something from you, too."

He arched a brow again in question, and I had to resist the defensive urge to fold my arms over my chest.

"I don't want to be picking you up off the floors and trying to put you back together again while we're here."

A muscle at his jaw twitched, but he nodded. "Deal."

"Really?"

"Yes."

I hesitated, thinking about my phone call with Leigh.

"Leigh seemed to think—you're not... this *is* fake, right? There's not some kind of desire for more on your end, is there?"

"No." His Adam's apple bobbed as he swallowed, then tipped his chin up and met my gaze directly. "You're right, what you've always said: I'm not very discriminating. And sure I'd be into hooking up with you because I've always thought you're hot, which you know. But I'm not a relationship guy, which you also know so... yeah, you can lay that worry to rest."

I rubbed at my chest, as if doing so would erase the disquiet that spread through it.

CHAPTER 21

Les

Since I'd known him, Evan had maintained the same morning routine. He got up, went for a forty-five minute run, then did another half hour of body weight exercises. Rain or shine, 365 days a year. The one time we stayed in a hotel without a gym and it stormed, he'd gone to a hotel a few streets over and convinced them to let him use their treadmill. It showed. He was fit as hell, and I used to think it was a vanity thing—because why the hell would someone go to all that trouble, otherwise?—but Evan didn't seem to care much about vanity or getting laid. So finally one day I asked him, and he gave me this vague spiel about it clearing his mind and boosting endorphins, but I didn't buy that, either. He had other obsessive tendencies, like making sure his clothes for a show were properly laid out an hour before call time or his guitar strings were changed after every other performance. He'd had the same suitcase since I'd known him, and he packed it exactly the same way, layering things in a specific system. I'd decided a big part of his running habit was a way for him to feel grounded in the constant change of our lifestyle—and maybe it was rooted deeper, in his childhood, because I knew he and his mom had moved from place to place a lot. But as long as he could find pavement or a strip of revolving rubber, his day started the same way no matter where we were. When I'd told him that, his eyes had widened and his mouth opened like he was going to protest, like the idea that he was that transparent or maybe neurotic was disagreeable to him. Then he'd closed his mouth and cocked his head to the side thoughtfully, and said, *"I guess you're probably right. I'm just surprised you even noticed."*

I noticed a lot about him, though. Probably more than he'd ever imagined.

For instance, when I walked out of my bedroom the next morning at 6:30 a.m., I knew he was going to be wearing the dingy green mesh running shorts because he'd worn the blue ones the day before and he had a steady rotation going on among four pairs of shorts that he'd probably deny if I told him I was onto.

He glanced up at me from where he'd leaned over tying his shoelaces, expression shifting into one of surprise when he noticed my running gear. "No, you're not."

"I ran track in high school you know." I went to the sink to chug a glass of water and felt his gaze trailing me, probably still in disbelief. I'd never once gone running with him, and I'd left my track career behind as soon as I'd gone to college. Who wanted to run around in circles when there was a bevy of mind-altering substances and sexual deviations to explore? I'd had enough trouble keeping up with my classes.

"Have your feet even seen a pair of running shoes since then? And how are you even awake? I'll bet the last time you saw this hour was also high school."

"Actually, it was three weeks ago." No need to tell him it was because I'd stayed up all night doing things that would just piss him off.

It occurred to me that maybe this was some kind of sacred time for him; maybe I was interrupting. "I mean, if you don't mind."

He gave me a wary look, as if he wasn't sure what my motivation was. That was fair. I wasn't sure, either, but I'd slept like shit last night and hadn't gotten much more on a page than a doodle that vaguely resembled his lips, so when I woke up to the sound of him moving around in the kitchen, I figured it was either go with him and remind my body that it had other capabilities besides fucking, partying, and music, or stare at the ceiling until he got back and dragged me into the basement for practice. Reluctantly proactive, that was me.

And besides, running was important to him, and he was important to me. After our conversation last night, I thought it might not be such a bad idea to show him that, if subtly. So far, it seemed to have gone right over his head.

Evan shrugged and straightened, catching his ankle in his hand for a quick quad stretch. I wasn't bothering with stretches. My legs weren't going to know what'd hit them anyway, so why bother with forewarning?

"Try to keep up," he said, opening the door. And then, with a challenging little quirk of his mouth that sent a jolt of heat through my balls, he shot off down the front walk.

I'D JUST ASSUMED THAT SINCE I'D BEEN A RUNNER IN HIGH SCHOOL, there'd be a little muscle memory involved, even a tiny bit. Something better than the internal shriek of my lungs and the burn of my calves and hamstrings that made me want to double over before we'd even gone a full mile.

I'd also assumed we'd be running along the main road. Wrong again. We got about a quarter of a mile down, and Evan veered off onto a trail I'd never noticed before. The terrain was uneven, but we were shaded by a thick canopy of green. The air itself smelled lush and ripe, full of color and life, and it was cooler than the asphalt we'd been running on. I kept up with Evan, just barely, though the glances he tossed me over his shoulder had shifted from amused to increasingly concerned.

Another tenth of a mile and he'd noticeably decreased his pace so that I was almost on his heels.

"I can keep up," I huffed out, ignoring another twinge in my shin. They were going to be screaming tomorrow, but at least the scenery was nice: Evan's legs packed with well-defined muscle and the way his running shorts draped over his tight ass would've given me a boner if my circulatory system wasn't trying to shut down.

"You're breathing like a guy with emphysema, and I'm pretty sure I heard your quads begging for mercy a few seconds ago."

"That was my stomach. It needs coffee," I panted out.

Evan glided nimbly over a thick tree root stretching over the trail, but when I tried to imitate his grace, the toe of my shoe caught and I went down hard—breath-knocked-out-of-my-chest, knees-skinned hard. Silver lining: the packed dirt floor of the trail was nice and cool against my sweaty cheek. I decided I'd just rest there for a minute.

"You all right?" Evan asked amid laughter, his shoes coming into view just in front of me.

"Just communing with nature." I groaned, rolling to my side as I caught my breath. "It's not funny. I could've broken a wrist. Unable to play or write—you going to take up the slack?"

"Eh, we'd figure it out." He extended his hand to me, and I hauled myself up.

"Wouldn't be able to jerk off properly—you going to figure that out for me, too?"

His mouth went slack, then curled up again. "Guess you'd have to live a monastic lifestyle for a while. You should try it. Very Zen."

"I need to bust a nut once a day, or I feel off." My brow ticked higher. "Don't look at me like that. You have your rituals"—I gestured widely at the forest around us, then his running gear—"I have mine."

He rolled his eyes and wiped some sweat from his forehead. "Whatever. It's moot anyway; you're fine."

I bent over, dusting dirt from the open scrapes over my kneecaps. Those were going to be fun in the shower.

"I'm good. Let's go." I started to brush past him to continue down the trail, but he caught the sleeve of my shirt and tugged me a half step back.

"Hang on." He reached out, fingertips curling under my jaw as he brushed his thumb lightly over my cheekbone. I winced as the salt from his skin leached into a cut I hadn't realized was there. But the sting paled in comparison to the sensation of his hand on my face, the almost tender way he touched me and the intensity of his stare as he examined my cheek. It sweetened the sting and made me want more. I took in a slow breath as my cock started to fill and the memory of his lips pressed to mine crowded every other thought from my head.

Maybe he was thinking the same thing, because his gaze transformed from intense scrutiny to a kind of hooded curiosity. I was careful not to react; after what he'd said last night, I was hell-bent on playing it cool. Two seconds later, he snapped his hand away. "Wash that good when we get back," he said, and then loped off.

By the time we got back to the cabin, my whole body was melting down. I left Evan to continue on with his push-ups, sit-ups, and whatever the fuck else he did to get those ripped arms, while I stripped my sopping-wet shirt off at the door, then went to bend my head under the kitchen faucet and suck up the equivalent of a small town's water reservoir.

After showering—unfortunately not together, as I often fantasized about—we reconvened in the basement. I sat on the floor and opened my notebook, paging through it, looking for anything promising among my dark scribbles while Evan tuned his guitar.

With a quick glance over at me, he reached for my guitar and tuned it as well. It was an unspoken, unacknowledged practice between us when we were writing together, and I never minded it because I liked watching him do it, liked watching how his fingers soft-shoed over the strings, the deft plucks, the tilt of his head as he listened to the vibration, searching for the perfect resonance. His gaze would drift far off, eyes narrowing. Elsewhere. Someplace where there were only sound waves and pitch. Evan said I looked like an angry scientist when I was writing, stabbing at the page with the pen, bleeding ink all over my hands. He looked like someone who'd reached enlightenment when he played, and there was a beauty in it that never failed to mesmerize me.

We were so fucking different in so many ways that sometimes I thought it was a wonder we'd come as far as we had.

Evan finished tuning my guitar and handed it to me where I sat on the floor. We ran through some of our first album to warm up. At the end of "This Time," his fingers hesitated over the strings, his mouth moving soundlessly, which usually meant he had some fresh notes wiggling on the line and was trying to figure out how to best reel them in.

He pulled a variation on a C chord, then dropped the note and slid his hand down the fretboard before dancing back up again through a series of minor chords that made my hair stand on end. It was dark and haunting, and it was definitely *something*. I listened, rapt, until he blinked up at me from beneath his lashes for my take. There was a tentativeness in his gaze that was so unusual, it was striking.

"Do it again," I nodded, and he did, and then one more time until I'd picked up on the chord pattern and played it back to him.

"It needs an anchor, yeah? It's just floating around there like a black balloon. Needs a string you can hold on to to keep it from floating off," I mumbled, letting my fingers run over the strings. We tried out a few combos, Evan running the notes while I layered in beneath until we found it: a steady, metronome bassline that held the roots of the song in place and let Evan's overlying chords dance lightly on top of it.

"This is really good," I said, and Evan nodded slowly.

"Just have to fill in the rest. Not sure if that's a chorus or verse yet."

"It's a chorus. Feels that way to me."

"You getting anything yet? Because I've got nothing for lyrics."

"Nope, but I can feel it." It was like a tickle at the base of my skull, like anticipation. An edginess that ran through my fingertips and trembled in my vocal chords. "What were you thinking of?"

Evan dropped his gaze to his guitar, then over to the stack of records with a shake of his head. "I dunno. Old things. When I was a kid." His lips pressed together, released. "You."

"Me?"

"Yeah."

I wanted him to elucidate and tell me what the fuck that meant, because what he'd played, it had pulled and tugged at me. It had gravity. It floated, then sank. It was hopeful and sad at once.

Stages

December 2016

Did you ever worry that when you transitioned to larger shows some of the onstage chemistry between you two would be lost?

Evan: Nah, not really. We've always been ourselves, and Les has that kind of peacock presence that scales up easily—

Les: A peacock, huh?

Evan: Don't even try to deny it. But that's what's great about... I mean, when I was doing shows on my own, it was very different, because I'm naturally quieter, I guess, and Les is so outgoing. He has a knack for drawing me out of my shell. We have fun up there. We always do, no matter where we're playing.

Les: What he's trying to say is: I help him be his best self, live his best life. Someone needs to give me my own talk show. I'm down to give away some cars.

Evan: That would be a disaster.

Les: A very entertaining one.

CHAPTER 22

Evan

We were walking along the downtown strip after dinner a few days later when Les bumped his shoulder against mine and leaned in, breath falling warm across my neck as he murmured, "Don't look now, but we're being followed."

"What? Who?" I resisted, just barely, the urge to crane a look around.

"Who do you think? That photographer."

My hands reflexively balled into fists at my side, but I forced them to relax, forced my shoulders to relax. Forced everything to relax. I couldn't do jack about my blood pressure, though. It was simmering. "That wasn't on the list, though, right? Just dinner?"

"Just dinner." Les nodded, seeming considerably more at ease with this situation than I was. The boundary overstepping annoyed me. For God's sake, we'd just spent two hours in a booth at an Italian restaurant doing something I was pretty sure the tabloids would call "canoodling." Touches to the arm, sitting next to each other, gazing deeply into one another's eyes. I'd drawn the line at kissing because we were in public. In the South, beyond the some- what protective boundary lines of the bigger cities. And while our publicist from New York might not understand that, Les and I did.

It had actually been kind of fun, though, and we cracked ourselves up at least a handful of times playing our parts. Once when Les leaned in to whisper that I was staring at him so intently he was worried I was about to have a stroke. Another time when he smeared a bit of oregano on his teeth and smiled smarmily, saying, "Kiss me, you fool." When I shoved my breadstick in his mouth instead, he bobbed his head on it lewdly. I figured that was the picture that would end up online. Then Les had reached under the table and dropped his hand ever so casually on my thigh and I froze up. Reading the tension in my expression, he'd let his hand fall away with one last light squeeze. His features were contemplative, though, and I didn't know what to make of it.

All of that should have been enough for the photographer, so I wasn't sure why she was still following us.

Les took his ball cap off and riffled a hand through his hair as I scoured the street beside us, searching for a cab we could duck into and make our escape. Ahead of us, a cluster of girls leaned against a storefront, peering into the glass. They glanced up at us as we closed in on them, then returned to ogling whatever was on the other side of the windowpane. Except one. Her eyes narrowed at the two of us just as I grabbed Les's elbow and started to cross the street.

"Where are we going?" he asked as we stopped in the center lane while a slow stream of traffic passed. An orange car braked for us, and I nudged Les forward until we hit the curb below a neon sign.

"A wax museum? Feeling the need to be among some fellow stiffs?" he quipped. He'd had more wine than I had at dinner because, well, it was Les, and he spoke with a jaunty smile that told me he was buzzed.

"There's an entrance fee, and it's dark inside. Not optimal for photos." I shoved a twenty-dollar bill at the sleepy-eyed attendant in the booth and pushed inside, dragging Les with me and mentally congratulating myself on my quick thinking.

Les touched the tip of his nose. "Aren't you clever?"

"Very. You're just better-looking, which apparently trumps in interviews."

"And life, really." He snickered.

"Sad truth."

The museum was broken into two rooms, and there appeared to be only one other couple wandering through it at this hour, which was exactly what I'd hoped for. It was dark and quiet and there was no one to pay any attention to us. My breaths came easier as we made our way from statue to statue. Dolly Parton, Kenny Chesney, Willie Nelson, George Jones. All the country greats. Tom Cruise. Taylor Swift. Les stopped in front of Dolly Parton, folding his arms over his chest and leaning in to inspect her like he was looking for flaws.

"I swear you're obsessed with her tits."

"Nah. She's got great legs, too." He gave me a flippant smile as he slung an arm around her shoulders, then pecked her on one waxen cheek.

"You know, if we ever get to meet her, you're going to embarrass us both."

Les arched a brow. "Please. If we ever meet her, I'm going to tell her that I can't think about my childhood without thinking about 'Yellow Roses' because my mom used to sing it every night before she put me to bed. And that 'Coat of Many Colors' is what made me want to write music."

My lips parted in quiet disbelief. Fuck him for surprising me with his sudden depth and sincerity. I was trying to think of what I'd say to her when Les glanced backward and said, "Three o'clock."

"You're fucking kidding me." But nope, when I glanced over my shoulder, the chestnut-haired photographer from dinner was making a beeline in our direction, camera already on the rise. I stalked into the next room, looking for an exit, Les laughing as he trailed after me.

"I'm glad this is so funny to you."

"I don't get why you're so pissed about this. Let's just see what she wants, because she's clearly after something."

"A bigger paycheck. And we did our fucking part. She needs to go away."

I wound around the displays and pawed through the thick curtains that draped the walls of the museum. There had to be an emergency exit, and I didn't care if it set the alarms off. Maybe the photographer could explain it to the owner. I just wanted to get back to the cabin.

Les hooked me by the elbow, velvet dragging across my face as I was pulled behind a curtain.

"This isn't an exit," I protested. We were in some kind of storage niche, and it was creepy as hell. A wall sconce emitting a pitiful amount of light revealed wax statues surrounding us in various states of undress and dismemberment. The headless torso of what I could only assume was Arnold Schwarzenegger flexed behind Les, who looked around with interest.

"She'll probably assume we found one, though, when she sees we're not out there. Then she'll go, too. Easy." He spoke in a low voice. "Ohhh, Demi Moore. Remember when she was married to Ashton Kutcher? I always thought that was fake, because I'd never have let that woman go. Take my picture with her!" He fumbled in his pocket for his phone.

"Les, you pretty much push your women and men out the door when you're through with them. Also, where are her legs?"

"I think that's them behind... no fucking shit, is that New Kids on the Block? Oh wait, maybe it's One Direction? Hurry up! Phone. Now. I need this."

He shoved his phone in my hand as I tried to shush him, but it was too late; a shaft of light pierced our stupid hidey-hole and backlit the photographer like something out of a horror B movie.

"Evening, fellas. Having yourselves a private tour?" The perky insouciance in her smile tempted me to snatch the camera out of her hands and break it against Arnold's mountainous bicep.

"Yeah, actually, so if you don't mind, I'm pretty sure you got what you needed at the restaurant." I did my best to affect a casual air, like we weren't cowering behind a curtain. Well, mostly me. Les still appeared enraptured by the discovery of Joey McIntyre. He had a lifelong obsession with boy bands that he'd told me about in great detail one night in Denver when he'd been out-of-his-mind stoned, and his depth of knowledge was frightening.

She shrugged lightly, completely unmoved. The wax museum was proving to be another stupid idea on my part. We should have just kept walking.

"I got some boring, lukewarm displays of affection, but nothing that'll sell covers and, therefore, make my trip here and my paycheck worthwhile, so..." Her smile sweetened. "I thought I might stick around for a while. See what's for dessert. By the way, you've been spotted." She hiked a thumb over her shoulder. "The sidewalk out front is filled with adoring fans and a few not-so-adoring ones. Seems your relationship has stirred up quite a vat of emotion."

I glowered at her, gritting my teeth, but Les touched my elbow lightly, then slid his hand up along my bicep and wrapped his arm around my shoulder affectionately. He plastered on his charming smile, the one that lit up his eyes and melted panties and boxers alike. Even if it wasn't aimed in my direction, it was still stunning. An unwanted heat spread over me as his fingers drifted over my sleeve.

"How about a deal?" he suggested.

The photographer cocked her hip, lifting an expectant brow.

"We'll give you something good and you prance yourself back out there and tell them we're not here."

"*Les*." That was me, trying to tell him we weren't going to bargain with fucking paparazzi.

"How good?" That was her, ignoring me.

"You'll have to change your panties afterwards, sweetheart." His voice oozed sex like syrup, and that did the trick. She swung her camera up, fingers flying as she adjusted the settings.

I didn't have even a second to formulate a protest before Les plowed into me, shoving me up against the wall. The flail of my hand sent one of Arnold's forearms flying off, and something in the wall lodged uncomfortably against my spine. A light switch, maybe?

But then Les's mouth hit mine like a shot of whiskey. Rich and dark, with the afterburn of his teeth scraping over my lower lip. One of his hands twined over my shoulder, sinking into the loose curls at the nape of my neck, and I grunted when he tugged and pressed harder against me. The heat of his body against mine, and the tongue that barreled into my mouth overwhelmed me with sensation. I stopped thinking. Stopped thinking about the photographer and Arnold's broken arm and the people outside. My lips parted on a groan, and Les deepened the kiss as I fisted the side of his shirt, low near his waist, balling up the fabric until my knuckles brushed his bare skin, and he shivered.

Les wedged his thigh between mine and forced my legs wider, his erection hard and forceful against me, the roll of his hips subtle but demanding in pressure. I couldn't help it; I reacted to the friction, felt my stomach contract as I rocked into him and he let out a soft moan, the pleasure in it transmuting and rolling through me like sound waves. God, was I still breathing? I knew that if I felt his dick like a steel rod, he had to be feeling mine and would know without a doubt how turned on I was. His tongue all but fucked my mouth, and then his teeth dragged over my lower lip, and just as I was about to give myself fully over to it, it was gone.

Cool air rushed the space between us as Les wrenched himself away and tousled my hair playfully before turning back to the reporter. I was left gasping and panting for breath in the vacuum.

"Better put on the brakes, because once this guy gets started"— he thumbed at me—"he can go all fucking night. He's seriously insatiable."

"Likely to fuck him right through this wall," I agreed, somehow managing a sober expression despite my aroused half-fugue state where the sensation of Les's mouth and weight against me pinged off every nerve ending in my body. I'd gone from zero to uncomfortably hard in a span of seconds.

From the corner of my eye, I caught Les pressing his lips together to suppress a grin as the photographer smirked, then waved a hand at us. "All right, all right. I've got enough."

"Sure you don't want to stick around and watch how I can make him speak in tongues?"

Oh God, I wished he'd stop talking.

The photographer arched a brow. "I'd be tempted to insert myself."

Les shrugged. "We've done it before."

"I don't like being third wheel."

I grabbed Les by the nape of his neck and squeezed before he could dig us deeper, ignoring how imagining what his mouth could do made my dick throb. "That's enough. Jesus."

The photographer winked smugly at us and vanished back through the curtain with a little farewell wave. From my new vantage point, I caught a beckoning sliver of red light beyond Demi Moore's legless torso. I started toward it and had just pushed through the doorway into another storage room with more wax figures when Les hauled me back by my waistband. "Not so fast, Romeo."

CHAPTER 23

"**W**hat? Let's go!" Evan was practically shouting, and he tried to jerk away to continue forward, but I kept my fingers fastened to his waistband, holding him in place as I stepped around to face him.

"Chill out, we're not—"

He lurched forward to try and pass me again, and I yanked him into me. He was going to drive me to desperate measures? Fine. I snaked my hand between us to palm his erection, attempting to ignore just how much touching him like that had my own cock ready to explode, because dammit, I was trying to make a point. He went stone still, eyes flaring wide, and we spent a handful of seconds staring each other down, his chest rising and falling in rapid breaths against mine. That close, I could see the heat in his cheeks, feel it rising from his skin.

"You want to take your hand off my dick?" he finally asked, giving me a cool expression that didn't quite dampen the color in his face.

"You're hard as a fucking rock." I was proud of myself for not moaning it, because God knew I'd dreamed of touching him just like this for months. Hell, years.

"Where are you going with this?"

"Where do you *think* I'm going with this? You enjoyed that back there." I inclined my head toward the room we'd just been in, in case he'd somehow forgotten the way he'd been rubbing up against me.

He pressed his lips together so tightly they paled, then he hitched one shoulder. "I wouldn't read into it too much, Les. Boners happen."

I snorted and shook my head, curling my fingers tighter around the hard heat of his bulge. The crinkle at the corners of his eyes was minute but telling. "You were into it," I said slowly, "with *me*."

"I know how to put on a show, same as you." His brows pinched together as his mouth turned down.

My grip on his waistband stopped him from going too far when he tried a different tactic and took a step backward. I let the hand on his cock fall back to my side but closed the distance between us, still determined to hash this out. "And you were into it with Ella and me, which is why it was so confusing that you were such a dick about everything the next day."

"I wasn't a dick." His tone was insistent, but the tiny thread of guilt in the eyes that darted away from mine spurred me on as I gave him a flat, unpersuaded stare.

"You said"—I held up a finger as I quoted him—"'That was something I'll live to regret.'"

"That doesn't sound like me being a dick; that sounds like evidence that I'm psychic."

Stubborn fucker. I cocked my head at him, one brow winging up. "And then you gave me the cold shoulder, and you did that for the next six months."

Evan scoffed with a choked-out laugh. "I did not."

"You did. Look, I get it. You were worried it would change our partnership, relationship, whatever."

"And it did." The conviction was back, the guilt gone, and I could tell in the uptick of his breathing that he was exasperated. Which was fine with me, because I was, too. It was about time we confronted this shit.

"Because *you* flipped out about it and made the last tour miserable trying to pretend it didn't happen. But it doesn't have to *be* a big deal. It wasn't for me. It was... fun. It was hot. I fucking liked watching you with her. I liked touching you. I liked screwing her with you. I liked"—I paused, because I was too close to telling him how much I liked *him*—"it with you." I watched Evan's face as I spoke, because there was a change happening. The cracks started forming when I said I liked watching him, and by the time I finished, he seemed almost hesitant. His shoulders had gone rigid as steel girders, and he glanced away from me with a flare of his nostrils.

I loosened my grip on his waistband and slid my hand behind the band of his boxers. The humid warmth of naked skin and the wiry curls of his pubic hair met the tips of my fingers as I brushed them lightly over his cock. He swallowed visibly, gaze shifting back to meet mine before he set his jaw as if steeling himself for something far worse than the potential of an orgasm.

"Do you like this?" I watched him, trying to read any minute changes, and he watched me back just as intently. His eyes were the stormy dark of clouds threatening to break. My pulse raced; I could feel it thundering at my temples and throat. When he said nothing, I let my hand dive deeper, hot skin against hot skin as I gripped his shaft between two knuckles and dragged a rough caress up his length. That tight set of his jaw broke open on a stuttered breath.

"Tell me the truth." I rubbed the pad of my thumb over the crown of his cock and felt a slight tilt of his hips in response. "Do. You. Like. This?"

"Yes." He exhaled, closing his eyes. Resignation and confession that stood my hair on end.

I reached deeper, cupping his balls, squeezing the heel of my hand against them, and fuck, I wanted to rip his clothes off right there and get down on my knees, same as I'd wanted to that night with Ella but had been too scared to push it. "Do you want me to stop?"

"Yes." A ragged sound that escaped him while his eyes were still tightly shut.

He seemed so desperate and conflicted that I stopped provoking him, removed my hand, and took a step back. "Porter—"

He shook his head, eyes flying open, his lips parting to speak.

"Hey!"

I whipped a glance over Evan's shoulder to find the booth attendant hobbling toward us.

Evan gave me a wild, disoriented look and then shoved me roughly toward the exit. "Go!"

I took off, Evan on my heels as I stumbled through the door, and heard him call out, "Your exits are supposed to be clearly marked!"

We hauled ass all the way down the alley, careening around the corner onto another street before I had to stop, bend over, and catch my breath because I was laughing so hard, mostly for the whole cockeyed situation.

"What the fuck's so funny?" Evan skidded to a halt next to me, then rested his back against the wall. When I'd recovered enough to look up, I noted he was hardly winded. Fucker could probably run a marathon right now.

"Your exits are supposed to be clearly marked," I mimicked.

"Well, they are. It's a fire hazard." He tried to conceal the threat of a smile by wiping the side of his hand across his mouth, but I'd caught it.

I pushed off the wall and scraped a few strands of hair from the side of my cheek. Then I reached for him, wanting to pick up where we'd left off, but he ducked away and started down the sidewalk, throwing his hand up to hail a cab. Whatever momentary interlude we'd had was clearly over.

I ambled after him, and when a cab pulled to the curb and stopped, he got in, scooting to the far corner without another word, looking out the window with his lips pinched in a thin line. We rode home in a thick silence that could've been a result of so many different things that I wasn't sure which angle to attack it from. Or if I even wanted to bother. He was clearly struggling with everything that had happened tonight, maybe even before, and I sure as shit wasn't a therapist.

Once we got back to the cabin, the stalemate between us seemed less oppressive since there was more room for it to breathe than in the cab. Evan pushed a cold bottle of water against my stomach while I peeled off my T-shirt. "Drink it. We have a lot of shit to do tomorrow, and if you're hungover, we'll lose half a day."

"I won't be hungover tomorrow. Fuck's sake, would you give it a rest?" I might be *slightly* hungover tomorrow, but I'd be up at the crack of fucking dawn and ready no matter what, just to spite him.

He folded his arms across his chest and gave me a look. All that was missing was him tapping his foot impatiently. After cracking the seal on the water bottle, I upended it, downing the whole thing in one long series of gulps under his watch. When I finished, I swiped my forearm across my mouth. Evan's gaze flicked down to my chest and then jerked up again. He lifted one hand to tug at the roots of his hair, then shook his head in what seemed like annoyance.

"My dick is attracted to you, yes," he said out of nowhere, and my pulse stammered before thrumming wildly in response to that declaration.

Unfortunately, he continued. "But I'm not a slave to my dick like apparently ninety-nine percent of the male population is, and everything else about you..." Another shake of his head. "So I don't trust it."

"You don't trust *me*, you mean."

"Tomato, tamatoh." He shrugged, then turned on his heel and walked down the hall to his bedroom, leaving me standing there in flabbergasted silence. Fuck me sideways; I had no idea it was possible to feel ecstatic and crushed at the same time.

If you could relive one show you've played, which one would it be?

Evan: The first one on our first tour.

Les: Really? We were so damn nervous, though. I thought you were gonna hurl on my shoes.

Evan: If I ever hurl on you, it'll be a direct hit, trust me. But no, in all seriousness, I'd pick that one. We'd played bars and smaller venues forever—college campuses, stuff like that. But right after our first album dropped, MGD put us on a big stage at a huge festival, and I guess that was the moment I really knew that everything we'd been working our asses off to achieve had finally arrived.

CHAPTER 24

Evan

For the next three days, I set my alarm and went running when it was still dark outside, before Les even had a hope of being up. Since the night at the wax museum, we'd spoken minimally. Maintaining a standoff in fifteen hundred square feet was no small task. That we managed to actually write through it was impressive, but we were hurting there, too. Our playing felt uninspired even though we were working on songs we'd already agreed were good. Les was either angry or letting me process, and I hated that both possibilities made my stomach knot up for different reasons—none of which I was allowing myself to address right then. We came to write an album, not for me to descend into some weird pit of emotional fuckery. It was so damn unlike me it was disconcerting. And it didn't help that every time I closed my eyes, I saw that penetrating stare of his as he'd shoved his hand down my pants at the museum, the quiet demand in his eyes. I couldn't have lied if I'd wanted to. And now I was trying to avoid having to do it again.

. . .

Les found me in the music room restringing my guitar and let out a bitter chuckle as he leaned up against the doorway, folding his arms over his bare chest. I couldn't help but look at the lean lines of his torso, the shift of muscle in his forearms as he crossed them, the ink all over his arms and pecs. It was as if once I'd admitted my attraction to him in my head, I couldn't stop noticing everything about him. It was annoying as hell, and I dragged my gaze back down to my strings, yanking out a loop of wire so hard that it snapped against my hand with a sharp sting.

"Fitting."

"What?" I kept my attention focused on my lap as I pulled out a coil of new strings and began sorting through them.

"Your shoulders look about as tight as those strings." He pushed off the doorway and came inside.

"I slept wrong last night." I rubbed the back of my neck as if to demonstrate. Hell, it felt like I'd slept on everything wrong, and the fact that Les could tell with a glance what most people wouldn't even notice got that prickle of nerves coursing through my body again. We knew each other too damn well, and while it'd been good for our music, it was wreaking havoc on my ability to detach from him when I wanted to.

"Feels like I've been sleeping wrong for months," Les mused, a smile playing over his lips as I glanced up. He brushed one hand over his bicep, goose bumps rising with the touch. "Cold down here. Coffee?" He turned away even as I grunted a *no*.

A few minutes later, he returned with a mug for me anyway, setting it on a nearby side table whose surface was liberally scattered with rings. "One sugar, splash of milk," he affirmed, without me even having to ask. Then he flipped through his notebook, tore out a page, and set it on the table in front of me before dropping onto the floor and riffling through a series of records I'd stacked there. "Hit a vein, I think." He jutted his chin toward the paper drenched in his cramped writing. "I've got a sound for it, too."

He hummed a few notes, the melody ascending and then dropping low. I set my half-strung guitar aside and reached for his, trying to mimic the sound of his voice as I let my fingers skip around and find the notes. "Like that?"

"Yeah, but maybe um..." He paused, head tilting side to one side, thoughtfully. "Drop it an octave and see."

"Yeah." He nodded when I did. "What do you think?" His eyes were wide and imploring. I'd forgotten how he could be when it came to music, the way he sometimes seemed like he was waiting for approval, and how his smile curved so gently when I gave it, as I did then. Because I was skimming the lyrics and hearing the melody in my head, and it was good. For as cocky as he was about other things, Les truly was a collaborative writing partner, always willing to listen and experiment.

I squinted at the page, then cut a look over at him that lingered longer than I intended. "This is about us?" I meant it as a statement, but it came out almost as a question.

Les did that side-to-side head-tilt thing again and scratched casually at his jaw. "Sorta."

"Dancing around your hard edges..." I read off the page, my gaze flickering up to find him watching me pensively. "That's what I'm like to you?"

"You're a lot of things, Porter." He shrugged and picked up his coffee, taking a long swallow.

I ran through the notes again, trying to expand on what he'd given me, and finally collapsed backward in a huff, giving up. Lately, it felt like I was the one stuck while Les churned along easily.

He read my frustration and reached for his guitar, dragging it from my lap. I thought he was going to pick up where I'd left off, but instead he laid it on the floor beside him, then crawled onto the couch, insinuating himself behind me. "I want to try something. I don't know if you've noticed, but you never touch anyone."

I hadn't really, but he wasn't wrong. Les was always touching people, throwing his arms around shoulders, showing affection or interest with a touch to someone's forearm or hand. I was careful of personal space, and I didn't like anyone I didn't know in my own, which had made working as a bartender an exercise in frustration.

When his hands landed on my shoulders, I flinched. Instead of taking it as a brush-off and retreating, though, he tightened his grip, digging his thumbs into muscle, pressing into the knots and rolling against them. I was about to shrug him off, but he pushed the heels of his palms into my shoulder blades and fuck did it feel good. I let my head drop forward a little and felt him sink more heavily into the cushion behind me.

"Good?"

I gave a tiny nod as he firmly prodded the top of my spine. "Yeah." It felt better than good, and if he kept going I couldn't decide whether I was more likely to fall asleep or pop wood.

"Remember when we played Gap Fest and there was a masseuse backstage?"

"Yeah. Didn't you sleep with her?"

Les laughed close to my ear. "No. I mean, I don't want to ruin your very flattering image of me, but I was about to say you should do this more often. I get that you have your routines and stuff, but you don't let yourself deviate and you never relax, and even if you're not going to relax about ninety-nine percent of your waking life — a masseuse kind of forces you into it for a while."

"What are you getting at here?"

He let out an exasperated huff. "That you should fucking relax for five minutes and let me do this. Your shoulders feel like rebar." His touch tripped up to the side of my neck, fingertips working the tendons. The warmth of his skin and the way he rolled his knuckles across my neck was almost orgasmic. I tilted my head to one side, then the other, directed by the pressure of his touch. When he moved on and closed his hands around my biceps, his torso pressed against me and I could feel him, hard and thick against me.

"Pretty sure masseuses aren't supposed to be sporting wood when they massage someone."

"That's why I'm not a professional. Sorry. It's an occupational hazard with me, I guess. I have a hair trigger, you know that. Do you want me to stop?" He paused, his hands still curled around my upper arms, but his grip loosening ever so slightly.

"No. Keep going." I tried not to think about how good it felt, because he wasn't the only one with a hard-on. Which answered my previous question; I was not at all drowsy at the moment.

He released one of my arms and put both hands on the other, initiating long, deep strokes from my bicep to my wrist, pushing at muscle, kneading tendons until my arm went rag doll floppy and loose. Then he did the other arm. Afterward, I felt him shift around, rising up on his knees behind me to tackle my shoulders again. His dick brushed against my back as he dug into me, and I wasn't unaware that his breathing had quickened. Mine had too and now I was so damn hard my pants were little more than a straightjacket on my cock.

When he reached for the hem of my T-shirt and tugged it up toward my chin and then over my head, I didn't resist, just lifted my arms, having slipped into some kind of trancelike autopilot mode that I'd blame on the insane eroticism of his touch. Air rushed cool across my skin, and his warm hands pressed flat against my ribs, dragging down to my lower back and then back up again with a friction that almost burned.

"Fuck, you've got a killer body. I've always been so jealous of that." Just the lust-heavy sound of his voice made me groan in reply, and I thought for the millionth time about how he'd kissed me the other night. When his boner brushed against me this time, I pushed back against him without even thinking twice.

He dug into my shoulders, finding a rhythm, pushing and pulling against me, his breath coming steadily but in heavy drafts. I was so fucking turned on I couldn't take it; I reached behind me, grabbed the back of his thigh, and yanked him hard up against me.

"Shit," he hissed out. "You fucker." He shifted again, tilting himself somehow so I couldn't feel his dick anymore. "I'm not trying to perv on you, I'm trying to relax you."

"It's kinda hard to ignore your dick."

"I get that a lot." He chuckled shamelessly. "Just think of it like... one of those massage wands in the SkyMall magazine."

"Those vibrate, though, don't they?"

"Keep arching your back against me like that and my wand will definitely be vibrating."

"There's something wrong with you." More mumble than words as I let my head droop forward again and my eyes fall shut to better focus on the pleasure radiating through me.

He walked the pressure of his knuckles up and down my back, his laughter low and sonorous when my spine swayed back and forth trying to anticipate his next move. My erection throbbed and was well on its way to full-blown ache. What was it with my cock and Les? For that matter, what was it with *me* and Les? Why was the worst option in the world the only one both my dick and I seemed to agree on?

"Want me to keep going?" He paused, his hands low around my waist, thumbs sweeping into the dimples at my lower back.

"Yeah."

"Yeah, like 'eh, this is okay' or 'yes definitely'?"

I twisted around to try and catch a glimpse of his face, because it struck me as such an unusual question coming from him. I thought he just wanted to hear some kind of verbal confirmation of what he was visibly doing to me. Because there was no fucking way he couldn't know or couldn't see the evidence trying to leap out of my pants. His eyes were glassy, cheeks tinged with color, and his tongue darted out to swipe his lower lip as his brows winged up, silently prodding me.

"Yes, definitely." I kept my voice as even as I could.

He nodded and lifted up on his knees again, tackling my shoulders with the downward force of his body through his arms. When I let my head droop forward, I noticed a tiny wet spot on my sweats where my cock was plastered to the fabric, and I wondered if that was the cause of the curse that slipped from his mouth next.

The whole ambience transformed in an instant.

I lifted my hips at the same time Les's hands landed on the waistband of my sweats. He shoved them down below my knees, then pulled me back against him, between his thighs. Resting his chin on my shoulder, he ran a hand down over my chest, then my stomach, stopping before he reached my cock. His breath tickled the side of my neck as he spoke, but there was no mistaking the desire in the velvety roll of his voice. "You want me to touch you?"

I figured the fact that my dick was twitching was answer enough, but apparently that didn't cut it. He wrapped his hand around me and gave my shaft a single, excruciatingly tight stroke that almost had me coming off the couch for more before he released me suddenly. My dick protested the brush-off with another hard twitch, a thick bead of precum squeezing from my slit.

"You want me to jack that fat cock, then you fucking say it."

I gritted my teeth and reached for his hand, but he swatted me away. "Goddammit, quit fucking around and jack me before common sense catches up with my dick."

He rumbled, a sound that was caught between laughter and purr. "Not gonna happen this time, sweetheart; I'm one step ahead. I'm about to get you off so fucking hard you'll be Jell-O."

"You always such a cocky fuck when it comes to sex?"

"Besides music, it's the only thing I know I do well."

It'd be funny if it wasn't so true, because when he gripped me again, his fist gliding along my length and twisting deftly at the top, it was fucking perfect. The pressure, the friction, everything. He pushed his thumb against my lower lip, and I opened to him automatically, taking it into my mouth and sucking while he growled against my throat. He dragged his wet thumb down my chin and then rubbed it over my head a few times, making me writhe.

"Spit." He cupped his palm under my chin, and when I hesitated, he said. "Don't think about it, just do it."

So I did. Then his hand was back on my cock, slick and hot and driving me mad.

"Fuck, I'm gonna come just getting you off," he whispered, and nipped at my earlobe.

I shuddered out a breath as his hand twisted over me, my hips chasing every stroke, his breath hot against my neck and his dick pulsing against my back. He stroked me slow, then fast, hard then soft until I was half-crazed at the variation, my orgasm constantly yanked to the foreground, then shoved to the background until there was nowhere left for it to go, and no matter how he touched me, I was about to explode.

I panted, letting my head fall back to his shoulder, and he braced his legs around my hips. His teeth sank into my shoulder, my collarbone, my neck, and I arched every time into his hand, nearly whimpering with the need for release. I was never fucking like this, had never *been* like this with anyone else—almost feral with how turned on I was, how much I ached over what he was doing to me, how perfectly he read my body.

"God," I grated out. I sounded desperate and whiny and so unlike myself. "Fuck, I'm gonna come." And then I couldn't stop talking, telling him *harder*, *faster* on harsh, guttering breaths. Les was right there with me, breath coming heavy and fast in my ear as he whispered filthy encouragements—how hard I was, how good I felt in his fist. And when he gripped my balls in his other hand and told me to give him the load I was holding back, I fucking lost it. My thighs quaked with the full-body shudder that coursed through me, and I blew hot in his hand to a string of curses he whispered against my throat. I felt the hard press of him against my back as my orgasm rolled through me, and then a bloom of wet heat as he came with muffled groan.

His legs sprawled on either side of me as we both went limp and collapsed backward into the sofa, the harsh rise and fall of his chest lifting me up and down.

After a few minutes, I rolled off to one side, hiking my pants back up over my ass and tossing my T-shirt to him so he could mop himself off.

"Shit."

"What?" I glanced at him in alarm.

"You came all over Bowie's face."

I looked down at the records scattered over the floor and there, streaked across Bowie's softly focused expression on the record sleeve of *Young Americans*, was a streamer of cum. My eyes went wide, and Les rolled off the couch, racked with laughter.

"Oh hell." I reached down and swiped at the record sleeve. "Fitting tribute?"

"Absolutely."

. . .

AN HOUR PASSED. TWO. WE'D CLEANED UP AND WORKED ON SOME songs, blithely glossing over what had happened earlier. Patches of uncomfortable silence were interspersed with comfortable conversation. All of it felt inherently unsteady, like the way Les's coffee mug was sitting at the very edge of the table, one clumsy movement from tipping over. That was more or less what the past six months had felt like, too. So when Les blew out a long breath, shoved his guitar aside, and sprawled on his side on the floor near me, saying, "We have to talk about this," I was relieved this time instead of angry. Maybe I'd needed that orgasm more than I thought, because I was definitely calmer now. I'd also spent the last half hour reliving the feeling of him getting me off and wondering how and if I could make it happen again.

"Have you always been into guys?"

That wasn't what I expected, though, so it took me a minute to reframe my mindset. All the while, he studied me passively. Not hurrying me, just patient interest.

"I'm not 'into' guys." He snorted and I held up my hand so he'd let me finish. "I'm not 'into' people in general that often, okay? You already know that."

"Have you been with a guy before?"

I schooled my expression, steeling myself. Of course he had to ask the fucking question. "Yes."

His jaw dropped as he sat up straight and stared me down like I'd brutalized a puppy or something. "Why haven't you ever told me?"

"Because it's none of your business really. How often do I talk about anyone I date anyway?"

He tipped his head to the side. "All right. Point. Still, it seems like something that would've come up somewhere along the way. I dunno, maybe one of the many times you walked in on me. Some solidarity or a thumbs-up and a 'hey, your oral technique looks great.'"

"You're usually on the receiving end of said technique," I pointed out.

"Okay, point again. But why?" Then he squinted one eye and

pursed his lips, like he was seeing right through me. "Wait. Who was it? Did he break your clockwork heart?"

I fought to ignore the jab. My heart was far from clockwork. It was a bastard. Fleeting images surfaced—a red skim of hair, a soft mouth, warm brown eyes. My best friend in high school. Until he moved away senior year and our friendship unraveled suddenly, painfully, like it'd never even been there at all. I told Les the first part, but he seemed unsatisfied by the answer. "What'd you do with him?"

"Mostly hand jobs, a few blowjobs. It was... high school." It had always been hurried and hushed. Like there was something intrinsically wrong with what we were doing. That was mostly on his part, though. I didn't have enough of a social profile back then to give a shit what other people thought; I was already invisible.

"Did you love him?"

Relentlessly, painfully. But I was confused, too. So much of high school was nothing but confusion to me. The social politics, the general obsession with body parts and who was sticking what in where and for how long. Music was easier. A place I could dissolve into. A place where I created the rules, the structure, the tone.

"He contacted me once. Sent me an email right after our first album hit it big."

Les's eyes widened. "Did you reply?" He lowered his voice as if we were in a crowd rather than in an empty room, and it was clear that he'd mistaken my reluctance to talk about it as embarrassment rather than hurt. "Did you see him again?"

"Nah. When I'm done, I'm done."

And then he sussed it out. "So he *did* break your heart. And that's why you haven't been with another guy since?"

I didn't say anything. Maybe it was easier to let him think a broken heart was to blame than to tell him the deeper truth. Because that truth was far more complex than some implication of self-imposed restraint after a soured relationship. The truth was I hadn't been attracted to another guy until Les. And if I was brutally honest, I'd never been attracted to *anyone* the way I was Les. And yeah, I'd only come to that conclusion recently after a shit ton of internal turmoil, but the force of it hit like an avalanche primarily *because* it was so rare for me to be truly into anyone. "Maybe."

"You're being really obtuse right now."

I felt the corners of my mouth turn up, and Les threw his arm across the couch cushion, leaning closer to look up at me, the green intensity of his gaze brightening like a flash fire. "I won't hurt you, you know."

"I know. Because this isn't real anyway." It was both true and untrue, but it was the best kind of answer for the ridiculous promise Les was making. How could anyone predict whether they'd hurt someone else? If someone had asked me about Luke in high school, I never would've thought it possible that we wouldn't somehow be connected for life, and what I felt for Les now was so damn complicated I was hesitant to label it. Les *got* me and I got him, but it was on this subdermal, subvocal level that didn't make logical sense to me. It was like trying to break down a song. If you went too far, it would lose all its magic, but it was also a necessity if you wanted to truly understand the structure and why the song worked in the first place.

Maybe I needed to try not questioning us. With music, my trust in Les's instinct and ability was absolute. But where I was concerned personally? Not so much. Yet, I couldn't deny that I wanted more of this. Whatever it was. Because the sad truth was, sex rarely felt as good as what had just happened, and I was jealous. Jealous of people like Les, who seemed to find pleasure easily, in any random hand or mouth or body, while apparently it took an act of God for me to even want it. That load I'd blown in his hand felt like it'd been building up in me for a decade. So yeah, I wanted more. A lot more. But that meant I'd have to make a concerted effort to keep it casual the way Les apparently could.

Les frowned and scraped his teeth over his lower lip but nodded after a moment. "Doesn't mean we can't have some fun with it. Like we just did, yeah?"

I licked my lips, and somehow when I said, "Sure, yeah. I'm down," it felt as if I'd passed through some door that slammed shut and disappeared behind me.

CHAPTER 25

I was cartwheeling inside the rest of the morning and into the afternoon. Evan might've been second-guessing himself over this morning, but clearly his body was into me. If I could just prove to him that there was no need for him to get all mired in over-thinking, maybe this whole fake relationship could become... Fuck, was I really considering that? Yeah, I'd been lusting after him forever, but it was always accompanied by the ice-water shock of reality reminding me that that was pure fantasy because Evan was never going to be into me in a romantic way. Not to mention my track record with relationships was pretty shitty. Regardless, I wasn't about to look a gift horse in the mouth. Or maybe gift dick was more appropriate.

We worked for another half hour until we had a loose chorus-and-verse structure for a couple of other songs. But no lyrics. "I think you should write them," I said. Evan watched my guitar bob and bounce on my knee, and I knew he could tell I needed a break.

"I can try, sure." He twisted his mouth up like he was considering it before he suggested we stop for lunch.

"Yeah." I nodded gratefully and slid my guitar into the stand next to me. "Was thinking I'd go check out Grim's. Dan said he'd be bringing in some new stock this week. Interested?"

Evan didn't even look at me when he shook his head, his focus back on his guitar, absorbed by a riff we'd been working on earlier. I'd hit a wall, but I hoped a change of scenery would be enough to put a few chinks in it and some lyrics would start pouring out of me later that afternoon.

GRIM'S PARKING LOT WAS TINY, AND MY THREE-POINT TURN TO back into a spot became a twenty-point tactical operation that resulted in me crawling out the passenger-side door of Evan's SUV. I grabbed my ball cap at the last minute and popped it on my head. Not that I thought I was likely to be papped at noon in downtown Gatlinburg, but lately, who knew, and music perusal? That was my sacred time.

When I pushed through the glass-fronted door, a couple of rusty bells emitted a pitiful whimper, and immediately the scent of dust, old paper, and plastic surrounded me. I inhaled deeply for the way it reminded me of growing up and all the music stores I'd loved. Most of them were long gone. Grim's Record Repository in Nashville was one of the few stalwarts left, and its owner, Daniel Grim, had opened smaller satellites here and in Knoxville and swore he'd die before his shops would.

I grinned when I spotted the man himself crouched over, sorting through a bunch of albums. I strolled down the narrow aisles, letting my fingers trail an uneven path over record sleeves displayed in the roughly constructed plywood racks. He had CDs and even some cassettes, but most of the central floor space was devoted to records.

"Old dude checking out Conway Twitty. There's a cliché," I teased as I stopped near his hunched back.

Dan glanced up with a smile and cranked his middle finger up slowly while he sang a few husky bars of "Hello Darlin'." Dude could sing, and he used to professionally but had quit years ago. He was handsome, too, and not even for an older guy, just flat-out handsome in a rough, world-weary way as if time and tragedy had sanded his features in some places and left him sharp in others. Like his eyes, which twinkled as I cracked up.

He grasped my hand and pulled himself up, and then me into a hug, which he tightened unnecessarily until my lungs compressed and I let out a wheeze.

"Feel that vise? That ain't old—that's the vigor of the seasoned."

Dan released me and I staggered back dramatically, earning a warm chuckle from him.

"How's tricks?" he asked, sweeping up a stack of records and setting them into the display bin. He nudged the other two stacks aside with the toe of his cowboy boot and tipped his head to keep an eye on me as he started walking up the aisle to the checkout counter.

I followed along slowly, skimming records as I went. "Same old. Working on the new album."

"Yeah? Got anything good yet?"

"I think so, but shit, I don't trust my judgment as much this time. I thought the third album was good."

"It was." He leaned up against the counter, pulling out a can of nuts from behind it and spilling a handful into his palm. When he offered them to me, I shook my head. "I think it was the timing when it dropped. The market took a hit, people were flailing. The collective consciousness was primed for something light and hopeful and—"

"*Black Dove* definitely wasn't that," I finished for him. Dan had all kinds of theories on music, and if I got him going, he could go for hours analyzing and tying an album's success or failure to fashion trends, politics, even the stock market on the day an album released. It was fascinating and maybe a little crazy, but I always listened anyway because Dan was Dan. He'd had a solid music career that he left behind to open a couple of record stores, so he knew his shit. And he was partially responsible for me and Evan getting together. I'd known him since I moved to Nashville and used to haunt his main store, digging through records, hanging out, or playing shows. I had a huge soft spot for him.

"What's the new stuff sound like?"

"I'm not telling you, because you'll analyze it against market trends or something and psyche me out before we can get it finished."

He grinned. "Fair enough."

He popped another peanut in his mouth, chewing it thoughtfully as he studied me, and I knew before he even opened his mouth again what he was going to ask. I started drifting over to one of the display racks because I was going to have to lie to him and I didn't want to. He was still pretty well connected in the music industry, and even if I wanted to tell him the whole story about what was going on, it was a risk with the way gossip was traded in Nashville.

"It true?" He fixed me with a gimlet-eyed stare, then cracked another nut between his teeth.

Yep, there it was. I turned my back to him and picked up a random record without even reading the label, because the dude had a penetrating gaze that might as well have been an X-ray machine for bullshit.

"Sort of." And that was all I gave him.

He grunted and I thought he read between the lines well enough because when I looked over my shoulder at him, he pulled his thumb and forefinger across the seam of his lips, like he was zipping them, and moved on.

"You looking for anything in particular today or just come down here to distract some words out?"

He knew me too well. "Kinda both. You have any Jessup Polk?"

Dan's eyes crinkled at the corners as they narrowed. "Shit, that's a rare one." He put a hand to his forehead, thumb and index finger running along his brows like he was trying to coax something out. He had a pretty damn good memory, could usually nail an album's release down to the exact date. "I think I've got one or two of his, but they may be at the main store. They're hard to find now. Want me to call and see?"

"Sure."

I wandered the aisles, watching him while he made the call. He was probably fifteen years older than my twenty-six, maybe a little less. Back when I first started out, I'd have slept with him in a heartbeat, but the one time I'd tried, he'd given me a gentle letdown. He had a rumored history with another of Nashville's greats, but it was all wrapped up in some convoluted love triangle that had involved the woman the other guy ended up marrying, and nobody really knew the truth as far as I could tell. I respected Dan too much to ask, though I was curious as shit. For as long as I'd known him, he'd been single.

HE FOUND ME STARING DOWN DOLLY PARTON. THE CUTOUT display version, this time. She wore a sparkling red dress and a smile the size of Nashville that I matched, thinking about the wax museum.

"Paying your dues?"

I clasped my hands prayer fashion and gave a short bow to her gleaming, dimpled smile and physics-defying tits. "Always."

"We've got it in stock at the main store. Only copy. I had Ru set it aside for you. I can bring it when I come back next week. Assuming you'll still be here."

"We will."

"I've never heard you mention Jessup before." Dan went back to eyeing me thoughtfully; apparently I was quite the mystery to him today.

"Evan was talking about him recently and I thought..." I thought what? I bit my lip. Shit, what I'd thought about was how surprised Evan would be. The pleased grin he'd give me that would be like moonbeams and starlight and the fluffy soft warmth of a good blanket in the winter. *Goddammit.* I cleared my throat. "I thought it might inspire him or something."

"Uh-huh." Dan emphasized the "huh" as if he'd made a discovery.

"What?" I feigned innocence, and Dan shrugged but didn't ease up on the scrutiny.

"Better be careful with that shit. Music chemistry getting all mixed up with hormones? Can get messy—"

Again, I thought of the rumors about him, but just then the bells on the door chimed and a guy around my age wearing a beanie and carrying a wooden crate tripped in over the threshold.

"Shit!" he shouted and stumbled another step forward, just managing to keep the crate in his hands, though a few record sleeves went skittering over the open top and slid across the floor.

"Goddamn, kid, you're killing me," Dan grumbled, and went to take the crate as the guy bent over to collect the records.

"Owen, Les. Les, Owen."

Owen righted himself, nodding absently. He started to speak and then stopped, his mouth half-open, eyes wide as he registered me standing there. "Oh." He tilted his head to one side, avian-like, then nodded to himself again, like he'd come to a decision about something. "Les. Yeah, hi." I guess that decision was to play it cool. I gave him a grin.

"Shit. I love your music. I heard you were in town. Working on the album, I guess? How's it going? I love your music." He smacked the side of his face. "Oh. I already said that. Well, you get the extended version. Bonus praise!" He wiggled his fingers enthusiastically, dropping one of the albums he'd picked up in the process.

Or not. Man, that was a lot at once. I cracked up and leaned over, sweeping the album from the floor and handing it back to him. "It's going all right, I guess?" Usually I was better at this, but Dan was standing behind him now, rolling his eyes and shaking his head as he clapped his thumb and fingers together quickly. I got the gist. A talker.

I pointed at the door. "Was on my way out, actually."

"Oh, right, sure. Yeah. Cool." Owen skirted a few steps to the side, still clutching the records close to his chest. "Come back anytime, though, seriously. I could pull some stuff we get in that you might like. I mean, I'd be guessing because obviously I don't know you personally, but just based on your music."

"Sure, that'd be awesome." I smiled my friendliest smile again and stepped past him. Dan held the door open for me, pitching his voice low as I passed. "He'd keep you all afternoon, trust me. Sweetheart, though." And then louder, he said, "Be good."

"To the bone." It was our common parting shot, and I cut him a wink before I headed down the sidewalk back to the car.

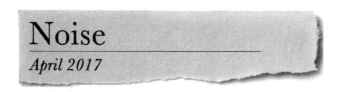

You've said before that "Violet Hour" from your second album was a surprise hit.
Evan: It was more aggressive than the other songs. At the time, the popular sound was more atmospheric and soft. So I was just surprised something that was a little grittier made it that far. Obviously we put it on the album because we liked it, but I don't think either of us thought it would top the charts.

How did that song come about?
Les: Evan left his favorite blankie behind in Nashville. He was quite distraught. I think the vocals on the track express it well.
Evan: You're such an ass. It was my pillow. And I wasn't distraught. And that's not at all where that song came from. Jesus fucking Christ, please don't print that.
Les: He was beating his chest. Wailing. Inconsolable.

CHAPTER 26

"**P**orter! Fuckin' A. Are you shaving your legs or what?" I nudged the bathroom door open as I yelled and was greeted by a waft of fragrant pine-scented steam as Evan poked his head around the shower curtain, his hair plastered over the crown of his head and dripping onto his shoulders. Goddamn, he was sexy when he was wet. *Down, boy.*

The glare he shot me didn't hold any heat. "I literally just got in. Antsy?"

"Little bit." We hadn't left the cabin in two days because we'd been locked in the zone writing. Evan couldn't care less about staying in. But me? I was restless. I needed sunlight on my face every now and again, needed to see other human beings. I was a social animal, and while Evan was probably the only person on earth I didn't get sick of even after weeks on end, being shut away in the cabin with him for days upon days was too chancy with everything that was going on right now. I needed to remember that what we were doing technically had an expiration date. That it wasn't real, as Evan had so plainly said. At least, not yet.

"Five minutes." Evan flashed me a smirk and pulled the shower curtain closed again. I was tempted to strip and get in with him, just to see what he would do, and I made a mental note to try it some-time. But not right then, because we were already late.

The past two weeks since I'd gotten him off in the basement had been busy with more than just music. I didn't think I'd ever given or received so many hand jobs in my life. I wanted more, but instinct told me to let Evan lead, give him time to situate himself in this fucked-up tapestry of a relationship.

Not that I was complaining, and I could tell he was still into it. The following day after we'd gotten off in the basement together, he kept giving me these looks until I'd finally come up behind him when we were in the kitchen after lunch and pressed my erection against his ass, covered his hand with mine, and pushed it down his pants. He'd shot a bewildered glance over his shoulder at first, but was soon jacking himself with my guidance all the way to a white-hot release. I'd come the same moment as he did, jizzing in my pants like a fucking pubescent boy. And the first time he'd put his hand on my dick, I almost came before he'd even fully wrapped his fingers around me.

I loved getting him off—watching his face contort, listening to him groan and curse while I stroked him to orgasm in the basement, up against the kitchen counter, in the hallway one time just because he'd aimed a cocky grin at me when I passed him on the way to the fridge. Last night I'd finally blown him. I'd attacked him while he was sitting on the couch off the living room checking our stats, as usual. I'd pushed the laptop off his thighs and started yanking his shorts down.

"You've got a problem, man," he'd said, even as he writhed under my touch.

"Yeah. I'm stuck in a cabin with a guy with a hot dick. I'm miserable."

He laughed and then stopped as soon as my fist closed around him. *"Fuck,"* he groaned, hips rocking into my hand. He threw his head back as I pumped him hard and slow the way he liked it, my lower lip caught between my teeth in concentration, when I realized he was staring intently at me through slitted eyes.

"What?"

"Your mouth."

My hand slowed. *"What about it."*

"I want it on me."

He didn't have to tell me twice. I swallowed him so fucking fast I think it caught him by surprise. He cried out at the wet heat and suction and twisted on the couch until I pinned his hips down to keep him still. Then he watched me hungrily as I lapped at his cock, groaning when I let his tip slip free and slap wetly against my chin before rubbing my lips over his head. I loved having him at my mercy. So often I felt like I was at his, but when I was getting him off, he was wholly, desperately mine to torture. And I took advantage of every second of it. He glided like satin in my mouth, and he didn't last long. One deep, hard suck and he filled the back of my throat, his thighs twitching in time to the spasms of his cock. And then we'd eaten dinner like nothing had happened and gone back down to the basement to hammer on the album some more. It was the weirdest non-relationship I'd ever been in. And, I guess, technically the only one. But fuck if I was going to be the one to burst our little pleasure bubble.

EVAN SLID INTO THE PASSENGER SEAT SMELLING SHOWER FRESH, dark blond hair slicked back from his face. I keyed in the address Maize had given me into my phone and pulled onto the street. Evan's phone rang and he tipped it toward me to show our manager's name flashing on the screen, then hit the screen to put the call on speaker.

"What's up?" he greeted Byron.

"Les with you?"

"Right next to me."

"How cozy." Byron chuckled.

"We're in the car, asshole."

He grunted, then said, "Dan called me asking about a secret show at Grim's."

"Huh?"

I winced. Dan had mentioned the possibility of doing a show

when I was last in his shop, but I'd neglected to tell Evan because I didn't think anything would come of it since we were supposed to be laying low and I wasn't sure how serious Dan was anyway.

"Said he mentioned it to Les."

Evan shot me an accusing look.

"I didn't think Evan would want to do it," I said, ignoring Evan as he tried to burn a hole through me with his gaze.

"You didn't ask me, tool."

He'd balked at doing anything more than required publicity, so how the fuck was I to know? "Well, *do* you?" I glanced over at him, searching his face for any evidence of interest in performing off the cuff. I'd be down, because I always was.

"I don't know."

"What do you think?" I asked Byron.

"I think it'd be a good move, get you guys out there but in the more controlled setting Dan could provide. Try out some of the new stuff. As long as you can keep your hands from each other's throats." If only he knew. Evan must have been thinking along the same lines because he barked out a laugh.

"We'll think about it and get back to you," he said.

Before Evan could even get started after he hung up with Byron, I was on it. "You made it clear you wanted to do the minimum amount of publicity."

"You could've at least asked."

I stared at him, trying to gauge whether or not he was really mad. He looked... irritated. But not angry. He massaged the space between his brows with the knuckle of his thumb. Yeah, irritated. Angry would set his jaw harder. He was considering it. Who would've guessed?

"You wanna do it," I said, unable to keep the surprise from my voice.

"I wouldn't mind trying out some of the new stuff." He shrugged.

"But... people. And... us." I gestured back and forth between us. "You know some way, somehow, some reporter's going to manage to catch wind of it and get in there."

"And they'll see us. Putting on a show."

My heart flip-flopped in my chest, but I nodded. A show. Right. That's all we were doing.

CONSIDERING MAIZE HAD PROMISED THE DRUM CIRCLE WOULD BE low-key, I was curious what she'd consider a blowout, because there had to be at least fifty people in the gathering on her front lawn when we pulled up. I'd been expecting something along the lines of ten. Maybe fifteen. I didn't even know there were fifty locals around Gatlinburg, much less ones under the age of fifty-five. We could hear the drums as we pulled into the long, winding drive, but now that we were next to the circle, the sound loomed and beat at the air around us. The thumping bass reverberated through the rubber tires of the SUV, and Evan seemed reluctant to undo his seat belt as I stopped the car and turned it off. I suspected he was thinking the same thing about the size of the crowd.

"Still want to?" I asked.

He hesitated, then nodded. "Yeah. It'll be fine. I know you're dying for a change of pace."

As soon as we got out, Maize detached herself from the big tom she was pounding on and came over, a warm, welcoming smile appling her cheeks. Evan laced his fingers with mine as I came around to his side, and I wasn't sure who was more surprised, me or Maize. But she didn't miss a beat, her eyes jumping from our twined hands to our faces as she leaned in and gave us each an air kiss. "Don't worry. I told anyone if they act a fool, I'm kicking them out. No one's gonna ask for autographs or get in your face. I promise."

And she was right. Aside from some initial staring, and maybe one or two folks who stopped playing momentarily, we were absorbed into the circle with no fanfare. Maize pulled Evan down next to her and passed him a bongo drum. The guy I sat next to jutted his chin over his shoulder, without breaking his rhythm, to indicate a couple of drums sitting just behind him. I snatched up a djembe and listened for a while before finding a place where I could add my own rhythm. I'd started as a drummer, so it was probably sacrilege that I'd never participated in a drum circle before. I'd caught one from my hotel room in Asheville once, but it was a completely different animal to sit in the middle of one and contribute. I felt an immediate sense of connection that wasn't unlike what I felt onstage, but it was somehow bigger, grander, because the audience and the players were one and the same. It was interactive and exhilarating, and I lost myself to the infinite feeling of it. I caught Evan watching me more than a few times, a studious half smile on his face as we played.

"You love it, don't you?" he said when the circle finally broke to tap into the kegs set out on the front lawn. He scooted nearer to me and spread out on the grass.

"It's a different vibe. Don't you feel it?" I was almost high with it, loving the peaceful backdrop of cicadas and the drone of crickets in the late afternoon.

He nodded. Maize dropped off a couple of Solo cups filled with beer, and I guzzled half of mine in one go because I was thirsty as hell. Evan watched me warily.

"I told you I'd DD, dude. I'm not going back on that."

He gave me a thin smile, and I set the beer down and sprawled backward in the grass. On impulse, I shifted, resting my head on the top of his thigh. His face registered surprise, and then mine probably did the same when he reached down to brush a few strands of hair from my forehead. He kept his hand on my crown of my head, playing with the ends of my hair.

"It's more diffuse," he said. "The energy, I mean. Distributed more evenly. I do like it. I'm kinda surprised we haven't done it before."

"That's what I was thinking earlier. It'd be sorta hard to do it now, though."

"I mean way back when, though, when we were first getting started. We could have."

"We were focused on writing and getting the record out." Probably to an unhealthy degree. Making that first album, I'd swear I didn't sleep more than a few hours the entire time we'd worked on it.

"Even that was different." He abandoned the ends of my hair to sweep his thumb along my eyebrow, the steady, soothing rhythm making me drowsy. I let my eyes drift shut, content.

"Because we weren't answering to anything or anyone but ourselves."

"I miss it," he said wistfully.

I didn't. I'd almost burned out at that pace, but I thought what Evan meant was that he missed that fresh energy of possibility, when it felt like the world was hanging on a string and if we could find just the right hook, we could reach out and seize it.

And then we had.

He combed his fingers through my hair, then tapped them lightly over my scalp, playing invisible strings. I wasn't sure he realized what he was doing, but it was nice as hell. Almost sweet, for Evan.

"What would you be doing if we weren't doing this?" I asked.

"Nothing. This is it for me. Music is the only thing I'm good at besides bartending, and I hated that."

I'd always struggled to imagine Evan as a bartender. It had seemed like an odd fit because he was such an introvert. He must have been thinking along the same lines, because as I opened my eyes, he smiled and said, "With music it works because I can keep a stage between me and someone else. A manager between me and reporters if I have to, and I can just ignore the paparazzi most of the time. But spending seven hours in a crowded bar slinging drinks to a bunch of drunk people—it wore me down."

"There's me, though. I'm up there on the stage with you. In the bus. In the cabin."

"You're different. And besides, I take breaks from you, too." He finished off his beer and set his empty cup aside. Almost immediately someone brought him a refill. He turned to watch them depart. "People are watching us."

I laughed. "Of course they are. You're petting me."

"I'm not—" His hand stopped moving over me for a second, then resumed. "Yeah, I am. Should I stop?"

"Not unless you want me to start nuzzling into your palm like a cat, which might draw more attention."

"Touch slut," he accused, and gave a short, sharp tug to the ends of my hair.

"Unapologetically, and if you pull my hair like that again, you'd better be prepared for what comes next, because that will definitely draw more attention."

He wiggled around a little, trying to subtly adjust himself, then cleared his throat dramatically. "What would you be doing?"

"Hmmm. I guess I'd be a corporate drone. I would've finished college. I'd be a face in a suit. Something in sales, probably."

He chuckled.

"What's the funny part? Me in sales, me in a suit, or me with an actual viable future outside of music?"

"The suit. Like some Men's Wearhouse off-the-rack."

"There's nothing wrong with Men's Wearhouse."

"Please. You bitched about a Prada off-the-rack once." Evan honest-to-God grinned one of those rare, delighted grins that was like a shot of epinephrine to the heart.

"Only because I can. And it didn't fit me right."

"You do a lot of things because you can. You smile and someone will give you their last dollar," he said, though it was more musing than disparaging.

I propped myself up on my elbow and brushed a kiss across his lips quicksilver fast before he could jerk backward. "Because I can," I explained when his brows rose. He hadn't jerked away, though, just gave my shoulder a light shove, making the beer I'd picked up again slosh in the cup.

"My music career wouldn't have gone anywhere, though," I said. "Not without you. Everyone knows that. Even you. Maybe I'd make some money off lyrics. But most likely I would've tooled around bars for another couple of years while I finished my degree, then I'd have been absorbed by the American machine. Gone on to live in a suburb, maybe put a drum kit and guitar in the garage that I'd go down and bang around on every once and awhile. I'd be just another paycheck." I swallowed the last of my beer and tossed the empty cup beside me on the grass.

Something passed over his face, unreadable to me, which wasn't unusual lately. His mouth went a little slack, like he was about to say something, and just then Maize called out to us with a big, swooping gesture of her arms.

Evan closed his mouth and hopped up, extending his hand out to pull me up, too.

THE SUN DROPPED BEHIND THE TREE LINE, LEAVING THE SKY GLAZED in a syrupy orange that darkened and turned the color of a bruise as night fell. Someone started a fire in the pit behind Maize's cabin, and we ate hot dogs coated in char from the open flame. Evan was laughing at something somebody whose name I'd forgotten was saying. He had a relaxed smile on his face that I couldn't stop staring at—one I'd seen more of over the past couple of weeks than I'd seen on our entire last tour. He sprawled his legs out in the grass, stretching his arms behind him to look up at the sky as the guy he'd been talking to drifted off, and I dropped down beside him with another hot dog. He shook his head when I offered him a bite.

"My mom used to take me on these camping trips every year. It was our big trip. A KOA somewhere. Usually in state, but God I loved it," he said. I'd once asked him about his dad, who ditched out before Evan was born, but he never cared to talk about it, said the guy left and that was it for him. I knew he gave money to his mom. I wasn't sure how much, but enough that she was able to quit one of her jobs. Evan had said she kept the other cleaning houses out of stubborn pride. When he'd told me that, I felt so shitty about hoarding my earnings, I started setting aside a quarter of it each year and paying it out anonymously to local charities. That was another reason I liked Evan. I was far from perfect, but he was the only one who ever made me want to try to be a better human just by being himself.

"Every year?"

"Almost. The only time we didn't go was when I was fifteen

and she used up all the savings to buy the Martin." Evan still brought that particular guitar everywhere. I knew the story. How he'd ask his mom to take him to the music store downtown every other week to play it because the sound was so much better than the shitty second-hand he'd saved up for by cutting yards and washing cars after school and on the weekends.

"We should do this more."

"Go to drum circles and eat hot dogs and drink beer?"

"Yeah. Simple stuff. I mean, doesn't it feel good?" The way he looked up at me then, with that loose, drowsy smile and the fire making his eyes glossy and large, hit me deep inside, spread warm through me like melted butter. It felt so damn good I could almost forget all the crap that had come before. And might be yet to come.

I WENT INSIDE TO GET A WATER BOTTLE AND USE THE JOHN AND GOT sidetracked on the way back by a cute little twink who asked me about fifty different questions about our music and touring. When the conversation turned to my relationship with Evan, I begged off and went back outside to find him. I was ready to leave, but Evan wasn't by the fire pit where I'd left him. Everyone had scattered wide over the lawn in little clusters. A girl with pink hair saw me looking around in confusion and told me he'd gone down to the pond with some other folks. Her blue-haired friend disagreed, telling me he was with Maize, who was showing him her chicken coop. I laughed at that and dug out my phone.

Les: *You better not be looking at other cocks with Maize.*
Evan: *Wtf?*
Evan: *Oh. Yeah. Already saw 'em. Stiff competition for sure. Jealous?*
Les: *I don't do jealousy.*
Evan: *Ever? I don't believe that.*
Les: *Seriously. Where r u?*

Evan: *On the dock. Come down. I think this guy is trying to hit on me. Need backup.*
Les: *Tell him your boyfriend will break his face. I don't care if he's a fan.*
Evan: *I thought you didn't do jealousy?*
Les: *I do it selectively when the person in question is my fake boyfriend.*

Lie. Total, total lie. I was seething with jealousy right then, wondering if Evan was actually serious and there was some dude down there hitting on him.

Evan: *Oh. Right. I forgot.*
Les: *No you didn't. But if you need a reminder, I'm more than willing to give you one.*
Evan: *Maybe. When we get back to the cabin? Because I might pass out.*

I looked around and caught sight of a greenhouse-looking structure off in the distance.

Les: *No. Now. Not willing to risk your lightweight ass passing out.*
Evan: *Maybe. Kinda busy here.*
Les: *Will. Break. His. Face. Get the fuck up here. Greenhouse. Five minutes.*

CHAPTER 27

I half thought Evan wouldn't show up. Five minutes passed. I pulled a few needles from the boughs of the pine above me and broke them between my fingers, inhaling the pungent scent. Another minute and I was just about to walk back toward the house when I glimpsed a dark silhouette weaving in my direction. Evan stumbled over something on the grass, and I chuckled as he closed in. "Got caught up on the way. Man, Maize is a chatterbox."

"You're drunk," I observed, amused. His hair was windblown, cheeks slightly flushed. Not that I minded. Hell, I wished I was there with him, but I was trying to show him I could be reliable and not a fuckup.

"I'm not." He bullied right on into me, knocking me into a tree trunk, then took a step back, shoving his hands in his pockets and looking around. "So."

"So," I repeated.

He cleared his throat. "Here we are in the trees, which is weird."

"You've never made out in the woods before?"

He shrugged. "Not that I can remember, nope."

"Oh c'mon, you're a country boy. Really?"

He tipped his head back, gazing up into the boughs in thought, then shook his head. "Nope, nothing. I was always working for extra money or playing music or... I didn't get invited to many parties. *Any* parties."

"Shit, that's kind of depressing."

"It is what it is." He shrugged, then laughed at my expression. "Are you really pitying me? Don't. I didn't miss out on anything."

"That's 'cause you didn't know any better." I reached out and caught his wrists in my hands. "Let's fix that."

He let me pull him closer, his chest bumping up against me, and when I hooked two fingers over the collar of his shirt and tugged, his mouth slanted hungrily toward mine, teeth scraping at my lower lip. I kept my grip on his collar and walked him backward across the grass until his back was against the greenhouse, the glass still warm when I pressed my palms into it, caging him in.

"Definitely drunk." My whisper came out a little garbled between the action of our tongues. He tasted like cinnamon and licorice.

Evan pulled back an inch. "Maybe that last shot was overkill. But I'm fine. Shut up before you ruin this."

I wasn't good at shutting up. "Ruin what?"

"What I'm considering doing to your cock."

I lied. All hail shutting the fuck up.

He reached for the string tie on my shorts and yanked it loose with one hand, pushing my shirt up with his other and pinching one of my nipples so hard I hissed out in pain. He chased the sting with the heat of his mouth, dragging his lips across my chest as it rose and fell with my shallow breaths.

"You're so easy to get hard," he mused, like this was some fascinating aspect of my character.

"Don't preen. I'm always horny." And when it was Evan, I was as combustible as gasoline near an open flame. I wasn't about to give him the satisfaction of telling him that, though.

"Yeah, I've gathered that over the thousands of hours we've been together."

"Shhhh. It's hotter when your mouth is closed."

"Yeah?" He tugged my shorts down my thighs, easing to his knees as he did so. "You sure about that?"

Who was this man and where could I get more of him? Should I start spiking his morning OJ?

His breath streaked hot over my cock, and as he looked at me expectantly, I realized I hadn't answered because I was fixated on the sight of him kneeling in front of me, his mouth a scant half inch from my raging hard-on. This was a sight I'd only ever dreamed of, so he'd have to excuse me for a couple of seconds while I made sure it was properly encoded into my spank bank for life. I'd be making frequent withdrawals in the future, no doubt, after we went back to the real world.

"I'm willing to reconsider," I said after a moment. "Open that pretty mouth, Porter, and make me reconsider."

I expected some kind of resistance, or some smartass comment. Instead, Evan kept his gaze fastened to mine as he leaned forward, dragged the tip of his tongue across my slit, and licked his lips.

"Shit," I hissed out. The look in his eyes was a perfectly sinful mashup of daring and desire, a little teasing, and a whole universe of sexy that was way hotter than I'd given him credit for in my jerk fantasies. "More," I demanded, my gaze dropping to his mouth as it hovered in front of my cock. I still couldn't believe this was happening.

He flicked his tongue against me again, and I shivered. Then he opened wide and took me to the back of his throat, and my knees almost gave out at the torturous wet slick of his lips wrapped around me. "God, that's good," I gasped, and he murmured something that translated only as vibration. Delicious, hot vibration that coiled around the base of my cock. I was sober as fuck, and the guy who could give me a contact boner the way some people got contact highs was on his knees going to town on my dick. I'd clearly died, and as it turned out, the afterlife was fucking awesome.

Also, I wasn't going to last long.

I braced my hands against the glass wall in front of me, leaning more of my weight into it as Evan licked up my shaft and pleasure roared through me. My hips rocked into the fist he wrapped around me, a low rumble escaping my chest while I tried to stave off my orgasm.

The next thing I knew, I was pitching forward.

I met resistance as I barreled into Evan, but it wasn't enough to stop me. He went sprawling backward, his hand snapping out and clenching the back of my thigh in a futile effort to steady us. But no dice. I ended up on my side in a heap, Evan on his back, groaning. The greenhouse door we fell through swung gently beside him, knocking against his knee.

"Fuck," Evan groused, and then looked over at me and started laughing. I wasn't laughing. My shorts were tangled around my knees, I could feel a bruise forming over my ribs, and my super-shiny fantasy moment had been cock-blocked by a fucking greenhouse.

I rolled onto my back and hitched my pants up, brushing away a frond of greenery that was tickling my cheek. I heard water trickling somewhere, and the air was humid and warm, pungent with the scent of dirt and plants.

"You okay?" Evan asked through his laughter, and I finally gave in and started laughing, too.

He helped me upright, and somewhere between my hand in his and him levering me up, we tangled together and started kissing again. Evan dropped his hands to my hips and shoved me up against a wooden counter laden with empty pots and a bag of soil that rattled and spilled over with my impact. His cock ground against my thigh as he licked my lower lip, reviving my dick. In seconds I was panting again. Slow kisses became deep strokes of our tongues, and I sucked on the tip of his, then latched onto his lower lip until he dug his fingers so hard into my sides I was certain there'd be marks tomorrow.

"Fuck, I want you." His voice was sweet ache and hunger, and it hit every damn nerve ending in my body, making them dance like light thrown from a sparkler.

"So have me." I didn't know if he'd meant it that way, but I was sure as hell game.

"Right here?"

"Yeah." I groaned and scrambled to kick off my shorts. I had no idea if he knew what he was doing, but I got my answer a second later when he spun me around. My palms flattened over the counter, fingers curling against the wood surface as he slid two spit-slick fingers between my cheeks, circling and rubbing my hole, then kneading the tract of skin behind my balls.

"Someone's been watching po—" My words dissolved into a hiss as he prodded the tip of one finger inside me.

"You make a lot of assumptions about me." The words landed close to my ear as he leaned in and licked a wet stripe over my neck.

"I'm usually right."

"Mmm." A nonanswer as he pushed his finger deeper inside me. I braced one elbow on the counter and turned a look over my shoulder. Evan's attention was fixed on his finger as he pumped it in and out of me, the other still gliding along my taint. The tandem sensations saturated my body in arousal, making my vision go hazy at the edges. When I reached my other hand back and spread myself for him, he inhaled sharply and jerked his gaze to mine, his eyes wide and unfocused with heat. "You really are shameless."

"And you love it."

He didn't deny it. "Where're your condoms?"

"You make a lot of assumptions about me," I threw back at him.

"I'm usually right." He grinned, stepping around my side to cup my jaw and draw me up for another searing kiss. God, he was good at it.

"Wallet. Lube, too," I managed around a moan.

Evan didn't go for them immediately. His brow furrowed as if in concentration, and he kept one hand spanned over my jaw while he continued to play with me with the other, teasing the muscle, plunging a finger inside, stretching and plying me in direct proportion to the pressure of his touch. And it wasn't expert, but it was fucking earnestly attempted, which was just as hot.

Outside, the drum circle started up again, and the tempo rolled through the ground beneath our feet. Evan picked up the rhythm and stroked me to it, his hips rocking gently against me, his touch a form of intoxication that blew any drug high or liquor buzz out of the water.

"Shit," I whispered, tipping my head back when he started trailing his lips along my jaw and down my neck. My dick throbbed and I wanted him so much my cells ached with the need to feel him thrusting inside me. Almost every time I'd imagined us together, it'd been the other way around: me behind him, pounding him senseless. I didn't typically like bottoming, so the force of my desire was electrifying. I had no idea if he sensed it or what—sometimes we were on a wavelength to a degree that was frightening—because he asked, "How long has it been since someone was inside you?"

"Years." And when I detected hesitation, I hurriedly tacked on, "I want it, though. Fuck, I want it like you wouldn't believe."

Evan's fingers worked me a few more times, and I was left pushing back into nothing when they abruptly retreated. I heard him pawing through my pants, and I collapsed over the counter, gulping air while he got himself ready.

"Yes," I groaned at the wet tip of his sheathed cock anchoring against my hole. He reached for my hips, sliding his length up and down my furrow a few times, his fingers tightening to keep me steady. He dropped his forehead to the nape of my neck and laughed. "Shit, this might be short-lived."

"It's okay, sweetheart, I won't judge." Even if he couldn't see my grin, I knew he could hear it in my words.

He clapped a hand over my mouth and nudged the head of his cock inside me. Not recklessly, but with enough force that I couldn't reply when he said, "Call me sweetheart again and you'll regret it."

When he pushed in deeper, I moaned into his palm, and he kept it pressed over my mouth so that every sound coming from my throat vibrated against his skin.

"Jesus," he exhaled softly, and I knew exactly what he meant. There was something eerily perfect about how he fit against me, the palm he had clapped over my mouth, and the seductive, swaying bassline of drums surrounding us as he fucked me.

I licked his palm, salty and tart, and he twisted his hand, sliding his thumb between my lips, running it along my teeth. I clamped down and sucked, and he exhaled another groan, his hips surging forward harder. Electricity streaked up my spine with every thrust. I twisted my hips a little and... *there*. A string of curses escaped me as Evan nailed my prostate over and over.

"Does it feel good?" I whispered.

He thrust into me faster, and his arm came around me, pulling me upright. "Yes," he grated out against my shoulder.

"Good. Do it harder and tell me how much you like it."

"Such a fucking talker. You're tight. So fucking tight, and..." His words came out with gaps between them, and then his breath hitched again. "Stop asking me to string fucking words together right now for fuck's sake."

The pots on the table rattled, soil spilling from the counter to the floor.

"Then get your hand on my cock and get me off. Maybe I'll shut up."

"Doubtful," he grunted in a tease, but he dropped his hand from my chest and slid it down my stomach to give my cock a few rough strokes. That was all it took. I came with a whimper and a full-body shiver, contracting around his cock as I slicked his fist with my load. I gasped out his name, babbled all kinds of nonsense, and felt him begin to shudder. My cheek smacked into the counter as he flattened my spine with a brutish shove of his hand, then drove into me hard, over and over as he shattered with a moan.

Our bodies heaved against each other as he draped gracelessly over my back. A minute passed, and then he pulled out of me. I rested my cheek on my forearm, watching from the corner of my eye as he bent to pick up the foil wrapper and wrapped it around the spent condom.

I was about to make a flirty quip suggesting he drink more often when my shorts landed on the counter next to me, and he said, "I'm ready to go once you clean up. I'll meet you out front."

And then he just fucking left.

I watched him go in bewilderment, then took stock of my surroundings. The moonlight pouring in thick shafts through the clear roof of the greenhouse, the marks in the packed dirt floor from our bodies, the dishevelment of my hair. The aches on my body from where I fell, the bruised feel of my hips where he'd gripped me, the throbbing echo of his dick inside me. And for the first time in my life, I felt fucking used.

CHAPTER 28

Evan

I couldn't stop thinking about wrecked bands. The Civil Wars, the White Stripes, No Doubt, Sonny & Cher, Oasis—and countless other musicians who churned out hits and soared on the charts and then went up in flames. Music was tricky that way. And worse when there were feelings involved. It wasn't like an office romance where you could switch departments or do your best to ignore someone. When you made music with another person, you were giving them a piece of your soul and stitching it to theirs. It was a vulnerable process that was both primal and carnal, which was exactly why the best songs resonated with people and took on a life of their own. It was procreation absent of biology, and that was why it was a phenomenally bad idea to go fucking with the dynamics if you could help it. Apparently I couldn't.

I could still smell Les on my skin as I stood in the front yard and waited for him. Still taste him while I watched him walk across the grass toward me wearing a dark scowl, his hands shoved deep in the pockets of his shorts. Still feel his body against mine, the warmth of him, the give as I buried myself in him. It was like nothing I'd had before and everything I wanted again. And I fucking hated that.

We said goodbye to Maize, then Les stalked ahead of me to the car. Five miles of silence became seven down a road of my own making. I had plenty of time to look for things to blame. The beers, the shots of Jager. But it wasn't the alcohol's fault for loosening me up enough to do the thing I'd been denying I wanted to do. It'd just been a primer.

"You need to fucking say something," Les said, cutting a look across at me that might as well have had teeth the way it gnashed at me.

"Like what?"

"I don't know. Something that makes up for you just tossing my shorts at me and dismissing me like a goddamn groupie." His hands tightened on the steering wheel. "I don't mind being used. I know the score. I do it plenty, so it's only fair, but I don't go out of my way to remind someone of their status."

"Why don't you mind being used, though?" That wasn't the question I should have been asking, but it was what came out.

"My body is just a fucking body, Porter. It has various holes that like to be filled and an appendage that likes to fill other holes. I don't get why it's a problem to enjoy that, to enjoy getting off and not make a fucking federal case out of it. There's zero reason that if we enjoy doing that together during this stupid mission impossible, that we shouldn't do it. But I don't want to anymore if you're going to go catatonic afterward. That's not hot. That's not sexy. It makes me feel like shit."

"Then we should stop." I made it sound so simple, and what was more, I said it as if it was, when it was anything but. Inside, my thoughts were festering, growing tentacles and suffocating me. Because while Les could be cavalier about sex, I'd tried and I wasn't good at it. And I'd rather have Les pissed at me over being a dick than me be heartbroken when this stupid ruse reached its expiration date and Les went back to his old ways on tour. But fuck, the way I felt right then, it was already too late.

"Done." Les clipped. He yanked the keys from the ignition once we stopped outside the cabin, then stomped inside.

. . .

I WOKE HOURS LATER, A GLANCE AT THE CLOCK SHOWING THREE IN the morning. My temples throbbed with a headache that pulled me out of bed and toward the kitchen in search of ibuprofen. Les's bedroom door was cracked, the room dark. I tossed a couple of pills in my mouth and chased them with two full glasses of water to clear the desert off my tongue.

I set my empty glass beside the sink and listened to the twang of guitar rising from the stairwell, then followed the sound to the basement quietly.

Ever have a flash where, for just a second, you see someone you're used to seeing daily as if they're new, like it's the very first time you've stumbled across them? Devoid of the little quirks and habits you pick up on over time, devoid of personal history. Just a stranger you glimpse from across a room. Just possibility. At the bottom of the steps, I turned, looking through the open door of the music room, and I saw Les just like that. It made my breath catch in my throat and my heart thunder in my chest.

He sat on the floor with his back to me, bare legs crossed as he softly strummed his guitar and hummed. His notebook lay open beside him, the white pages glowing beneath his dark scribbles, and the sliding door a few feet from me was open, letting in the sound of crickets to accompany the low croon of his voice. I'd never heard the song before. His naked back was slightly hunched, ink and imagery moving and shifting over muscle. I knew which of his tattoos had stories, and the stories behind them, and I knew which ones he'd gotten just for the hell of it. And now, I knew what it felt like to be inside him, to have his body in my thrall at the same time I was undeniably under his spell. It was addictive and intoxicating to a frightening degree. I'd always felt close to him; even when we were arguing, there was a bond that was almost brotherly. Now there was something new, something different. A place I wasn't sure I'd be able to return from. Deep-seated, overwhelming desire.

I stood in the doorway listening until his back straightened, as if he sensed my presence, and he turned a look over his shoulder to find me.

"It's good. New?"

He gave me a muted nod. "Came to me the other night. Been working on it ever since."

"When were you going to share it with me?" I rested my head against the doorframe, my gaze pinned to the back of his neck where a tendril of ink disappeared into his hairline.

He seemed noncommittal and wary of my presence, one shoulder hitching up as he set his guitar down and replied, "Maybe tomorrow."

I wandered deeper into the room and dropped down to the floor across from him with my back against the bottom of the couch. "So you're just having what, an impromptu practice session at three in the morning?"

"I do this almost every night. Why do you think I sleep so late?"

I had no idea, other than guessing alcohol was involved. He laughed softly at my expression. My teeth sawed at my lower lip, and he kept watching me like he was waiting for me to tell him why I'd interrupted him.

"I'm jealous of you, you know," I confessed.

He barked out a short, doubting laugh. "Why?

"Because you're not afraid of anything." He'd never seemed to care what people thought of him, wasn't afraid to bomb an interview, or of getting too attached to anyone. Wasn't afraid to fail.

"Jesus. You have no clue." He sighed and bent his knees up, resting his forearms over them. "I practice everything before I show it to you to make sure it's not complete garbage."

"I don't think you're capable of writing garbage."

"Oh, I am. You just never see it."

"Why not? You hear my garbage all the time."

"Why do you think, Ev? I want your respect. I want you to think I have some clue as to what I'm doing. I constantly feel like I have to measure up, earn my place."

Anytime we were working together there'd be these moments when he'd pause looking at me, like he was gauging my reaction. I always thought he was just a glutton for praise or that he was waiting for me to catch up or add something to the song. But now he was telling me point-blank that he was looking for my approval.

Thinking about it made me feel things I didn't want to feel toward him. An intimate tenderness that simultaneously broke my heart and made it clench up. "What are you even talking about? You've already earned your place a million times over."

"Tell that to the label," he mumbled.

"What does that mean?"

He bit his lip and shook his head. "It means just what I said earlier tonight. You're the real breadwinner here. You're the one with the pipes and the mad guitar skills I can't even hope to ever live up to. I have lyrics, a decent voice, and passable talent. All of which require *you* to make them better. If you decided tomorrow you wanted to go back to writing, too, you could. Easily. You're the full package, Porter."

His voice, so raw and vulnerable, sank into me like stones. I wasn't even sure where to start. "You're selling yourself way too short," I began, looking him dead in the eye and hoping that my sincerity came across. "We're a team, and I'd never have come this far without you. I'm not going to abandon you."

He grunted something and picked up the guitar again.

"Can I look?" I reached for the notebook, wanting to see what he'd been working on. The hook he'd been humming looped around through my mind, searching for some kind of grounding wire.

He pulled the notebook just out of reach and shot me a small smile. "No. It's not finished, and you've seen enough of my raw parts for one night."

My chuckle brought his gaze to me again, fierce and glittering. "You know what I mean," he tacked on.

I took a deep breath. "I'm sorry about tonight. I didn't mean to make you feel used."

"There's a way to do it without making someone feel used, you know." The raised eyebrows that followed told me I wouldn't be so easily forgiven.

"Yeah, well, I guess I'm still learning." I needed to tell him why getting this close to him was a bad idea. Why it was a bad idea that he was under my skin and constantly on my mind. That I wouldn't want to let go and that one thing I knew for certain about him was that he was never meant to be tied down.

But he started strumming his guitar again, and when I tried to speak, nothing came out. I leaned back against the couch, listening to him caress sound from the strings, the progression smooth and soothing and nothing like the electric feel of his bare skin under my palm when I reached out to touch his arm.

"Come to bed." I left it open to interpretation, because if he got up to come, I knew I'd take his hand and pull him into my room, and though I didn't know what would happen after that, it was frightening how much I wanted just the touch of his hand and the feel of him at my back.

He shook his head resolutely. "Gonna practice a little while longer." And when I stood up, he said, "You're right, though. We should just stick to the original plan. Messing around was a stupid idea."

It should've made me feel better. A decision had been made. We were in accordance, on the same page. But it didn't. Not at all.

You've talked before about the writing process and a certain cabin you travel to when you're in the final stages of planning an album. Do you plan to continue that?

Evan: It's kind of a superstitious act now, I guess. So yeah.

Les: We work on new stuff constantly while on tour, but the cabin is where we really try to lock it all down and nail it to the wall.

Evan: [laughing] You make it sound so... murderous.

Les: That's what weeks in a cabin with you drives me to. Murderous intent.

Do you two get cabin fever? Stir-crazy?

Les: Evan doesn't. He's secretly a hobbit. Me? Sometimes.

CHAPTER 29

We hadn't done any advertising, but the turnout for our secret show at Grim's was overwhelming, which I guess should have been encouraging. That was the Southern grapevine for you. Dan had to turn people away and call in a couple of his local contacts for extra security. He usually hosted a few small shows a year for local artists, so he had the organization down to a science. Porter & Graves had only ever played at the main store in Nashville, but I was impressed by how Dan had transformed the Gatlinburg satellite. The displays were all rearranged to create the effect of an open glen amid a forest of records and CDs. He didn't bother with chairs; people just packed in to the central pit. At the front, our equipment was set up on a barebones platform that mimicked the one at the main shop. It was only about a half foot off the ground, but on either side, two burly biker-looking dudes watched over it.

My heart thumped with a mixture of excitement and anxiety the same way I used to feel when I was playing in bars. When you're that close to your audience, you can watch their expressions, which always psyched me out as much as it was rewarding. I could see them wince if I hit a note wrong as well as I could see their faces light up at their favorite song.

Evan and I waited in the storage area at the back of the store while Dan took the small stage, giving a rundown of the show to the audience, talking about how it was all about the music. I knew he was trying to keep the show focused, considering all the publicity we'd been getting lately, and I appreciated that, but it did nothing for the nerves darting through my system like fireflies.

"All right?" I asked Evan, mostly to distract myself. He'd been fiddling with the tuning knobs on his guitar for the past five minutes and looked up at me now distractedly. We'd been careful around each other for the past few days. There was a sense of tension underpinning everything, but it was different somehow than it was on the tour. More potent, it teetered between us, lingering in every glance we exchanged. But we were both stubborn as hell, and I only excelled at playing along because I'd had so much prior practice ignoring my impulses where Evan was concerned. Unfortunately, I didn't have my usual fallback of booze and sex to distract me, so I figured I was only good for another couple of days before I'd end up doing something stupid and messing things up even more.

I was totally regretting the whole fake boyfriend thing because instead of curing me of my Evan obsession, it'd just made it worse. I'd had a taste of him now, and I wasn't ready to let that go anytime soon. Pushing back the other night when he told me to come to bed had been a Hail Mary play to collect myself and go on about business as usual. I was trying.

"Nervous as shit." Evan laughed, and just the sound of it after so much thick silence flooded me with relief. "Isn't that stupid? How many hundreds of shows have we done?"

"Yeah, but none since we agreed to this dumb charade."

Evan rolled his shoulder through a wince and nodded. "It'll be fine, though. They won't care." He sounded like he was trying to convince himself. "Shit, there are whole fandoms devoted to AU pairings. If we were fiction, we'd have been one long ago."

"Like Spock and Captain Kirk."

"You're giving me that stupid smirk because you're thinking of me as Spock, aren't you?"

"Yep. And those ears." I snapped my teeth at him, and his laughter hit me like spring air.

Dan walked off the stage and into our impromptu backstage area, giving us the thumbs-up. "You're good to go. Any funny business and I'll chuck 'em."

THE SHOW WAS OFF FROM THE GET-GO. THE SOUND WAS GREAT, AND the audience was enthusiastic, but Evan and I were out of sync.

We ran through some of our older hits first. The first two songs went fine, but when he started "Chanteuse," I lagged behind a half beat and had to leap to pick up, which threw off the opening verse. We stopped and laughed through it, Evan cracking a joke about vacation making us lazy to smooth things over. Then it happened three more times, and this time it was his fault. He was too mired in his head. I could tell because he wasn't doing his usual thousand-yard stare over the heads of the audience, but was focused hard on his guitar, instead, as if it had wronged him. We barreled through without stopping again or calling attention to our fumbles, but Evan kept glancing over at me, so then I started to become all too aware of my timing and psyching myself out.

We played the next batch of songs, cutting in some of the new stuff we'd been working on. The crowd seemed to like it—heads were nodding, they were dancing, there was plenty of applause. I watched faces the way I watched the slot machines in Vegas, scrutinizing expressions with my stomach in a knot, waiting for that perfect combo that meant a jackpot. Just before we took our first break, I did my ask-the-audience bit and, no surprise, the dude I'd pointed out asked for "Blue." Fucking "Blue." I had zero interest in playing that damn song right then.

I shook my head and chuckled. "Aww come on, man. It's been done to death. Pick something different." The whole room got eerily quiet, and Evan's mouth dropped open like I'd committed the ultimate faux pas.

The guy I'd singled out darted a nervous gaze between the two of us, clearly uncertain of how to reply. Evan strummed the opening chords of "Blue," leaning into the mic. "He's fucking with you. We'll—"

"We've got something new," I blurted without turning my head to the side so I wouldn't see the daggers Evan was undoubtedly shooting at me for veering off course. I felt it anyway.

"So you pick. 'Blue'? Or something virgin no one else has heard, yet? Not even... Evan."

The audience exploded at the prospect, cheering and pumping their fists, and it was only then that I dared a glance at Evan in time to see a brief flash of horror he masked quickly with a smirk. Evan hated surprises, but I was willing to bet he'd hate giving that fact away to the audience even more.

"How fresh are we talking here? Fresher than yesterday?" he asked, trying to suss it out.

"Fresh as last night."

Evan let out a low whistle, and there was scatter of laughter through the audience. Behind his loose smile, I could sense his anxiety. "Keeping me on my toes, huh?"

"I like to watch you dance." Someone catcalled as I winked at Evan, then turned back to the crowd, strumming the opening notes. I'd had the basic melody stuck in my head for days, but it was only in the small hours of the night before that the lyrics had come:

I am smoke and fire
And you're the coming rain
The thunderhead in the distance
That will wash me clean again.

The chord pattern was simple enough that Evan would be able to pick it up after a single verse, and he did, weaving in a basic harmony when I hit the second.

The audience loved it, and I had to admit it was a decent song, especially once Evan got involved. I could tell the moment he fully settled into it and got comfortable. It was hard to explain, but it was as if I could hear it click into place for him by the way his fingers started running wild over his guitar strings, pulling out notes that wrapped around my score and squeezed it until the sound spun out into beautiful chaos. On the final chorus, Evan's voice came in high over my rich baritone, and the last few bars haunted the air like ghost notes hovering over the crowd.

A prolonged silence followed, and for a second I thought I'd misjudged the reaction, then they went apeshit. The volume of applause in such a small place was crushing. I basked in it for as long as I could and then disappeared backstage with Evan for a break before it stopped, sweaty and high with the residual adrenaline of absolutely nailing it. In an hour I'd have the musician version of a hangover, but I didn't care. It felt so damn good in the moment.

Evan was another story.

"What the fuck was that?" He tore his guitar off and dragged me out of earshot of Dan and the few other people backstage.

"Improv?" I ducked my head into the hole of my T-shirt to mop at the sweat on my brow, "They loved it. God, you killed it, and when you twisted your voice up there at the end? Ugh, it was brilliant. I'll never get how you do that shit."

"Why didn't you mention the song before, though? We could've worked on it this afternoon."

"I was just going to save it and then—Ev, we were flailing up there. It felt like the set was about to come apart."

"You flubbed our first opening, and yeah, I screwed up the next few parts but—" He threw his hands up, then raked them through his hair and I had to curl my hands into fists to resist reaching out to straighten the disheveled strands.

"I was trying to get you out of your head and me out of mine. And it worked. Perfectly in fact, if you were listening."

Evan paced alongside a bunch of old amps and record crates and rubbed a hand over his eyes irritably. "What if it hadn't, though? Because that could've easily been a disaster."

I caught him by the arm and held him still, putting my hands on his shoulders as I spoke, trying to counteract the edginess I could feel under my fingertips with the softness of my voice. "I can't tell you how I knew it would work, but I did. You're brilliant under the gun even if you think you're not. Even if you think you need all this time to work shit over. Fuck, I—" I paused, wanting to make sure what I was about to say didn't come out wrong. "I guess maybe I just wanted some proof that we still had it on stage after everything that's happened lately. And we do, Ev. That was the proof."

He sighed, his expression softening, and when he leaned forward and rested his forehead against my shoulder, it felt so fucking good to bear his weight. But it was brief. He took a deep breath and then a step back, shaking out his hands like he was casting off extra energy. "Okay. I'm good. Let's finish this."

It happened near the end of our last set, and despite Dan's assurances, it shouldn't have been a surprise. Every one of our shows came with its fair share of commentary and shouts from the crowd, and this one was no different. All night we'd been bantering back and forth with the audience, joking around between songs. Usually what came from the crowds was flattering stuff, and a lot of times related to music. Other times it was off-the-wall shit from a random troll or someone who was fucked up that we'd ignore until it faded to background noise of squealing fans and random cheering. But sometimes someone would say something loud enough and at just the right time for it to reach us onstage clear as a bell. Some chick once yelled out that she hated my haircut. It came at this really weird lull between songs at a smaller venue, and I'd had no idea how to respond. *"I'm sorry?"* I'd said, and everyone had laughed, the girl included, especially when Evan tacked on, *"I don't know if you know this, but his hair actually has a fan page. You should lodge your complaint there."* My hair actually did have a fan page at one point. I thought it was defunct, though, now.

Crowd dynamics were weird, and they were especially noticeable tonight when Evan and I were only about five feet away. So when some dude about seven heads back yelled out, "Who's the catcher?" everything got eerily silent again the way it had when I'd refused to play "Blue" earlier. I didn't have to glance at Evan to know he was scowling, and I was readying a light quip back when someone else shouted, "What the fuck does it matter?"

The security guards beside the stage glanced at me, and I shook my head.

"I've got this," I said. I had a great speech for such occasions because the question was universal and annoying as hell, not to mention fucking personal. I didn't ask someone what position their girlfriend liked it best in. That shit would get you looked at weird. Okay, *maybe* I'd asked it a couple of times, and I understood the curiosity. But still.

Evan cut in before I could get started. "No you don't. I do." He glared at the guy. I could see his pulse hammering at his throat. "That's the stupidest fucking question we've ever been asked in all our years of making music together. Congratulations. Now get the fuck out."

I stared in shock as he spoke. He sounded so matter-of-fact as he said it, but there was a poisonous lilt to the words I'd never heard from him before, and the way he was standing, with his hand strangling the neck of the guitar and the slight tremor that passed along his jaw, told me he was furious. He'd never snapped on stage before. I relaxed slightly as the guy started through the crowd for the door when he saw the security guards heading in his direction. Then he fucking piped up again. "I guess that answers that."

Nice. Power dynamics. I had a speech for that, too, but I didn't get the chance because, quicker than I could comprehend, Evan wrenched his guitar over his head and took off, barreling through the swarm of people on a mission to... I didn't even know what. A ripple ran through the crowd, and the security guards at both ends of the venue started pushing toward the center. Chaos exploded and I couldn't tell what the hell was happening. Everything became a tangle of limbs and motion mixed with a lot of yelling and scuffling. I lost track of Evan, and when I started to rush into the fray, a strong pair of hands latched around my shoulder and dragged me backward.

"I'll find him, go out the back," Dan growled. I ignored him and started forward again only to be yanked back roughly by my T-shirt. "Don't make it worse. Go on."

The front doors crashed wide, and the fire alarm went off as someone shoved the side exit open. People poured out in droves as I snagged our guitars and jetted backstage.

EVAN HAD A THIN CUT ON THE CORNER OF HIS MOUTH, A GOOSE EGG on one temple, a scrape on his cheek, and the knuckles of his right hand were swollen. He wore a scowl a mile wide as he slumped into a chair at the back of the shop, plopping the ice pack Dan brought him against his temple before he let his head fall back against the wall and closed his eyes. Security had pulled him from the melee. Dan had talked the other guy, who was in equally rough shape, out of pressing charges by mentioning the words "inciting a riot." I had no idea if that would really fly, but it seemed to have worked, because the dude had stumbled off without another word when his friends collected him, or so Dan had said. The guy had clearly been on something.

Dan had apologized profusely, and I'd apologized in return because shit, I knew the last thing he needed was a stampede where someone got hurt in his shop. Luckily, security had managed to break up the fray, and most people had stayed out of the way and pushed for the exits as soon as the fighting broke out.

"What the hell kind of Jekyll and Hyde bullshit just happened?" I didn't say it angrily, but it was forceful because Evan's reaction was so uncharacteristic.

His head snapped toward me, and he gave me a slow blink, like I was an idiot.

"That? That was exactly why this whole charade was a stupid fucking idea in the first place. From now on we're going to be fielding dumbass questions like that, and guess what, when it 'leaks' that we're not a couple anymore, it's going to be a whole other set of questions."

"Yeah, well, it's kind of what we signed up for." I wasn't disagreeing with him, but it was what it was.

"No. I signed up to make music, not to be asked whether or not I'm taking it in the ass. I don't even know why they care."

I slid down the wall to sit next to his chair. "Because you're you, Porter. You put out music that resonates, that people feel to their core. They want to know what makes you tick and how you fucking do it. It's fascinating to them. Getting all the little details, they can share in that. It reminds them you're a human, too. Because otherwise? You're an enigma. You rarely talk about anything personal, so it's exciting to feel like they've been let in. Why do you think I air all my laundry in public? It's not just because I don't give it a shit. It's about counterbalance, too, and it's part of why we work so well, I think. Tonight will get spun however it will, and we can just let it. Because none of it fucking matters as long as you and I know the truth and know what we are."

"Yeah, well, I'm starting to question that, too." He let out a rough exhale and dragged the ice pack over his eyes.

My breath felt as if it'd been sucked from my chest. I reminded myself that he was just reacting to the situation and he'd cool off. But before I could do anything else, he tossed the ice pack aside, launched off the chair, and cut out the back door into the night.

Dan grabbed me as I started to follow.

"What is it with you and grabbing me tonight?" I asked, struggling to wriggle free from his grasp. He was a strong dude. "He has the fucking car keys."

"Give him the space. I'll take you back."

We stared each other down, and eventually I shook my head petulantly.

"I know whereof I speak," Dan said, fixing me with a sage expression as I rolled my eyes.

"Fine, oh wise one."

Dan and I went to cool off at a bar, and even though I didn't necessarily want to, I forced myself to stop after one beer because if Evan was at the cabin when I got back, being hammered definitely wouldn't help. It was strange as hell to not only be the sober one, but the level-headed one. I didn't think I cared for it one bit.

The SUV was in the driveway when I returned, and I lingered outside for a minute after Dan dropped me off, just looking at the front door. I kept having this one thought that made my stomach flutter; I'd gotten so used to being shuttled around on a tour bus, or in a town car, whatever, that seeing the SUV in front of the cabin struck me as so perfectly domestic it would almost be funny if the current situation didn't suck so much. Because I wouldn't mind having something simple like this with Evan, wouldn't mind getting off tour and getting in a car together and then walking into the same house with him. In fact, I'd— I stopped the thought before it could begin to sprout and take root. It was never gonna happen. Tonight was another reminder of that.

In the kitchen, I stopped and guzzled some juice from the fridge, spying a tiny orange glow out on the deck as I drank.

Evan had kicked cigarettes soon after we'd started writing together, but when I got outside, there he was smoking, a small mound of butts in the ashtray as evidence he'd been there for a while.

"Trying to make up for lost carcinogens?" I asked, then snatched the cigarette from between his fingers.

"Funny coming from you." His gaze remained fixed on the horizon.

"Yeah, well, do as I say and not as I do. Or something." I took a long drag off the cigarette, then pinched out the butt and pitched it into the ashtray. Evan watched without comment. "Let me ask you something."

He groaned. "If it's about whether I'm a pitcher or a catcher, I'm fucking leaving."

I blew out a little chuff of air that wasn't quite a snort, wasn't quite a laugh, then twisted to face him, leaning back against the rail of the deck. "What do you want?"

Evan lit another cigarette and, after a moment, came to stand at the rail next to me. I turned and rested my arms against it, and we both gazed out into the darkness of the forest beyond. The cherry of his cigarette flared when he inhaled, shadows painting themselves into the hollows of his cheeks. I stole the cigarette again, took another drag, and scraped a shingle of ash onto the railing before handing it back.

"Like on a grand-scale level or right this very second?" he finally replied, glancing over at me.

"Whichever?" Whichever got him talking, whichever got that dark expression off his face.

He exhaled in a noisy rush of air. "Sometimes I want to throttle you."

"I'd let you." I kept the tease playful, encouraged by the sight of his expression downgrading from glower to frown.

He switched the cigarette to his other hand, freeing the one next to me, then reached up and closed his fingers around the side of my neck, his thumb pressing gently into my windpipe. "Unsurprising. You like all kinds of kinky shit." He angled toward me, his hand shifting and tightening. A tingle rose through my jaw and spread over my cheeks before he released the tension of his grasp slightly.

"How do you know?" Another squeeze, this time brief, and when he traced his thumb down my Adam's apple to the hollow of my throat, I shivered in hopeful anticipation. "Just a heads-up that you're making me hard, so congrats on being right. Apparently I'm into being mildly throttled."

Evan barked out a rough laugh, letting his cigarette fall to the deck and crushing it underfoot before sliding his hand down my shoulder, as if he intended to let it drop back to his side before a last minute change in course brought it back to my neck, where he tightened his grip again.

"What are you doing?" I didn't move, didn't want to, but I was curious.

"I don't know." He gave a brief shake of his head. "I don't even make sense to myself anymore. I was so pissed at you for springing that song mid-show, but you were right. It was good. It got me out of my head, and once I got over panicking about it, it was exhilarating in that free-fall, *oh-shit-my-stomach's-floating* kind of way. Like when we first started working on songs together. And then that asshat made that dumb comment, and even if I was still aggravated at you, I hated how what he said implied you were less than me." He tilted his head to the side to look at me, and the vehemence in the blue eyes that had provoked our greatest hit crashed over me with such force I almost stumbled backward. "Because you're not. Les, you're so fucking not. It's bad enough if you think that about yourself, but if someone else ever even remotely suggests it, it makes me want to hurt them."

I couldn't speak, could barely even breathe, and not just because his hands were moving over my skin, alternately applying pressure and then releasing and tracing gently, like they were directly connected to his emotions. I swallowed hard. Fuck, I was not going to tear up in front of him. I refused.

He blinked up at me and huffed out this self-aware laugh as he glanced at the one hand he still had around my throat. "I still want to choke you, too, I guess."

"You're being pretty diplomatic about it, though." I brushed aside the threat of tears and gave him a small smile. "It's kinda like an indecisive mix of murder attempt and massage."

"A relaxing murder."

"Name of our next album."

We both laughed. It was weird and a little awkward just standing there with Evan gripping my throat, but somehow erotic, too. Awkward eroticism. Was that a thing? My dick said it was. I sensed we were hanging on the cliff's edge of something, but Evan wasn't sure how to tip us over, and after our last hookup, I sure as shit wasn't going there.

"I should stop fucking with you," Evan said. Softly, like he was telling himself, and yet he didn't move away. His thumb turned little circles in the hollow of my throat, his fingers tightening again, this time to knead the back of my neck.

"I'm not sure I want you to," I whispered.

"Which part, the massage or the choking? Are you a secret masochist?" He ran his thumb along the midline of my neck all the way to the underside of my jaw and tipped it up until I saw stars, literally, the bright canopy above filling my vision. I swallowed hard again, my voice coming out husky. "Right now I'm good with either, but if you go the choking route, you should probably know you're not in my will, though you're welcome to my notebooks. I think my ghost would be cool with some posthumous fame." I probably had a bit of a masochistic streak in me, but mostly I had a strong desire for Evan to keep touching me — in whatever form that came. If he wanted to throttle me some more, so fucking be it.

"I'd credit you in the liner notes of course." His voice came to me as a distant drawl, and I felt a wash of heat across my throat when he brushed his open mouth over it. A whoosh of cold air followed as he turned me to yank my T-shirt up. I lifted my arms so he could pull it over my head.

"If you didn't, I'd haunt you." This might've been a good place to ask him again what the fuck we were doing or remind him of everything that happened the last time we screwed around, or even our commitment to not mix our public charade with some kind of private one. But I didn't. I was too turned on by this amazingly strange thing that was happening between us and too desperate to see where it would go to say a damn thing.

CHAPTER 30

Evan

H ave you ever had a moment when you're sick of yourself? Sick of how your mind works, sick of always trying to think ahead, of trying to plan, of waiting for the other shoe to drop, and you want, for just one fucking second, to be different? I was at that moment. I had no idea what I was doing, but I couldn't stop. Les's warm body was a magnet for my touch, and as soon as I pulled his shirt off, my hands went roaming over his bare chest, examining the valleys between his ribs, tracing whorls of ink, rubbing his nipples to hardness against the pads of my thumbs. His breath stuttered when I pinched one.

"Hurt?" I asked, bending to chase the sting with a brush of my lips.

"Yeah, a little. Good hurt." He shuddered through a nip of my teeth. "Addictive hurt."

And wasn't that almost a metaphor for the last six months?

Les twisted around to put his back to the rail, gripping it hard with his hands on either side, and I caged him in, caressing the backs of my knuckles up the side of his throat, making his head tip to one side and a soft hum of sound vibrate against my fingertips as his eyes fell shut.

"Maybe you're not going to kill me after all, just rub me into a coma," he murmured, a drowsy smile tilting the corners of his mouth.

I pinched his nipple again, and his shoulders jerked. "Or not."

And then I kissed him, slowly, like I could trap the flavor of that sedate smile and hold it on my tongue. When I danced my fingers over the fly of his jeans, his eyes flashed open and widened, his pupils large in the darkness.

"Can I?" I asked, tracing the edge of his button with the corner of my thumbnail.

He gave me an abbreviated nod. "Right now? You can do whatever you want, sw—Porter."

"Nice save." I chuckled.

"Old habits."

I yanked his button free and pulled down his zipper, finding his dick long and thick behind it. "What is it with you and underwear?"

"They get in my way. Obviously."

I couldn't disagree. It was sexy as anything seeing him half-undone, popping through his jeans as I reached my hand out and ran my fingertips over the head of his dick. I could tell he was trying to be stoic, but when I wrapped my hand around his silky shaft, so fucking warm and stiff, he exhaled in a hard gasp of air.

I stroked him faster, marveling at his body lighting up in front of me, writhing, pushing, pulling, and clearly aching for my touch. He threw his head back, and his chest rose and fell with sharp, panting breaths. Then I gripped him hard, squeezed up until the tip of his cock swelled and precum beaded along the slit. He winced at my roughness and staggered out another breath when I released him. Guess I was still choking him one way or another, and goddamn was it making me hard. I shifted my stance, my dick rubbing uncomfortably in the confinement of my jeans.

"Shit, yeah," he whispered, lowering his chin to gaze down between us, then nodding to indicate my straining fly. "Let me see you."

I obliged immediately, without even thinking about it. Did Les even know how much power he had over me? He eyed my exposed cock the same way he watched me play sometimes, a mixture of appraisal and appreciation. "Stroke it. Like you're stroking me." His fingers tightened around the railing, squeezing hard as he watched me stroke him and myself at the same time. "Yeah. *Fuck*." One of his hands flew from the railing to ball up tight in my T-shirt, then released and dived under the fabric, gripping my rib cage firmly for a bruising second before drifting over me in a light caress that sent a tantalizing shiver up my spine. He slid his arm up through the neckhole of my shirt and clamped around my throat. Payback, I guess. Gradually, I inched forward until I could take us both in one hand, and his forehead bumped mine. We stayed like that for a handful of seconds, just listening to the pattern of our breathing speed up and coalesce in harsh exhales. It took only a fractional movement for his lips to meet mine. He licked the corner of my mouth where the cut was, then my lower lip until my tongue surged forward to meet his and taste him. Smoke and the salt of my own skin still lingered on his mouth. It wasn't enough. None of it was.

Les growled when I pulled away. Actually growled with such a dissatisfied rumble that I laughed.

"If you're about to flip out right now Porter, I'm gonna finish myself off and jizz on you anyway," he warned.

"I'll try to wait until after." I released my hold on both of us, grabbed his loose waistband, and tugged as I turned toward the sliding door that led inside.

"Try to wait until never. Where are we going?" He was right on my heels, sneaking a hand down the back of my pants as we went.

"Bedroom."

"What for?" Desire made his voice thick, but I could sense a hesitation in it, too. And hope.

"What the hell do you think for? Sex does happen in bedrooms, doesn't it?"

"And on porches, living rooms, kitchens, outdoors…"

WHILE WE'D BEEN STANDING THERE ON THE PORCH MUTUALLY captivated, I'd figured out what it was that had all my nerve endings singing and flushing my brain with those feel-good, crazy-making chemicals. It was having him under my command. Having him respond so viscerally to my touch. It was similar to when we wrote songs together, an effortless call and response between us. And I wanted to give the same to him.

We got to his bedroom and shed our clothes in seconds, then stood there staring at each other while I tried to figure out how to get from point A to B, because I could tell Les was still intent on letting me lead. He spoke softly as he stepped closer and ran a hand down my shoulder. "You can fuck me again. I'll bottom for you, I don't care." He caressed my forearm, then took my hand in his, twining his fingers with mine. "Shit, I want you so fucking bad, I'll take you however you'll let me."

The note of plea in his voice wrecked me. I shook my head. I wanted to feel his power, wanted him to talk to me the way I'd witnessed him do with others, wanted to feel possessed by him, marked by him. Fuck my own fears about what came after.

I took a shaky breath and said, "I want you inside me. You asked me what I wanted. This is it."

His fingers tightened on mine, but he didn't move as his gaze searched my face, I thought, for any evidence that I hadn't meant what I'd said. But he'd find none. I wanted this.

After a moment, he released my hand. "Lie down." His voice was a low-timbred purr that rode the surface of my skin like a shock wave and turned into a shiver at my shoulders. I turned and lay facedown on the bed, and Les crawled on behind me, sitting on my calves, his hands spanning low across my back. "I'm gonna make this good for you, I promise."

"Don't baby me." My voice came out muffled by the comforter, and I turned my head, craning a look back at him, the dark swathe of his hair shadowing his face, the full lips and tensile strength of his hands gripping me. "I don't want to be babied. Fuck me the way you fuck everyone else."

I caught his smoldering gaze flickering over me a second before I lowered my head to the bed again.

"I can't, Ev," he said softly, "You're not everyone else."

The mattress shook as he got up. Hearing the click of a cap, I tensed instinctively, but then his hands glided over my hamstrings, over my ass, and up my back in long, lingering strokes that dug into muscle and relaxed me. I thought it'd be lube on his hands, but it was some kind of oil, silky and soft.

"Goddamn," he breathed, sounding so reverent that my breath caught in my throat, and the joke I'd been about to make died there. When his fingers slid between my cheeks, I tensed up again. His chuckle poured over me as warm as the oil he was slicking me with, and he palmed my ass with both hands, kneading and squeezing until I blissed out again. His touch was so damn good, so firm and confident and attentive, like he was reading every twitch and movement of my body and responding accordingly, tuning himself to me. His thumbs spread me wider and finally brushed over my hole in slow successive strokes that had me soaring.

"Oh fuck." I gasped as the very tip of his thumb pressed inside me.

"Yeah. Just wait. Fuck, I can't believe I get to…"

Les trailed off, draping over me, the head of his cock sliding back and forth in the seam of my ass, pressing me into the mattress as we both groaned.

"Turn over," he demanded.

"Why?"

"Because I'm a greedy asshole and I'm going to make you look at me while I fuck you through this mattress."

Fuck if that didn't make my balls tighten up. I rolled onto my back, and he pulled my legs atop his, spreading me. I'd have felt far too exposed and embarrassed if it wasn't for the wolfish way he watched me as he wedged himself between my bent knees. He took my cock in his hand again and stroked it, arousal coursing through me like a faucet turned full blast. With his other hand, he worked my hole, plying the muscle patiently but firmly. I clenched reactively and gritted my teeth as he slid the tip of his finger inside.

Les gave me a lopsided smile. "You're gonna have to relax, or you'll break my dick off."

"Trying," I ground out. *Relax.* I remembered the word, right?

He withdrew his finger until I let out a slow exhale, then eased it slowly back inside. This time I made a concerted effort not to tense up and was rewarded with a burn that diminished and became pure warmth. His expression was fierce and determined, lips pulled in, a discerning slant to his brow like he was still reading my every expression. "So fucking tight and warm. Can't wait to feel you around me." That helped. He pushed deeper, then added a second finger, glancing at my face as I winced through the sting. "It'll ease up. Just wait."

I gave him a short nod. His fingers glided lazily in and out of me, then he twisted his wrist and something happened. Something good. Something that flared inside me like a lightbulb flickering before blazing to life. A slow, delicious, pleasurable tingle that had me arching off the bed in pursuit of more. "Holy shit."

"Mmm. Found it."

"Shit, what are you doing?" I panted. Then, when he hesitated: "Don't stop!"

Les braced himself on one hand, scooting back, then bending over and licking a wet stripe up my cock, kissing over my stomach, my pecs, my throat, all the way to my mouth, which he claimed in a slow kiss. His fingers pushed against me, twisted and caressed that white-hot spot inside me until I felt like I was melting. He rumbled against my mouth. "You like my fingers in you? Like them fucking you, stretching you, getting you ready for my dick?"

I groaned. *This*. Yes. *This* was what I wanted. Pure, unadulterated, filthy Les.

"Fuck. Yes," I rasped out, and he sucked at my tongue, grinding his dick against my hip, then slid down my body, all the way to the floor, pulling me to him. He spread me again, and when his tongue flicked against my hole, I bowed upward, only to have his hand clamp down on my abs and force me back down.

"I know what you need." That voice that ran over and under mine onstage, chasing my high notes with mellow lows, my low notes with fever-pitch highs. I believed him in that moment. He knew exactly what I needed, and I groaned at the promise of fulfillment.

"Uncharted territory for you, I guess?"

I grunted an affirmative, and he kept rimming me, licking me, using his fingers and mouth on my ass and my cock until I could hardly see straight. My muscles shivered like a bowl of Jell-O on a rickety table, and my entire body physically ached with the strength of my desire.

There'd once been a week where Les followed me around with his phone, reading highlights from posts about him in the groupie forums just to annoy me. *Beautiful cock, wicked mouth, devil's hands, but what he can do with it all is even better.*

I didn't know why that specific comment had stuck with me. I'd laughed it off at the time, told him I doubted that was the case, but I thought of it then as Les kneeled in front of me, so in his element, turning me inside out one touch at a time. He somehow managed to be both appreciative and commanding, both dirty and sweetly sensual all at once, and fuck if that crazy combination didn't make me a believer.

"Ready?" He kissed the inside of my thigh and stood up, stroking himself, eyes blazing down at me, burning me up, driving me out of my head with arousal.

I nodded because I couldn't speak. I was all shivers and jolts and tremors of pleasure.

"Good, because you're going to give me what I want. What I *need*. Because you're wrong. There's no difference for me when it comes to you, Porter. I want you. I need you. Same thing."

Holy mother of God, he was going to kill me with the sincerity leaking from his tone, the vibrant intensity of his green eyes. I was starstruck, moonstruck, whatever it was you called the almost other-worldly euphoria rushing through me.

Les fit a condom over himself and crawled onto the bed, urging me back from the edge as he knelt over me and swallowed my panting breaths in a deep kiss. At the brush of his tip teasing my hole, and I moaned, ache and nerves rolled up in one big ball of scorching *need*.

"Fuck. Do it," I whispered into his mouth, desperate.

A burning fullness, that was what I felt first, and it seemed infinite, made my lips peel back from my teeth and my forehead break out in a sweat that Les soothed his hand over. His gaze fixed on me, watching every reaction intently even as his mouth dropped open and he groaned out a sound like he was breaking. "Oh God, you have no idea how much I—" He pressed a hard kiss into my shoulder, then my throat, and I curled one hand through the strands of his hair and clutched his ass tightly with the other, squeezing him to show I could handle it.

Les moved inside me slowly, inexorably slowly, like he was patiently waiting for my body to catch up with what was going on. Which was good because I struggled at first, the pressure uncomfortable, the fullness overwhelming. I tried to keep my breaths measured as he seated himself deep inside me and went still. He kissed my lower lip, sucked on my tongue and began moving inside me again—slow even strokes that rolled through my body like the best kind of wave, pleasure breaking over me. I was so turned on I couldn't think coherently, couldn't make my mouth function other than to kiss him. But that was all right because he said enough for both of us when he whispered my name and told me how good it felt. And finally, everything settled into place and my body opened fully to him.

"Touch yourself," he commanded.

I reached between us to fist my cock, and God did the twin sensations of my hand and Les inside me feel incredible. My hips moved instinctively, rocking me into my hand, rocking me onto him, and with my other hand, I tugged at the roots of his hair with every thrust, drawing gasps and grunts and other lewd sounds from him that sent me spiraling toward orgasm.

Les braced on his arms, gaze fixated on the place where our bodies joined, watching as I stroked myself faster. The smack of skin on skin filled the air, and I could tell he was close. I'd seen that look on his face before, that lost-to-the-world, jaw-hanging ode to explicit pleasure. This time, it was because of me, and I couldn't take one more second of being devoured by it. A shudder ran through my thighs, and Les grabbed my hips, bending in close to me and growling out against my lips. "Want it. Lemme feel you come apart."

I was toast. I blew apart at the seams with a shout, clutching a fistful of his hair and yanking his head back as my orgasm turned me end over end inside and exploded from the tip of my cock in hot streaks that painted my abs and chest. Les dropped down on top of me, wrapping his hands under my shoulders and sealing his body tightly to mine.

"Goddamn, Porter," he gritted out as he pummeled my channel through a series of aftershocks. I felt him tense up, his cock pulsing inside me, and he dug his fingers into the meat of my shoulders as he came on a guttural moan.

I couldn't move and I didn't want to. I soaked in the feeling of him as he grew heavy on top of me. We slowly extricated ourselves from the various ways we were tangled, in no hurry. I let my fingers drift from his hair and trickle down the side of his face in a soft caress.

Les released his grip on my shoulders but kept his arms around me as he kissed the side of my throat and then my jaw. I wrapped an arm low around his waist and sighed when he eased out and rolled off me and onto his back beside me. He put his hands up to his face, rubbing at his cheeks. "Fuck, I think you just destroyed me."

"Same." He really had no idea. I laughed and touched the stickiness on my chest as he snapped the spent condom off and laid it across his thigh. "I don't think I can move." My cock softened and my breathing slowed, and drowsiness hit like a sledgehammer.

Les knotted the condom and tossed it onto the floor, rolling into me. "Good, because I don't want you going any-fucking-where."

I didn't want to go anywhere, either. Ever. I wanted to stay in this room cocooned in the deep sense of intimacy between us, safe from the outside world, safe from tours and albums and sales reports. Safe, even, from me.

Do you have any idols?

Les: Daniel Grim.

Evan: Is he aware of how intense your crush on him is?

Les: He has to be. I've been around him drunk too many times. Answer the question, who's your idol?

Evan: Probably Johnny Cash.

Les: Ugh. What a standard answer. Give 'em something good. C'mon.

Evan: All right. You.

Les: What? Really?

Evan: No. [Laughing] I had to drag you away from a hot dog cart the other night while you were singing Meatloaf at the top of your lungs.

Les: Psht. I'll bet you ten bucks Cash did that at least once.

Evan: But he probably wasn't wearing a fishnet shirt.

CHAPTER 31

T ypical wake-up scenarios for Les Graves:

- Hungover + way too fucking early
- Hungover + way too fucking late
- Somebody I didn't want still in my bed still, in fact, in my bed
- Cold shower + being flung in tour bus because... late + Evan angry at lateness

I had my first ever Disney wake-up the next morning. One of those where the sun streamed in through the windows, clear blue sky visible beyond the panes, birds fucking chirping with their chests bellowed out and friendly eyes on display.

Nix the last part. Fuck birds. There was a pair outside the window engaging in world war three and raising a holy ruckus. Nature lover, I was not. But the rest was true, and the best part was the man still in my bed, his face buried in the pillow, sleep-warm back exposed.

It was 9:00 a.m. He'd skipped his run.

It was 9:00 a.m., and I'd slept all damn night.

"What's that noise?" Evan grumbled, his voice muffled.

"Birdageddon, part five million. There's gotta be a nest out there because I hear them every morning." I reached out, rapping hard a couple of times on the window beside the bed. The cacophony outside quieted for all of ten seconds.

"Maybe they should consider counseling."

"Maybe someone should stick them in a cabin together. Let them duke it out in a confined space until they end up in a full-on fuckfest."

"Duking it out?" Evan laughed softly and rolled onto his back, glancing over at me with a smirk. "Is that what last night was?"

"Duking, choking, fucking. Same idea. You started it." But that wasn't what last night was really. Last night was Cinderella at the ball, getting to dance all night with the prince without ever hearing the stroke of midnight. I'd be keeping that analogy to myself, though, since I could just see Evan using it against me for life.

Evan groaned and rubbed the heels of his hands against his eyes. "I did. I didn't mean to; that's not what I—but yeah, I did. I definitely fucking did."

I rolled onto my side, studying him, that sexy natural pout, the sleepy gaze, looking for the signs of our own small apocalypse—a regretful expression, a tinge of fear in his eyes. "Is this the part where you're going to panic? Let me know, because I can go make myself some breakfast or something, take a long shower, clean baseboards with a toothbrush, watch paint dry."

He snorted lightly, turning to face me, and I slung my leg over his outer thigh.

"If I'm panicking, I think the correct response is to talk me down. Isn't aftercare a thing?" He gripped my thigh and squeezed it once, then stroked the length of it idly.

"Aftercare?" I laughed. "It's not like I had you shackled and was caning you into subspace, although I think I could totally be into that with you."

"Pretty sure I'd be the one caning you."

I shrugged one shoulder agreeably. "I'm in. Especially if there's leather involved."

We fell silent, and it wasn't that the air grew thick or uncomfortable, but I got this idea that we were both suddenly very aware that we were lying in bed naked together, and very aware of how different it felt this time.

Evan inhaled deeply and made a face. "Okay, yeah. I might panic. Shit."

I scooted closer to him, and he watched me warily, skeptically.

"Turn over," I told him.

"No. Why?" He was getting cagey. I didn't want that.

"Fuck's sake, Porter, I'm not about to stick a knife in your back. Relax."

He sighed and rolled over, putting his broad back to me. I caressed down his spine then fanned my fingers wide, stroking the muscles upward, rolling my thumbs into the nape of his neck until he groaned and I could feel some of the stiffness dissolve. Scooting nearer, I pressed my chest to his back, wrapping one arm around him as I spoke close to his ear, loving the goose bumps that studded the side of his neck in the wake of my breath. "I'm not going to let you panic this time. We're going to talk this through logically."

Evan groaned, and not the sexy you're-killing-me groan I was addicted to, but the oh-shit kind. "I'm having sex with my bandmate and best friend. We owe our label an album. We're currently faking a relationship for a PR boost with plans to terminate said fake relationship before we go into the studio. Except it's hard to call something fake if you're fucking. And it still has to end. How do you logic through that clusterfuck?"

"Who says it has to end? That decision was made because we insisted on an expiration date. That part's on us." I proposed this lightly, almost tentatively, and Evan twisted around in the sheets to study me.

"Are you suggesting we... what, date? Be together?"

My expression deadpanned. "You're saying that like it's offensive to you, which is a little insulting considering you were moaning my name into my own mouth not five hours ago."

He grimaced. "Okay, fair. I apologize. I can't lie and say I don't feel something for you. I do. I feel a lot of things. Shit, we're together constantly. I feel closer to you than I've ever felt to anyone else. When you kiss me, when we touch it's... something else. Something I haven't had with anyone else. Addictive and... shit, more than a little scary. But we're in a vacuum here. This is suspended reality." He yanked at the covers and rolled over again to face me, a quiet intensity in the gaze that searched my face. "What happens when we leave and I go back to my house and you go back to yours? What happens when we're out on tour? What happens when you're surrounded by chicks and dudes clamoring to fuck you and I get jealous? Or you're hammered out of your skull and pull that shit where you take it out on me? I could handle it before because it was just annoying—although, to be honest, increasingly concerning. But I couldn't handle it if we were together, because I won't be able to distance myself from it."

"I don't want to fuck anyone else, Ev." But I stopped there because I had no idea how he'd react to the news that I'd been lusting after him for months and months, that everyone else was a pitiful attempt to get him out of my head. "And I'm working on the drinking. In case you haven't noticed."

"I have." His expression softened and he reached for me, running his hand down my side. "But like I said, we're in a vacuum. It's all around us on tour."

"Look, I don't know how it'll all play out, but I don't want to stop, okay? So could you give me a real shot at trying to prove it can work? Give me until we go to the studio, and if you're not convinced, then we let the hammer fall as planned and I promise to respect your decision." I shouldn't promise that part. I couldn't even think it without feeling nauseated. Because now that Evan was in my bed, I didn't want to let him out. Ever. Metaphorically speaking. Literally too, maybe, except my stomach started grumbling, so after we went back and forth some more, I finally crawled out of bed and went to make us breakfast. That's right—I was gonna cook for him. One fuck and I was domesticated. In another week, I'd probably be begging to fold his laundry.

. . .

BY MIDAFTERNOON THAT DAY, WE HAD A ROUGH SKETCH OF THE new album, ten songs that were more or less complete and the beginnings of two more—one being the song I'd broken out at Grim's the night before. *Jesus, was that just last night?* It felt like a week ago. Time had a way of slowing out here, and I was starting to get used to it. I liked having Evan all to myself.

"Come with me to Grim's. Dan's got something there waiting for me," I said when we decided to take a break.

"A fist to the face for that shitshow?"

I grinned. "No way. Though I thought he was going to destroy that jackass."

"I didn't see what happened to him. That biker dude pulled me out of the pit and dragged me out back." Evan slid his guitar into its case, then extended his hand to yank me up from the floor.

"I didn't see much, but Dan had the guy locked up, and the other biker dude had to pull him off."

"Dan doesn't give a fuck, does he?"

"Not even one."

I was worried there might have been damage, too, but when I'd texted Dan earlier that morning, he'd said it was all good, and when we walked into the shop late that afternoon, everything was back in its usual place, the only sign of last night's show a single busted display rack Owen was bent over fixing when we came in.

He slid a new wood slat in place and gave us a bright smile when he saw us, eyes running up and down us both curiously. "Back to bring more chaos?"

"Nah. Just picking up something Dan said he'd leave for me," I said.

"Oh yeah, right here." Owen dropped the hammer he'd been holding and popped up, darting to the checkout counter.

Evan wandered off down the aisles, poking through the racks while I followed after Owen.

"The show was killer last night, in spite of everything." Owen glanced up at me as he rummaged behind the counter. "Really digging the new stuff."

"Thanks, man. Hope everyone else digs it, too." My attention turned to Evan, tracking him around the store, watching as he caught his lower lip in his teeth. He narrowed his eyes as he picked up an album, studied it, then put it back down. Watching him debate over a record sleeve shouldn't have turned me on, but it did. I embarked on a tasty fantasy of sitting his sweet ass in a chair and making him watch me strip down and jerk myself until he couldn't take it and bent me over said chair and fucked me mercilessly. The fantasy burst when I realized Owen was still talking to me.

"Do you have a certain time of day you write?" Owen had these big, beautiful eyes that blazed with sincerity as he spoke. He really did seem like a sweet guy.

"Nah. I'm a slave to the muse, I guess, and sometimes a deadline." I chuckled.

He laughed and nodded. "I've got some stuff I've been working on. I know how it goes."

That happened a lot, and I tried not to be a dick about it because Evan and I had both been there. I listened as Owen talked about the album he was working on, which actually didn't sound half-bad. The premise was intriguing, at least. He handed me a bag from behind the counter with the album I'd requested in it, then tore a sales slip off the pad and started writing on the back. "Web addy for some links to rough demos, if you want to give it a listen," he explained. His smile was infectious and brightened further as I folded the slip of paper and tucked it in my pocket.

"I'll do that," I promised.

"'Course... you could come listen in person sometime." His tongue darted out to wet his lips as both eyebrows rose hopefully.

"You have a show soon?"

"No." He colored faintly. "I meant at my place." He inclined his chin a fraction, whatever hint of sheepishness he'd just displayed now overridden by that defiant lift, a hint of both challenge and promise in his eyes. Shit, I was slow on the uptake today. Owen was cute, but no way. I'd told Evan the truth; he'd destroyed me. New territory for me, because I rarely said no. Rarely wanted to.

"Not a fucking chance." Speak of the devil; Evan's arm latched around my waist and squeezed like a boa constrictor. His tone of voice had "mine" stamped all over it. Vocal territoriality. I could get into that.

Owen's cheeks flamed in full blush, and he shook his head quickly. "My bad, dude. I thought that shit was fake."

"What gave you that impression?" I was curious, even if he was kind of right.

"Adam Slade had this whole piece on PR hacks that was up on Tattletales this morning. I mean, he didn't call it out blatantly, but he suggested it, so I just thought..." Owen winced and fidgeted.

"Was your cock in my ass last night, or did I dream that?" Evan said, cocking his head to the side like he was confused.

My jaw threatened to drop. "It was definitely buried deep inside you. And you're *definitely* being a dick right now." I picked up my bag from the counter and leaned in toward Owen. "Sorry. He's not usually a dick, and I will listen to your stuff, but by myself. I don't know what that article says, but trust me, it's an oversimplification."

OUTSIDE, I STARTED LAUGHING. "WHAT THE HELL WAS THAT?"

"I want to know what this article says." Evan glowered as he reached into his pocket for his phone.

"All right. Can you drop the alpha-hole mode for a while? Dude was just flirting." And then I got it. "Shit, you were jealous. Awww, sweetheart."

"I warned you," Evan groused as I chuckled.

I darted after him as he stalked toward the car. Halfway through the parking lot I shouldered into him. He huffed out a breath, his expression heated and stern when I clenched his shirt in my fist.

"I had no interest in hooking up with that guy, Porter. I can still taste you, and as soon as we get back to the cabin, I'm gonna help myself to more."

His eyes flashed as he pushed me off him, but that shove came accompanied by a smile and the quick streak of his mouth across my jaw. He was slow to release the waistband of my jeans.

When we got back to the cabin, I fully intended to strip him painfully slowly and ride him until we both fell apart.

Except that didn't happen, because Evan looked up that stupid article on the ride home.

CHAPTER 32

Evan

"He could have said a lot worse, I guess." Les tossed his plastic bag of records on the floor and flopped onto the couch. He plucked restlessly at some loose threads on the worn plaid cushions.

"I haven't gotten all the way through it, yet." I had the article open on my phone and scrolled down to continue reading. "'This time-honored tradition of PR stunts that manipulate the listening public for ratings stretches from movie star pairings and reality shows and trickles all the way down to beloved alt-rock musicians who pride themselves on their gritty, honest, down-home sound, yet have no problem faking a relationship in the hopes of boosting lagging sales.'" I glanced up at Les to find his expression souring. "'I'm looking at you, Porter & Graves, who've been careful not to precisely confirm one thing or another, but have been conveniently spotted around a small Tennessee town in very cozy company with each other.'"

"Technically it's supposition," he said. And it felt like we were back at the beginning.

"Technically, his evidence is as solid as your dick down the back of his throat," I pointed out.

"He didn't say that, though, the fucker. Would've jeopardized his journalistic integrity. Fuck him."

"Too bad you did." I didn't mean for it to come out as snappishly as it did.

Les made a face. "He's just bitter because I didn't return the favor. And stop harping on me about that. It's over and done with."

I continued to quote, "'And while it's easy to buy into a high-profile, top-of-the-tier pair like bubbly film star Leah Price and crowd-pleasing pop singer, Justin Wolf, pairings like mercurial, megawatt creative Evan Porter and his bad-boy, train-wreck-waiting-to-happen counterpart, Les Graves, is a ridiculous notion that asks us to suspend far too much disbelief. Porter is too calculated and business-minded to get involved with that mess.' So yeah, he's definitely a little bitter."

Les bolted upright on the couch. "That piece of shit. That's gotta be slander."

"It's op-ed and we're public figures. He's untouchable on this." I tried to hold back my amusement at Les's sudden indignation, but it was helping me avoid thinking about how quickly this was all getting out of hand, both in public and private.

"Sounds like he's got a boner for you. Maybe you should've been the one sucking his cock."

I took the verbal jab on the chin while Les paced in front of the couch, biting the corner of his thumbnail so hard and fast, the sound of his teeth clicking filled the air. "So what do we do now?"

I was none too pleased about it, either, but my irritation went further back: Les letting the guy blow him, the path that led us to this ridiculous stunt in the first place. And yet... how could I be angry over the events that landed me in the arms of the one person I thought I might be falling in love with? *Holy fuck, did I really mean that?* It was a paradox.

"I'm calling Levi." I closed out the article and tabbed through my contacts to distract myself from my racing heart.

"I was just about to call," Levi answered.

"Did you know this was coming down the pike?" I was oddly suspicious, an uneasiness in my stomach whose origin I couldn't explain, and the way Levi answered didn't help. Why hadn't he called me first thing?

"What? No!" he said emphatically.

"If I find out this is all part of some larger scheme, I'm done," I warned him.

Les watched me carefully, one eyebrow cocked, a stern set to his mouth as I paced listlessly.

"That's ridiculous, Evan. We're on your side. On both of your sides," Levi was quick to add. "But this is really no big deal. It's one opinion piece, and there's plenty to suggest you two are together. We're still on track to quietly drop news of the breakup to a few sources just before you go into the studio."

I snorted over the fact that my publicist was having to reassure me that the course of my fake relationship with my bandmate was on track and proceeding smoothly toward its demise. This was insanity, and yet, I couldn't help but say, "And what if we don't want to do that?"

Les's eyes went wide. Mine probably would've, too, and I wasn't really sure where I was going with that because whatever Les and I were, I was nowhere near ready to make a public declaration about it, but the flabbergasted silence on the other end was worth the two seconds of vindictive peace that rocking the corporate machine gave me.

When Levi replied, after a lengthy silence, he sounded hesitant. "We could certainly work with that, if you'd like to keep up the charade. Or... maybe it's not a charade? It's... um... yeah, we could work with that." He picked up speed, and I could tell by the rapid way he spoke he was starting to get excited. "Actually, that could be really great. It opens up a whole new avenue of publicity to mine."

I tossed the phone to Les in aggravation. Les's attention was still fixated on me, but now he seemed wary and confused. His brow furrowed as he spoke. "I think what Evan's saying is that we need some time to think about it, so we'll just sit tight right now and not worry about the article."

"Good plan. I'll check in tomorrow and you can let me know

what you're thinking. The more heads-up we have, the better. If you want to continue the relationship, I'll need to get on the ball. This could be huge."

Damn, the guy was all kinds of fired up now. So much for rocking the corporate machine. Talk about backfire.

After he ended the call, Les canted his head to one side, studying me where I stood at the kitchen island, my fists clenched on top of the counter. "What...?"

I shook my head. "I don't fucking know. I don't know anything." I searched his face, his expression, looking for a sign... but I wasn't sure what I was looking for. I was uneasy all over. Something felt off. "Did you know about any of this before?"

Les flinched like I'd thrown a punch. Then he barked out an incredulous laugh. "Yeah, Porter, this was all a part of my grand scheme to get you in bed."

My brow cocked up, and he gave a disbelieving shake of his head, ground-eating strides carrying him to confront my frown. Somehow the intensity in his movements comforted me.

Les gripped me firmly by the biceps, and he was close enough that I saw the tiny pores on his face, the thick fringe of his lashes, the eyes behind burning with a fury that made my next inhale slow and measured and relieved. I licked my lips and kept quiet, and it was only after I'd done it that I realized what a tell it was. Even right then, in that moment, when everything inside me churned with doubt, I wanted him. I thought maybe I'd wanted him for much longer than I'd ever allowed myself to believe.

"I've been along for the ride, same as you, and I have a very distinct memory of you underneath me, begging for it, wanting it. Did I make that up?" His nostrils flared as he inhaled, and for the first time, I glimpsed the fear behind the frustration. It made something inside me go very still.

His expression softened when I said, "No. It was real. Shit, I don't know. I guess this is the clusterfuck I was talking about." I didn't want to argue with Les. Hell, I didn't know what I wanted right then besides to go back to this morning when we were lying in bed together.

"It's real to me, too. Fuck, Porter." He shook his head as he squeezed my shoulders hard, then released me and took a step back, like he was drawing his next breath from the space he created between us. His fist rose to rub at the spot between his dark brows, his eyes clenching tightly as he shook his head again.

When he looked up at me, his face was drawn, but his eyes were clear. "I don't know what all of this is to you, if it's just a convenient exploration, or... I've already told you—maybe not in so many words—but I've got it pretty fucking bad for you, Porter, and I don't know where it leaves us in all of this, but it's the truth. Fuck. I don't think I've felt this way about anyone since I was... I don't even know. Maybe ever. Goddamn."

"Les." This was anything but a convenient exploration. In fact, it was incredibly inconvenient. My heart stuttered. I felt it like a skip in my chest. Or a kick. And I had no idea what to do with the confession he'd just given me. It wasn't an *I love you*, but it rubbed elbows with the sentiment, and now he was squirming, looking at me like he'd made a mistake. Les Graves wasn't meant to squirm. I took a step forward and reached for him, skimming a touch over his shoulder.

He looked up at the ceiling and laughed. "Oh shit. This is perfect. Fuck, I probably deserve this."

"Les." More forcefully this time. His gaze dropped back to meet mine, and I could see the shields going up behind it. "Give me a minute to process."

He nodded once, averting his eyes and shaking free of my touch. "Sure. All the time you want." He still wouldn't look at me, but when he turned to go, snagging a water from the fridge before thumping down the stairs to the basement, I let him.

I picked up my laptop and took it with me to the couch, checking our numbers before frustration had me shoving the laptop aside and throwing my head back against the cushions. I stretched my legs out, glancing down at the floor to see what crinkled, and picked up the bag from Grim's, dumping the contents on my lap.

Jessup Polk. A rare pressing of his debut EP, and two more I wasn't even aware existed.

I turned the sleeves over in my hands, then rested my forehead against the cool, cardboard surface. The sound of Les playing rose from the basement, the sweet melody draping over my shoulders. Fucking Les. He got me every time.

CHAPTER 33

I went back and forth with myself trying to decide whether I regretted telling Evan how strongly I felt about him. *I love you* had been on the tip of my tongue, but I'd restrained myself at the last second, biting it back the way you would a curse, still afraid I'd scare him off or overwhelm him. And I was *still* scared I'd said too much. But in a way, it was a relief to have it out there. His reaction hadn't been ideal, but then I'd dropped it in a stressful situation, so what did I expect? The article was annoying and pissed me off, mostly because it once again put Evan on a pedestal and made me sound second-rate. I didn't hate Evan for that, though. And shit, Adam Slade was right. I'd done nothing to show anyone otherwise.

After I cooled off downstairs and reread the article, I decided it didn't matter. What mattered were our fans, and I hoped this new album would prove we were worthy of the support they'd given us so far, regardless of what Evan and I were doing in our personal lives. It wasn't like we were murdering kittens or anything.

Evan was trickier. I'd meant what I said when I told him to take his time, and yeah, I could have said it with a little less bitterness, but I was being honest. We would always bicker. That was the nature of us. But as we worked through another couple of songs later that afternoon—songs I'd had no trouble writing, since I was practically bleeding out my feels by that point—I noticed we were cohesive again. At least, musically speaking. I wasn't going to press him on anything else, no matter how much I wanted to. I resisted the urge to touch him, which was hard because I constantly wanted to touch him now—wanted to feel his skin against mine, smell him, wrap myself in him. I did my best to keep my actions and words light and innocuous, and it was such a mature response I was kind of amazed at myself, really. I thought Evan was, too. I caught him studying me at intervals, his eyes narrowed, like he was expecting me to fly off the handle at any moment.

By evening, we'd run through the entire album and were trying to pregame an order for the songs—and also a title for the album—when I looked up to find Evan watching me again, his brows furrowed over his straight nose in a fierce blond bunch. I loved his nose, the slight natural flare of his nostrils giving him this dignified profile, how the heavy line of his brows intensified him. He was an intense-looking guy in general, but especially so in that moment.

"You solving the mysteries of the universe over there or what?" I rocked my pen back and forth in my hand a couple of times before settling it between my teeth. The plastic end was all chewed up. I went through a pack in a week, discarding them when the ends were so mangled and sharp I couldn't chew on them anymore. Evan had a cigarette stuck behind his ear that'd been there all day, some quirky battle of willpower taking place within him. He touched it lightly before replying. "How many notebooks do you have?"

I thought about it. "Twenty or thirty since we've been writing together, I think." I had a weird organizational system that probably wouldn't make sense to anyone else, but there were notebooks allotted for each album, some that I used on tour that got transferred into the album notebook if I thought the lyrics were worthy, and some that just kind of floated around and acted as a journal for the time period. I'd tried writing on a computer or my phone before, and it didn't work. I needed the physicality of a notebook and pen. Needed to see the ink bleed on my words. There was a kind of catharsis to it.

Evan shook his head, exhaling a chuff of breath. "You realize we've written this album faster than we've ever written anything before?"

"Guess we've had a lot to say."

He quirked a smile at that. "Remember the first time we met?"

I nodded, putting my pen down in my notebook and closing it. I was lying on the floor on my stomach, and Evan sat across from me, his guitar on his lap. He was so rarely without it. Even when we weren't actively playing, it was in his hands. It was like twisting a lock of hair or twiddling your thumbs. Some people did that. Evan plucked at the strings of his guitar.

"Jensen's. God it was hot that night." The AC in the bar had felt like it was pushing out lukewarm air.

"And smoky. Could hardly see the stage." He twanged a few ominous notes, making me laugh. "I kept hearing about you. This drummer from Virginia who'd just up and decided he wanted to play guitar, instead. All my bartender buddies would whisper about you, usually the chicks. Talking about your perfect hair. I think it was actually Mo who told me your own stuff was good. Then Dan mentioned you and said you'd be playing soon and I should check it out."

Evan already had a label interested in him, I remembered that, but they'd wanted to pair him with a lyricist, and Evan had felt uncertain about it.

"You were wearing a T-shirt with something really stupid on it."

"I will end you." That's what the T-shirt had said. It featured a squirrel brandishing its tiny fist. Thinking about it made me laugh. "I love that shirt." Still had it, in fact.

"I thought 'what kind of jackass gets up onstage in a shirt like that?' You looked like you'd just rolled out of bed."

"I think I had."

Evan tried to suppress a smile but failed, and it came out as this small, affectionate curve that I wished I could keep there for the rest of his life. "But then you played, and you talked to the audience. Small crowd, but they fucking loved you. Loved how you joked with them, how you'd try to play anything, even if it was terrible."

Someone had requested Barry White's "Can't Get Enough of Your Love" that night. It had been... interesting. Evan must have been thinking the same thing, because he tipped his head back against the chair and laughed, the sound full-throated and infectious, and I adored the rumble of it even more than his smile.

"I murdered that song."

"You did, oh shit. The way you tried to beatbox through the opening." He put his hands over his face, his shoulders shaking.

I snickered. "You should've been there the night I did 'Like A Virgin.'"

"You could do it right now?" Evan played the opening chords, brows hiking up in invitation.

"I'll spare us both."

"But you were good," he said, sobering. "*Are* good." He bit at the inside of his cheek, an action that hollowed out one side of his face and made his cheekbone stand out in stark relief—a tic of his I'd always found incredibly sexy. For fuck's sake, he'd turned me into nothing but gooey caramel filling.

"You told me my arrangements were off and they were losing impact, but my pipes were good and my lyrics were amazing." I'd remembered those words exactly. I'd known who Evan was back then. Everyone did. But we'd never spoken. He had a devoted following on the circuit and was known for being dry and serious. I'd had no idea why he was talking to me since I'd just started out. Evan ticked a look down to me as I added, "You were right. You usually are. It's annoying."

He blew out a breath, fiddling with the strap of his guitar, then raking a hand through his hair. "Not always." He smeared his palms up and down his face, then just sat there like that for a minute, and a split second of fear rushed through me like water let out of a dam, sudden and all-encompassing. He was going to tell me something I didn't want to hear, I was sure of it.

But he only smiled and shook his head. "You wreck my brain, you really do. And you drive me up the wall, and I know I do the same. But shit, I want you. I keep thinking about that. The past few days, it's all I can think about. Can't make sense of it. But I don't want to stop this."

It was a confession, not a dismissal, and though it lacked the three words I craved hearing from him, the naked look in his eyes was enough. I was straddling him in seconds, pushing the guitar out of the way, taking the strap over his head, and running my hands over him like they'd been itching to all day. He stilled them with his own.

"I don't know what this means for our music. The publicity or whatever, but I'm willing to give it a shot. I kinda can't… not."

"We'll figure it out," I said, then hooked a finger under his jaw and kissed him.

His hands landed on my hips, squeezing tight, relaxing, then squeezing again before holding there, a kind of Morse code of desire that transmitted shivery joy all over me.

I peeled his clothes off slowly and kissed him everywhere, touched him everywhere. And when he was naked and sprawled, arching his body into my mouth and my hands, I held him down and straddled him, burying his slick cock inside me so slowly that old tufts of carpet caught in his nails from where he clawed it. I wanted all of him, every square inch of skin against mine. We gasped and rocked together, and when I yanked him upright, he wrapped his hands around my waist, licking and biting at my pulse while I whispered filthy combinations of word and sound that soared through him and bled out as heat in the cheek I cupped in my hand.

His orgasm caught me and pulled me under, and I rode the quake of his thighs and the pulse of his cock until I spilled against his abdomen. And I was certain, as I had never been of anything else in my life, that this was how we were meant to be.

Is there a certain song you're most proud of?

Evan: They're all like children in a way, I guess? Not that I've ever had any children.

Les: That you know of…

Evan: That, yeah. Shh. But personally? "Collide."

Les: Oh wow. I thought you'd say "Blue" since it's killing the charts.

Evan: Remember writing "Collide," though? We started with one line.

Les: One measly line, yeah. That's all I had.

Evan: And then we just went back and forth, handing off words and notes, just throwing stuff out there. That thing composed itself. We were just along for the ride.

Les: Yeahhhh. You're totally right. And we came up with the same-sounding chorus at the same time. That was some eerie synergy.

CHAPTER 34

W e slept in Evan's bed that night, and the next morning was just sunlight and bird chirps, minus the territorial war still ongoing on my side of the cabin. I woke happy. So fucking happy. I couldn't remember the last time I'd woken with a genuine sense of joy. Always there was this vague dread and pressure, and this morning there was only the warm scent of Evan's skin at the nape of his neck where I buried my nose and fell back asleep.

He was gone when I woke again. Running, I figured. He'd already made coffee, so I whipped up some breakfast before going down into the basement to tool around for a while. I had one more song that had been in my head, and I thought we could tack it onto the album as a bonus download. It was called "Hard Ache," and it was for him.

Push me pull me, I'm out of control...

I rapped my pen against the notebook, then scrawled the last verse.

"Something else?" Evan asked, appearing in the doorway, drying sweat from his hair with a towel. He was drenched and looked delicious, color high in his cheeks, blue eyes bright and awake, and wearing a grin that seemed tailor-made to get me hard.

"Maybe." I gave him my best sly smile and laid my notebook over my lap.

"Do I need to be awake at 3:00 a.m. to hear it?"

"Nope, I'm saving it for the studio. You can hear it then."

Evan wanted to get into the studio as soon as possible, while the energy was still fresh, so we'd agreed to take only a single week off to do nothing once we got back to Nashville in a couple of days before going into the studio. Of course, I'd let my imagination go wild concocting ways we could fill that downtime.

While Evan was in the shower, I called Byron and let him know we wanted the studio time, so he could set it up. I was still talking to him when Evan finished up and strolled down the hall with a towel wrapped loosely around his waist and his shoulders dewed with water droplets. His fucking body was going to be the death of me. He tilted his head at me, chin jutting to the phone in inquiry, so I put the call on speaker.

"Ev's out here now," I said.

"Porter. How goes? Les was just telling me the album's in the bag and it's good stuff. Got anything I can take a listen to?"

Evan glanced up at me to check before he said anything, and I nodded. I'd been known to be superstitious about letting people listen to the rough cuts we laid down prior to going into the studio.

"Can send some over in a little bit. You heard from Levi, lately?"

"Not in a couple of days. Itching to end this charade?" Byron chuckled.

"Um," I said smartly, but Evan was on it.

"We'll talk about it when we get back."

"You don't want to tell him?" I asked when Byron hung up.

Evan made a face and shrugged. "I don't really know how to say it."

"How to say you're crazy for my cock-o-puffs?" I grinned.

He rolled his eyes and poked me hard in the chest when I

reached for his towel. "Your contribution was an 'um,' wordsmith. Let's go get lunch. I'm starving."

WE ATE AT DORA'S KOUNTRY KITCHEN, AND I FORGAVE HER FOR the *K* because Dora was a sweet old gal who loved to tease me, and who also always gave me an extra-large serving of hash brown casserole. Evan and I had discovered the place the first time we stayed at the cabin, and though Evan turned his nose up at the grease-slathered *everything*, I ate there at least twice a week when we were in town.

Afterward, we strolled slowly back toward the public parking lot down the street, Evan grumbling about how full he was.

"You're never satisfied. You were hungry, I bring you a feast, and then you complain about being full."

"Bring me." He chuckled. "Like you cooked and served it to me yourself. Right."

"I could do it. You truly have *no* idea what lengths I'll go to to get your pants around your ankles."

He hummed a light noise, mouth quirking up in a close-lipped smile as he nudged his shoulder against mine. I knocked his back with a little more force, and his smile broke into a grin.

"Kinda wish we could stay a little longer," I said. For a Saturday midafternoon, downtown was pretty quiet. Dora had said Dollywood was having some big-deal family day, and there was also some kind of camping or whitewater convention going on. It was nice, though, just walking beside Evan with no place to be. Not that Nashville was bad. It was a hipster city in many respects, and unless you were down on the strip where most of the tourists hung out, people left you alone, I thought because they figured they were cooler than you anyway. Everyone was a musician about to break. Everyone was on their way somewhere. But the thing was, there were parts of it that felt incestuous. Everyone knew everyone else, and also their business. The gossip trade was an industry of its own, and cutthroat. I guessed it was like that in other big cities, but I had no idea. I just knew it felt stifling sometimes when I'd hang out with someone and they'd mention so-and-so saw me at Fido earlier in the day drinking coffee with Jesse Rutgers and was I *really* talking to that hack musician? Were we going to work together? Etc., etc. So yeah, being apart from that was nice, and I'd just started nurturing a crazy spark of an idea about me and Evan investing in some sort of compound outside of the city when my faraway gaze came back into sharp focus on the figure waving excitedly at us as she came down the sidewalk.

"Oh for fuck's sake," Evan said, which was exactly what I was thinking. *Ella.*

I lifted my hand and gave her a tight smile, hoping she'd just pass on by. Definitely too much to hope for.

Her cheeks were flushed as she stopped in front of us, forcing us to stop, too. She brushed a honey-gold strand of hair from her forehead. "God, I forget how cute you guys are in the flesh."

"You're a sweetheart," I said, pulling her in for a quick hug. Evan just stared at her with his hands shoved in his pockets.

Time to make this short and sweet and get the fuck out. "We're actually on our way—"

"Oh yeah, sure, no worries." She detached from me and peered at the both of us. "Wow," she breathed, looking at Evan, "you're really throwing some hardcore death stare my way." She turned to me next. "And you didn't answer my last text. Did I piss you off somehow?"

Evan chortled and shook his head. I shot him a glare.

"Nah, it's all good. Just been caught up in a bit of a media circus."

"Yeah…" She winced. "I didn't realize it'd get so out of hand."

"Yeah, so thanks for that," Evan said, still glowering.

Her jaw slackened with the confusion behind her eyes, and she glanced at me again, as if I were the key to interpreting Evan's animosity.

"It's not her fault, dude—" I started, which was true, but I didn't get to finish because Ella interrupted with the words that blew my world up.

"I thought you said it was okay?" Her gaze slid uncertainly toward me.

"Um." That was all I managed. Words were not my friend that day, and the rest of my brainpower was devoted to trying to manifest the powers of telekinesis and open up a hole in the sidewalk to swallow her up. Hell, maybe the both of us. I cringed preemptively.

"What did you say was okay?" Evan's gaze darted over to me and pinned me like a rivet through leather as Ella looked between us, her eyes widening as he spoke.

"He said that I could—"

Fucking hell. "I told her it was okay if she did a tell-all with that tabloid. But I didn't say *anything* about us being together."

"I didn't say that!" Ella protested. "I mean, not in so many words—they just assumed it and asked me a lot of questions about how you guys acted around each other. Then they took it totally out of context. I had no idea you guys really were together." She paused, looking between us. "Or... you're not? I'm kind of confused, honestly."

Evan's lips pressed together so hard, I thought if he opened his mouth, his teeth might have turned into diamonds. And then, without another word, he wrenched his hands from his pockets and stalked down the street toward the car.

"Oh God, I'm sorry," Ella said, clapping a hand over her mouth.

I shook my head quickly, then called out over my shoulder as I started after Evan. "It's not your fault. Gave me the most intense few weeks of my life." Maybe the best, too, but now I'd be paying for it.

EVAN SHOOK MY HAND OFF HIS SHOULDER AS SOON AS IT LANDED and kept marching toward the car.

I trotted after him. "Porter, Jesus, come on. It's not that big of a deal. She was short rent money because someone stole her purse, and I *didn't* tell her we were together. I just told her it was cool if she sold the story about hooking up with her." She'd called me repeatedly that day and finally left me a tearful message in the evening. And yeah, I'd been a little drunk and maybe not thinking clearly about Evan and his privacy issues, but it seemed mostly harmless and I figured we'd get a little sales spike out of it that would make Evan happy. Two birds, one stone, everyone was satisfied.

He pulled the keys to the car out but paused with them in his hands, then whipped around to face me. "You keep saying that, but it is. It's a big fucking deal to *me*." His eyes narrowed into shards of ice so cold that even the sweltering July heat couldn't touch it. "Did you know Levi wanted to set up this whole fake relationship thing? Were you part of the fucking plan all along?"

The force of his accusation hit me like a punch to the gut. I took a step backward, my mouth falling open. "Are you fucking kidding me? No. What the fuck?"

"How am I supposed to believe that?"

"Because I'm fucking telling you."

"You didn't tell me you gave Ella the green light to sell my fucking sex life. You didn't tell me about Dan wanting to do a show at Grim's. How else do I know what you've not told me, or what you've lied about. Oh my God." He paled and went quiet. The detachment in his eyes when he looked back up at me did brutal things to my soul. "This, us? Is this even real for you? Holy shit am I an idiot."

I couldn't believe for a second he'd give any credibility to the idea that I'd been in on a fake relationship setup with Levi. Much less that I was lying to him about feelings I'd been hiding just trying to keep our band intact. It gutted me and I snapped. "Fuck you, Porter. *Fuck you.* I'm guilty of telling Ella to do the article, but I did that for *you*. I thought it'd help our ratings—those precious numbers you're always obsessing over. So that's my bad, yeah. But I did it, Evan, fuck... I did it because I'm *in love* with you. What you're suggesting about Levi, that doesn't even make sense, and if you think it does, you don't fucking know me at all."

"You're right about that last part. I guess I don't." His hands knotted in his hair, and his eyes squeezed shut; then he released a long breath and opened the car door.

"I'm done," he said, and I didn't have to ask what he meant.

I launched at him as he slid into the car. I needed him to calm down, needed him to listen to me. He snarled as he forced me back, his eyes dark with fury. "Leave me the fuck alone, Les, or I will hurt you." He meant it, too; his elbow cocked back and his hand tightened into a fist, and I could see the momentum gathering, anything I might say enough to snap the thin restraint.

But a fist to the face would've felt better than watching him slam the car door shut.

He left me in the parking lot. The sun blazed down, and I might as well have been standing in Antarctica. A few people had gathered on the sidewalk. I ignored them as I pulled out my phone and started walking toward Grim's.

Owen gave me a ride back to the cabin. Evan was gone, of course. With all his stuff, with the car.

Tattletale posted pictures of us arguing in the parking lot that night, which I was sure Adam Slade loved. I didn't know who took them. It didn't matter. None of it did.

I called Blink and told him to book a red-eye to Vegas the following evening.

CHAPTER 35

S lippery Nipples, Mind Erasers, Jager Bombs. Thin rails of coke like white jail bars on the mirror. Powders and pretty pastel pills. Hash in an orange pipe. I didn't care what it was. I just swallowed, sucked, and snorted it all. Streaks of light, a city from a window with rain sliding like sludge down the pane. I went to sleep dancing on the axis of the world, and woke with it drilling into my temples.

Where the fuck was I?

My head boomed in time to the pulse of rising panic, like a giant gong ringing against my temples. I scrabbled through sheets and pillows, knocking over ashtrays and empty bottles in search of my phone and found it on the floor. A desperate glance out the window showed me a neon dawn. Vegas. *Of course.*

I had about a million and one text messages, most of them from Blink and Mars. None from Evan, but my call log was filled with outgoing calls to him. *Fuck me.*

Rushing around the trashed hotel suite, I scouted every surface for something to take the edge off, my hands shaking. Something to calm my stomach, my head. My heart. And when I came up empty, I dropped onto the couch and folded my arms over my knees. I lit a lone cigarette I found on the coffee table and massaged my forehead with the heel of my hand.

Nausea surged through me after two inhales, and I barely managed to stub the cigarette out and make it to the trash can before I was hurling up shit I didn't even remember eating.

When I'd finished, I was trembling and cold and fuck, I was alone. Really alone.

I punched Blink's contact on my phone, and he answered on the first ring.

"Dude, where have you—?"

I cut him off with an unintelligible croak, then tried again. "I need you to come pick me up."

Something in my tone made his reply come out softer. "Where are you, though? I've been looking for you for a day and a half."

"Isn't that the question?" I mumbled, and scrabbled around some more, pawing over surfaces until I found a notepad with the Tropicana logo on top. I gave him the name, and he promised to be at my door in a half hour. I'd had to go physically look at the door to tell him the room number.

Before I hung up, he said, "Bro, you might want to stay off the internet."

Shit.

Of course that was the first place I went after I hung up. I didn't have a computer, any of my clothes, a suitcase. Apparently I'd left everything at the hotel Blink and I originally checked into. But my phone was enough. The screen had a nice new crack in it that cut up through the center of the face that popped up. My face. My Facebook page. My level of intoxication was so evident I could practically smell the booze rising from the screen. I should've put the phone down and not looked, like Blink had advised me, but I couldn't. A train wreck–style allure took hold of me as I scrolled through the pictures to see just how badly I'd embarrassed myself. It was quickly evident that I hadn't just gone off the rails, I'd chewed through the bastards and dragged the twisted metal carcasses of them after me.

Bellagio, 8:00 p.m., Saturday. Blink in the background, a bunch of glowing drinks with smoke pouring off them in the foreground. Faces I didn't remember. Shit, I hadn't just lost a night; I'd lost an entire day and two nights. That was a new low.

My descent was hard, fast, and reckless. And catalogued almost hour by hour via my own uploads to Facebook. Fucking hell, I was my own worst enemy. A publicist's nightmare come to life. Every hour of my misery was accounted for in confessional style. The second to last picture I'd posted was a blurry shot of a bathroom floor covered in scattered paper, dark with crosshatches of ink. My notebook. I panicked all over again.

I tore through the suite to the bathroom. No notebook, but there was a residue of a bubble bath ringed around the tub and an empty bottle of champagne next to it.

A knock at the door pulled my attention away from the meltdown in progress, and I flung the door open to find Blink looking tired and surly. Also, worried. There was a bruise on the right side of his jaw, but somehow it was the concern in his eyes that made my breath hitch and my stomach drop to the floor below me.

"My notebook," I said, and when my voice cracked, I realized it wasn't necessarily about the lyrics on the page, it was about Evan. It was about that notebook being the only catalogue of us I had left.

Blink put one hand to my shoulder and pushed me backward, closing the door behind him. "I've got it, man. It was in the other room. Picked up all the pieces, and I think most of it can be taped back together."

I dropped onto the couch, elbows to my knees, bunching my fists in my hair.

"I fucked up." In so many ways.

"Yeahhhhh." Blink drawled the word out. "But that's kind of what people expect." I loved him a little more for his honesty even though it fucking hurt, and he'd clearly thought my primary concern was the publicity, when really it was hurting Evan more. "It'll blow over fast."

"The tabs pick it up?"

"A few. Some of the Facebook photos. It's not terrible, though.

Not the worst they could do, and give it twenty-four hours and something else will come down the pipeline and it'll be forgotten."

But not by Evan, who'd just received yet more evidence of exactly how much of a fuckup I was. As if he needed it. Blink was saying all of that just to make me feel better. I could tell by the expression on his face, but I appreciated the effort anyway.

I scrubbed at my face and drew in a deep breath. "I want to go home."

Blink nodded slowly to that. "That's a good idea, yeah."

"How did I get here?" I asked. When I searched my memory, I came up with zilch. I stood up and walked around the suite, gathering various belongings of mine as Blink trailed after me, righting a few turned-over lamps and picking up empty bottles that he pitched in the trash.

"Dunno. I mean, I guess you walked or took a cab. I lost you when the Bellagio ejected you."

"Shit."

"Yeah, you were a hot fucking mess and making a scene, and I was trying to talk the manager down. Thought maybe if I could get him to listen, I could calm you down. Thought about giving you some shit to knock you out, but by that point I didn't know what the fuck all you had in your system, so I was scared to do that. Turned out it didn't matter. You punched the fucking security guard and took off."

I cringed listening to the account, and then my gaze landed on the bruise at his jaw. "That how you got that piece?"

Blink grimaced and looked away, bending over to pick up a throw pillow that was lying in the middle of the floor.

"Nah, man, that was you. Way earlier."

"I punched you?"

"Yeah. Shit." He straightened up, holding the pillow in front of him like a shield before he glanced down and realized what he was doing and tossed it aside. He stared at me, jaw working as his tongue pushed against the inside of his cheek where the bruise was. "I tried to kiss you, dude."

"What?" I nearly lost my grip on the shoe in my hand.

"Wow. Yeah, you really don't remember shit. Maybe we should just leave it at that."

"Maybe your ass better fill in the details before I give you a matched set." It was an empty threat. I could hardly get my jeans up over my thighs without stumbling. My equilibrium was off, and I probably wouldn't be right for another couple of days the way this hangover was going. "Why the fuck did you try to kiss me?"

He gave me some kind of look, like making him talk was physically causing him pain.

"Dude, I've had a hard-on for you forever. 'Blink, get me this.' 'Blink, I need that.' 'Blink, my head is on fire and I'm gonna die.' Why the fuck you think I was so quick on the draw?"

"Umm, 'cause we're paying your bills?"

Blink snorted. "Not anymore."

"What's that me—wait. One thing at a time. Back up."

He gave me a *do-I-have-to* look, but I set my jaw, and even though I was trying to reel back through every interaction with Blink ever—of which there were a lot, because I was almost as close to him as I was Evan—there was nothing, fucking *nothing* I could think of that would have ever tipped me off that he was harboring some unrequited crush on me. "I thought you were straight."

He lifted his palms and waggled his fingers, giving me a miserable half smile. "Surprise."

"Jesus."

He shrugged. "I keep it to myself."

That wasn't for me to argue with him about. He flopped down on the bed, covering his face with his hands, and spoke between them. "So yeah. I was hammered, too. Not like you, but yeah. I decided it was an opportune time to make my confession. It wasn't. It definitely wasn't."

"Did I kiss you back?"

"No. You punched me. That's what I'm saying. Started spouting all this bullshit about how you're going to be celibate now."

"Incredibly poor timing on your part."

"The worst," he agreed.

I finished buttoning my pants and sat down on the bed next to him. Blink didn't move, just kept talking through his hands, telling me about the clubs we'd gone to before and after, how I'd apologized later on and we'd ended up having some kind of heart-to-heart about how stupid I was over Evan and whether it could ever work out or not. Because apparently I'd been in the euphoric delusional stage where I thought everything would work out if I could just get Evan on the phone to listen to me.

"I tried to take away your phone, but you would've really lost your shit."

By then, I lay sprawled on the bed next to him. Every detail he recounted just dragged me lower. I didn't even want to get up off the bed. I wished I could just pull the covers over my head and suffocate myself.

"I'm sorry. That probably sucked for you on so many levels."

"Yeahhhh." He inhaled deeply and let the breath out slowly. "But whatever. It's done now. Evan called me when I was on my way over, asked me if I'd found you, and when I said yes, he said 'good' and that I was fired."

"What? He can't fucking do that."

"Honestly, dude, maybe it's for the best. This whole situation has turned black, and I can't keep up with the partying anymore the way I used to. I'm just... I'm tired, man. Tired of it all." He turned his head to face me and gave me a weak smile.

We lay there in mutually miserable silence for a while, then I pushed myself upright. "Let's go home."

I pulled him up after me, ignoring the way my limbs shook and shivered, and we collected the rest of my clothes. I didn't know what I'd been doing in that hotel room, but the proliferation of empty booze bottles, plastic baggies, and broken furniture suggested I'd thrown myself a righteous pity party. I was amazed I hadn't woken up with a stranger—or strangers—since that was usually how I soothed a wounded ego, but when I asked Blink, he shook his head quickly and said I'd pushed everyone away unless they wanted to drop something down my throat or give me something to put up my nose. And then I was amazed I'd even woken up at all.

Once we checked out of the Tropicana, I waited in the town car with my head slumped against the window while Blink went into the Bellagio and packed up the rest of my shit. I was worthless, practically immobile. Any movement made my stomach somersault dangerously. The driver had rolled down his window, probably to diffuse the scent of booze permeating the air around me. Blink had Mars handling getting us some plane tickets out of there, and honestly, I wasn't even sure I could fly, I felt so fucking awful. It was a gorgeous day outside, blue sky, laughter and chatter filtering in through the window. Happy couples and families walking through the portico, down the sidewalks, and I felt like my skin was made of ash and neon, my bones so brittle they would crumble with a breeze.

When Blink got back down to the car, the driver hopped out to load my suitcase into the trunk. Blink slid in next to me, and when the driver glanced over his shoulder to confirm we were heading to the airport, I stopped him with a shake of my head, then turned to Blink.

"Will you get Byron on the phone?"

Blink made the call and handed the phone over to me.

"We need to talk," Byron said.

"Yeah, I know. But not right now. I can't even fucking see straight. I need you to do me a favor."

There was a pause, then a leery "All right."

"Find me a fucking rehab within two hundred miles of Vegas."

He muttered something that might have been "Thank fucking God," then said he'd call me back.

Twenty minutes into our ride to the airport, he did. "The Reserve. Had to pull a lot of shit to get you in there so... you're going to show up, right?"

"Yep, on the way now." I paused to tell the driver where we were going, then came back on the line. "Have you talked to Evan?"

"Yes." Byron's voice was still wary, like he'd been afraid I was going to ask.

"I'm guessing from that short answer, he doesn't want to talk to me."

The line went silent, and I shrunk in on myself further. I expected as much, but it still sucked.

"I think you should both cool off for a while, Les," Byron said after a few moments. "Let everything die down."

I exhaled a long breath, chin tilting in a nod he couldn't see. "Tell him I'm sorry."

"He knows." I didn't know what that meant, but I didn't ask, either. I got off the phone, and Blink handed me a bottle of water. I managed a sip and then crashed hard in the back seat.

Do you get homesick being on the road for so long?

Evan: Yeah, definitely. I'm a homebody at heart.

Les: Not often. Anywhere I lay my head is home. What? Why are you laughing at that? We moved a lot when I was a kid, you know that! I'm a wanderer.

Evan: No no. I'm just thinking about the last place you "laid your head."

Les: Where?

Evan: I don't think they can print it.

Les: Ohhhhh, yeah. Shit, okay. Let me just say no, then, and leave it at that.

CHAPTER 36

Evan

Thirty-three missed calls from Les. Correction: ignored calls.

Twenty-two of them were apologies of various intelligibility. Eight told me how much he missed me. Two were obvious butt dials, nothing but the pandemonium of slot machines and overly loud voices in the background.

1. *Answer the fucking phone, Porter.* Pause. *Goddammit. This is fucking stupid. Fuck you.*

2. *I shouldn't have said fuck you. I'm sorry, but come on, Porter.* Pause. *Evan, just answer the phone and let's talk about this. I fucked up, yes, but I wasn't in on anything. I wasn't in on some conspiracy to... whatever it is you're thinking, you paranoid bastard. ...I take back the bastard part. You're not really a bastard. Uptight. Not that that's entirely bad. It's not an insult. Jesus, what the fuck am I saying? You're uptight, but I'm cool with it. It's hot. Most of the time. Not so much right now.* Long silence. *Ugh!*

11. *Do you know why I never let you see my notebooks? Because if you knew how much shit I write in there is about you, you'd think it was pathetic. Or creepy. I guess it's a little of both. Shit, Ev... you turn me inside out. I miss you, man. Like you*

wouldn't believe. Romantic bullshit, like how you smell and taste, and dumb stuff, too, that I'm not even going to tell you about. Well, I would if you would call me back. Call me back and let me tell you. Shit, just let me hear something other than your voicemail. Pause. *What? No. I'll be there in a minute! Evan, come on.*

17. *Blink just kissed me and I fucking punched him in the face. I feel bad, but what the fuck? That was out of the blue. He says he's been twisted up over me for years. I had no clue. Poor fucker. Haaaa. I really could start a Lonely Hearts club now.* Pause. *I think I've crossed the emo threshold. It's dark over here. Smells like coffee and cigarettes and the rubbery soles of checkered Vans. But you should know, I didn't want to kiss him. Or anyone. Fuck him. Fuck them all. I don't want to be with anyone else, Porter. Just you.*

32. *I'm sorry. I'm so fucking sorry, Evan.*

I'D LISTENED TO THEM ALL THE WAY THROUGH THREE TIMES BEFORE forcing myself to stop. By then, the fury I felt at him had waned to a simmer, but just when I'd start to actually feel bad for him, it'd bubble over again. Good. I needed that. He'd given me exactly the kick in the ass—and stomach, and heart—that I needed to remember why getting involved with him beyond the music was a stupid idea in the first place. He was a disaster. And like an idiot, I'd let myself get wrapped up in him.

The problem remained that as mad as I was, there were parts of it I didn't regret. Being with him, wanting him, feeling so turned on I could hardly stand to be around him without touching him, feeling like I was no different than the rest of the horny world—the part where, for three weeks, I remembered what it was like to be head over heels for someone. That had been priceless. If only Les hadn't been the one to get my motor running. I hated him for making me feel that way and then ripping it apart with something so stupid.

Regardless, I was done. So fucking done. I'd called Byron on the way home and told him I quit. He'd flipped out like I thought he would and told me to at least take twenty-four hours to think about it. I'd told him I would, but that the answer would be the same. And it was.

I HAD A WEEK OF QUIETLY TORTURING MYSELF AT HOME IN Nashville before Byron called me in for a meeting, and when I walked into his office on Music Row and found not only him, but Levi and Kenny, our A&R guy from MGD, I knew something was up.

Blink had texted me the day before to tell me Les had checked into rehab, to which my only reply had been "about fucking time." I didn't regret firing Blink. I thought he was an enabler of the worst kind, and if Byron or MGD had something to say about that, fucking fine. But no one even mentioned Blink.

I walked into the conference room, and all three of them stood and came forward to shake my hand. Byron's receptionist asked if I wanted anything to drink, and when I declined, everyone moved to sit again. Byron looked distinctly uneasy, which put me on edge.

"So we find ourselves in an interesting position, Evan," Kenny said, cutting to the chase. "Byron tells us you're not interested in continuing on as Porter & Graves, but you and Les have the next album written already, correct?"

"Yes." I hadn't planned ahead, which was a mistake, so my tactic was to say as little as possible and see what direction this meeting was going in.

"My thinking here is we proceed with the album and they record separately, if Evan is okay with that," Byron said with a glance over at me. He and I had discussed this on the phone before, but I hadn't been able to come to a final decision. And we hadn't talked to Les about it yet. I thought we'd have more time. Les and I had always been in the studio together, and it almost shocked me how wrong it felt to hear Byron suggest otherwise. But I got it. It was a practical solution and would fulfill the contract in technical terms. It didn't take into account touring after that, though, and I didn't think releasing an album without a tour to promote it would fly with the label. I couldn't imagine six months on a bus with Les right now.

"That's certainly an option," Kenny said. "I have another one for you to consider, as well." He leaned forward, lacing his fingers on the conference table.

From the way Byron's eyebrows shot up toward his hairline, this was news to him. My interest was more cautious.

Kenny continued. "In lieu of a fourth album from Porter & Graves, you fulfill your portion of the contract by delivering us a fresh album. In addition, we'd be highly interested in two additional albums after that. So essentially a three-album contract, for which we're willing to offer—" Kenny held up his finger, withdrawing a folded paper from the breast pocket of his coat and sliding it across the table. It landed between me and Byron. I skimmed through far enough to find the numbers as Byron looked on. Then he pressed his lips together and looked over at me.

Six figures, within kissing distance of seven. It was more than I knew what to do with. I didn't even know how to digest the amount.

I glanced up and met Kenny's eyes as he smiled. "There's a signing bonus included, which isn't mentioned in that contract."

"How much?" Byron asked, kicking back into business mode.

"A hundred K."

Our career as Porter & Graves was good. I'd made enough to buy my own house, have a personal assistant, and pay off my mom's mortgage, but this contract was... this was a nest egg for life, insurance that if I was smart with the money, there was never a chance I'd have to go back to scraping by. Ever. God, it was tempting. But there had to be a catch.

Kenny must have sensed my wariness. "You're the powerhouse, Evan, the voice and the sound. And reliable. We'd really like to keep you. I've got artists and writers already falling all over themselves to work with you. One in particular I'd like to point you toward. I think you would both get along really well. She's a writer and singer, too." Just like Les, but he didn't say that, seeming to want to avoid mention of Les altogether.

"Amanda Faulks," Byron said immediately.

Kenny grinned. "Yes."

"We'll need time to talk about this." Byron looked over at me to see if I had any input, but I wasn't opening my mouth about that until I'd talked to him more in private.

"Of course. Take some time. And while you do, I'd love to set up a meeting between you and Amanda," Kenny said, glancing at me.

"What about Les? He just gets discarded? His name is on the original contract, too." I had a weird feeling in my stomach, some combination of butterflies and discomfort.

Kenny's smile was less patient this time. "We'll work that out with him ourselves and compensate him fairly."

Why did I get the impression that it would be both less than fair and probably involve some strong-arming? Still, was that really my problem now, anyway?

"They're wanting to make you and Amanda The Civil Wars, version 2.0," Byron said, once everyone left.

"Obviously." I chewed on my lower lip and shook my head. "I don't even know her. They sort of made it sound like I could operate solo, too, though."

"Yeah. But do you want to?"

"That's how I started." I wasn't sure, though. The game had changed drastically since I'd woken up this morning, and it was hard for me to get a read on what my standing was.

"Amanda's really good. The two of you would probably work really well together, like Kenny said. She's driven."

I knew of Amanda, and Byron was right. She was good. Better than good. She was up-and-coming and had stubbornly refused to ink any deals with major labels, so if MGD was dangling her in front of me, they must have done some ninja-level wooing.

I planted my elbows on the table and tugged at the roots of my hair, trying to make sense of the tangle of thoughts and emotions inside me. "I keep thinking about Les."

Byron winced in sympathy. "Yeah. It puts me in a weird position, because I represent you both, and for you, this deal is good, and if you're telling me you're not going to work with him again, I have to advise you to take it. I'll do what I can for him."

I looked at him sidelong. "They underestimate him. They always have."

"Agreed." He nodded. "But they're the ones with the bank account, so that's on them. I'll do my best to get him set up elsewhere if he wants, or if he wants out of the limelight, there's serious loot he could make just writing."

I knew Les, though, and he loved performing as much as he loved writing.

I launched from the chair and started pacing, staring out the window at the tiny parking lot and the row of buildings that made up the heart of Music Row, remembering when we'd first walked into Byron's office, the thrill of knowing we were on the cusp of something good. Les had made me take a picture of him at the entrance, smiling so big and bright that even the stupid face he tried to make as I snapped the photo couldn't overshadow his evident joy. "Fuck. These are great options. I've basically been given carte blanche to do whatever the fuck I want, so why don't any of them feel right?"

I got the impression that Byron was choosing his words carefully when he replied. "The two of you have been working together on a deep level for years. Any change is going to be uncomfortable and feel drastic after that kind of partnership. It's something of a rarity, whether you fully understand that or not, to have the kind of partnership you and Les have. So think about it. Whatever route you go, I'll support you fully. And I do think you should meet with Amanda and see what kind of vibe is there so you'll know."

I put my head in my hands and stared down at the contract on the table. I'd told Byron the gist of what had gone down at the cabin. Not the nitty-gritty, but he got it. I thought that was why I felt his hand on my shoulder a handful of seconds later as he said, "I think you need to take more time. Only you understand the true scale of a decision like that."

I MET WITH AMANDA THE FOLLOWING WEEK IN A FUNKY RECORDING studio tucked away in Berry Hill behind a vintage shop. She was talented, smart, organized to a degree I could appreciate, and ambitious as hell, just as Byron had said. And she had that same enigmatic quality Les had that demanded your attention.

Right away, she filled me in on how she'd been building her following through targeted efforts that only appeared organic from the outside. Behind the scenes, she and her manager were busting ass. She'd followed our rise, taking cues from what worked and noting what didn't, slowly positioning herself in the industry. Unlike us, when the big labels came calling, she refused them outright, and they'd been chasing her ever since. It was a good tactic, and she had a huge following on every social media platform she'd dipped her fingers into so far.

She was everything I'd heard she was and more. Her songs were incredible, and her voice was amazing. We tooled around for a couple of hours, kicking some song ideas back and forth, before I finally got around to asking, "If you're so hell-bent on being stubborn, why'd you agree to meet with me?"

She leaned back in her chair and smiled, combing a strand of hair behind her ear. She was pretty in a haunting way, not classically, but a beauty with an echo that'd stick with you long after you walked away.

"Your show at Grim's Gatlinburg. Someone posted a video of it, and that song—" Before she even said it, I knew the one she meant.

"That was actually Les's idea. I'd never heard it before. Ever."

"I could tell." She paused. "There was this tiny moment when a flicker of panic passed over your face. I bet no one noticed it but me, but then you just locked into the song and it was phenomenal, and I thought, I want to write with somebody like that. I want to make music with somebody like that—somebody who gets me and what I'm about so instinctively that it doesn't matter what the song is or what goes wrong, you can be relied on to pull it off every time.

And it would take time, I know, to get to that level, but I think we could. It gets lonely sometimes, you know?"

I knew. Busking on Second Avenue, scorching under the sun, then playing the bar circuit that night before crashing in bed and doing it all over again, week after week, had been lonesome business. I understood completely, but I couldn't help thinking of Les. What we had, what we'd built, and fuck if my heart didn't start aching all over again.

I might be the voice and the sound, but Les was the soul of our music, and I didn't know if I could just cut him out and replace him with Amanda. It felt like cheating, somehow, and I left the meeting with no more clue of what I was going to do than I'd walked in with.

CHAPTER 37

I stood in line for breakfast behind Mason, a twenty-three-year-old trust fund baby with an oxy habit who was on a shower strike for some reason. He smelled like a dumpster left out in the middle of a desert for a month, and as he pushed his tray down the line, stabbing his finger in the direction of whatever he wanted, he canted a look over his shoulder and sneered at me.

"You're ripe, dude," I sneered back, and accepted a bowl of eggs from one of the line servers.

"Write a song about it, pretty boy."

I chuckled bitterly at his glare. Mostly, we all got along. Everyone was too busy with the demons breathing down their own necks to bother being a dick. That didn't mean there wasn't drama every day—someone breaking down, threatening to leave, or actually leaving. I kept my breakdowns locked up tight, but Mason had singled me out in our first group session my first day. We'd gone around the circle introducing ourselves by our first names, followed by the line, "And I'm an addict."

"You're that swishy singer," Mason had snapped out, giving me one of those false smiles that I thought was meant to make me feel like I was an infectious disease. It was clear he was using *swishy* as

a slur, but was too much of a wimp to use something outright hateful.

"Mason," Warren, our group counselor, had warned him with a sigh. *"Check the judgment calls."*

"Bi." I'd been hard into my hangover then, and my nerves were shot, nausea roiling like a whirlpool in my stomach. I was sweating buckets, but fuck if I was going to let some asshole sitting next to me in a rehab tear me down. *"And for fuck's sake, do you know how many douches like you have said the same shit to me and then begged me for my attention when we were out of earshot of everyone else? Get a new fucking game."*

I'd gotten the warning that time.

There were some decent folks here, though, like Mike and James, who I joined at a table after getting my breakfast. James was a producer. Mike did something in technology in Silicon Valley that didn't make sense to me, and when I'd given him a confused look as he'd tried to explain, he said, "Just think robots."

The days moved in predictable patterns, and we shuffled from group meetings to classes to individual therapists with three meals in between. I missed Evan constantly.

The first five days there, I focused solely on not cutting out through one of the side doors and calling an Uber to come get me and take me to the nearest airport. Or back to Vegas. I could live without drugs, but the prospect of never drinking again was unimaginable. Who wanted to live a life like that? I felt as if I'd joined a monastery.

I kept mostly to myself. I recognized a few other people in there. Showbiz types, musicians who'd suspiciously vanished off the scene, but I didn't want anything to do with them. I just didn't care. About anything.

By the seventh day I was resigned to being there and seeing it through. I wasn't excited about it, but shit, I didn't have anything else going on. I didn't have a band. I didn't have Evan. I was a binger, a glutton, an impulse with a pulse, a button too easy to push. None of that was news to me. But I'd always accepted it as my nature, and I didn't think twenty days in rehab could change my course. Not when the times I'd been intervened on before had done little more than make me switch my intoxicant of choice from pills to something more socially acceptable that I could buy off a grocery store shelf.

WHEN I GOT UP TO MY ROOM THAT NIGHT, I WAS RELIEVED TO HEAR the shower running because, lucky me, Mason was also my roommate. I'd gotten really good at ignoring his voice, but his scent was harder to deal with.

"About goddamn time," I shouted, no clue whether he'd hear me or not. I stripped down to my boxers and collapsed into bed. The days were long here, beginning at 5:00 a.m., and so monotonous that I longed for the ten-o'clock hour when we were allowed to return to our rooms and either sleep or read from the facility's library of paperbacks. I flipped through a Dan Brown book I'd gotten sucked into.

Forty-five minutes later, the shower was still going, so I got up and knocked on the door.

"The fuck you doing in there?" I sounded more hesitant than harsh, because my stomach was buzzing with uneasiness.

No answer. I knocked again—pounded, really—having visions of finding Mason's lifeless body inside. People shared stories about suicide attempts and a few completions, even if the facility searched our suitcases and made us use plastic forks and spoons.

The lock clicked from the inside, so I turned the knob and pushed, exhaling in relief to find Mason sitting against the wall in a thick cloud of steam that whooshed out around me. He still smelled like ass.

He looked up at me, his eyes bloodshot and his skin blotchy.

"Want me to get someone?" I asked.

He shook his head roughly. "Fuck that."

"What are you doing?" As the steam cleared, I noticed both his and my toiletry kits were upended, toothbrush, toothpaste, combs, and other stuff all over the floor. No razors. We got to shave once a week under supervision. His tube of toothpaste sat next to him. He

293

nudged it. "Trying to will a tube of toothpaste into being a razor." He gave me a thin, bitter smile and showed me his wrists. They were abraded and red, lined with shallow gouges where the edge of the tube had dug in just enough to well thin ribbons of blood.

I sat down across from him, putting my back to the sink counter. "They're going to kick you out for that when they see it."

He shrugged. "This is my eighth rehab. Someplace else will take me. Or my parents' money, at least."

I didn't like Mason, but shit, he looked and sounded wrecked, and it pulled sympathy strings I wasn't aware I still had. "Couldn't you just try to get clean?"

"I have. Fuck. The first three times, I tried." He glared at me. "I tried fucking hard, and it didn't work. They say I don't want it enough. Maybe they're right."

I bit my lip. "I don't know, does anyone come in here wanting to get straight?"

"Sure. Mike does. He wants it so bad it's like a halo around him; he's always talking about plans for the future, wanting to come back and speak as someone in recovery in five years, ten."

"Warren would probably say that's dangerous projection." We all knew the recidivism rates. They pounded it into our heads daily, right next to the idea that thinking we had addiction licked would be our downfall.

"Fuck Warren, too."

My chuckle earned me another hot glare. "Sorry, I'm not trying to be insensitive, it's just... I don't know."

"Did you want to come here?"

I had to think about that for a while. Eleven days in and I felt clear-headed the way I'd felt at the cabin, which made it all the easier for me to think maybe I hadn't been doing so badly after all. That was how addiction worked, though. I'd been paying more attention this time.

"Yes and no. As soon as I got in here, I started to think I hadn't been so bad off. Also, who the hell wants to entertain the idea that they can never put another drink or drug in their body again? At the same time, I was afraid if I didn't do something now, I'd do something worse later and then be worse off than when I came in. So it's not like I came in here with pure intentions, like 'yeah, I want to get clean and sober forever and ever.' I just felt backed into a corner, and I'd already gone right and left so many times that I guess I figured maybe it was time to try going up. People always forget that up is an option. Not just sideways or down."

Mason snorted. "I'll be back in again. Somewhere, somehow."

"Maybe I will, too." I shrugged. I didn't know what the right answer was; I was just relieved as fuck he wasn't a dead body on the floor. "But I hope not. I don't really have anything else to lose at this point." That wasn't true. I could lose my house or my belongings, but I'd already lost the thing that mattered most.

"Your music's not bad, you know," he said. "My ex loves you guys."

"I can't tell if that's supposed to be an apology for being a dick, but if so, accepted."

"It isn't, but take it however. I'm an unapologetic dick."

Oh, how familiar that sounded. So much so that I smiled. "You still smell like shit, and you need to take that fucking shower."

He threw his head back and laughed, and then when he sobered, asked me if I'd stay.

"Sure, as long as it's not some sexual ploy, which would be way too predictable since you've got sexual hang-ups coming off of you about as strongly as BO."

He rolled his eyes at me, but I remained where I was while he stood, pulling his shirt off. His abdomen was littered with scars, hundreds of them that I caught just before I turned my head away as he shucked his pants and stepped into the shower.

THE NEXT MORNING HE LEFT, NO WARNING. I CAME BACK TO MY room during a break between sessions and all of his stuff was gone. I couldn't stop thinking about him that night, wondering where he'd gone, who had picked him up, when he'd be back. Or if he would. And it made me think about what I'd been doing while I was here, how I was coasting along and just getting by, counting down the days until I could leave. I was scared of who I'd be when I left rehab and scared of what I'd become if I remained the same. I didn't know if there was a middle ground between that, but I didn't want to be Mike, setting myself up for a hard fall, just as much as I didn't want to be Mason, cycling through free falls. And if I didn't want to be either of those things, it seemed like maybe it was time for me to start listening to everything the counselors were saying and actually try putting it into practice.

That afternoon was when I had my first taste of real peace. They called it riding the pink cloud, but they could've called it anything for all I cared.

As I sat in group a few days later, Hannah, one of the counselors, rapped lightly on the door and stepped inside. "I need to see Mr. Graves, please."

Warren nodded, and I stood, walking out of the room feeling like I'd been called into the principal's office. I figured it probably had something to do with Mason leaving, and my conscience was clear on that. I'd thought of him often over the days after he'd left, and what I'd said to him, but I couldn't think of anything I could've done differently. His demons weren't mine to fight.

But when we walked into the front office, Hannah pulled me into her cubicle and indicated I should sit down in the chair across from her desk. I licked my lips and tried to clear the dryness from my throat, wondering if I was about to get kicked out for some reason.

"We do make exceptions to our outside contact rule on occasion, and after talking it over with your manager, we decided this would be one of them, if you want to take the call? It's Byron."

I nodded mutely, warily, and she picked up the handset of her phone, pressed a button, and held it out to me. Once I took it, she stood and left.

"Byron?"

His throaty, warm chuckle poured over the line. "How are ya, kid?"

I felt the sting of tears in my eyes and prickling in the back of my throat just hearing his voice. I couldn't answer immediately. *Lonely*, I wanted to tell him, and sad and aching and so fucking sorry for my stupidity.

Taking a shaky breath, I tried to compose myself. "Still here."

"I know, and I'm impressed. Proud of ya, Les." He cleared his throat. "Listen, I'm not gonna beat around the bush. I talked to Hannah and we figured it'd be best to give you this news while you were still in, just in case, uh… well, just because."

"I'm not a suicide risk, for fuck's sake."

"OD, suicide, drunk driving, all of them mean dead. You get my point here?"

"Yeah," I grumbled, feeling even more worthless. "Carry on."

"MGD is offering to buy you out of the rest of the contract."

"Okay," I said cautiously. I couldn't honestly say I was surprised they wanted to drop me.

"And they're offering Evan a separate deal. Possibly pairing up with Amanda Faulks."

My heart thudded once and then split apart and sank in my chest. It felt like it dropped all the way to my toes and puddled out onto the floor. I guess a part of me still hoped Evan and I could work together in the future. A blindly optimistic part of me, but nonetheless. Somehow it was worse that he might want to work with someone else.

"Is he going to take it?" I tried to keep the quaver from my voice.

"I don't know. He's thinking about it. They gave him the option of you two completing the album and recording separately, but I get the idea he wasn't too keen on that. You can contest that, though, contest for the completion of your original contract. But if he does want to go with Amanda, I want you to be prepared. I've been talking to some other people, and I've got a few other labels interested in you. Soundhouse is really interested in having you on as a writer."

A sigh leaked out of me, all the defeat I felt contained in the breath. "So someone else can sing my stuff."

"That'd be an option. But we might be able to get you back onstage if you wanted that. Blue Moon's lead guitarist just quit. You're strong enough to do it on your own, though, at this stage. If you wanted to, I mean."

I held the phone to my ear and curled over, resting my forehead on the edge of Hannah's desk and closing my eyes. "I can't make that decision right now." I couldn't even imagine striking out on my own. I didn't have the same drive Evan had, or any kind of business savvy. The best thing that had ever happened to my music was that Evan had appeared when I was just starting out and made me realize just how blindly I was fumbling along. Working with him forced me to focus and gave me the kind of structure I'd never been good at finding on my own. Imagining trying to go it alone without him? It felt like drowning.

"I understand."

I groaned and wiped at my eyes. "But Evan should do whatever is best for him, whatever he wants to do. Whatever the two of you decide. I'm not going to fight the contract. Or him. I just want him to... I just want him to do whatever's best for him. Whatever makes him happiest."

"I'll pass it on," Byron said gently. "You should stay, see this through. It's the best thing for you right now. I know it's hard, but try and hang in there."

"I will." That was one thing I was certain of. I didn't have anywhere else to be anyway.

Evan, what drew you to Les's music?

Evan: The first show I ever saw live was Ben Folds. The venue was tiny, and we were all crammed in close to the stage. I could almost hear the sound of his breathing, and he had this quirky presence about him. Great fucking musician, and when he sang, I felt the words. It's hard to explain, but I went to plenty of shows afterwards where it was just a band playing or someone singing and there wasn't anything extraordinary about it.

Anyway, I'd heard about this college dude, Les Graves, who was making the rounds, so I went to catch his show on a random Wednesday and… it was one of the few times since that Ben Folds show that I got the shivers. I could feel the lyrics like they were hanging in the air in front of me. There was this immediacy to his music that hooked me. What?

Les: I don't think you've ever told me I got to you the way Ben Folds did. Damn, you've been holding out on me. I'd like to request my own tour bus now, since I'm clearly a precious commodity.

Evan: [laughing] That's exactly why I've never told you.

CHAPTER 38

Evan

"I've been hearing some rumors," Leigh said when I answered her call.

"Yeah, what else is new? I'm nothing but rumors at this point." I tucked the phone against my shoulder, balancing a stack of mail under my arm and shifting my guitar case around as I fit my key in the lock and opened the back door to my house. Rita tipped me an upnod as I came in, then rushed to take the mail from my hands.

"Meant to get that on the way in and forgot," she muttered. Rita had been my PA for going on two years. It felt weird to call her a housekeeper—which was what I'd originally hired her for—because she did so much else, like handling my mail and bills while I was gone, so I just called her my PA.

I told Leigh to hang on and set my guitar case down. "Anything important I need to know?" I asked Rita, muffling the receiver.

"It's hot as hell outside and you're wearing jeans." She grinned, the thick wrinkles at the corners of her eyes deepening.

"Yep, thanks for that," I deadpanned, and she waved me off with a wink.

"I'm fixing to do the bathrooms and kitchen, then head out for the day."

I nodded and headed into the spare room I used as an office.

"Sorry about that," I said to Leigh. "So, rumors. Rumors you want corrected, or…?" I hadn't spoken to Leigh since her phone call to me at the cabin the first time the shit hit the fan.

"I don't know. I guess it's none of my business. But I have something I want to show you. If you'll be around later, I could stop by?"

I dropped into my desk chair and sprawled, lifting my T-shirt up to the top of my chest to cool off. Jeans really had been a bad idea. Just the walk from the driveway to inside had me dripping sweat.

"Sure," I answered. I didn't have anything else going on. I'd been practicing some with Amanda but was pretty certain I couldn't work with her as a long-term replacement for Les. She'd been cool about it, or seemed to be, and said the only way she'd sign with MGD was if it was with me. But I just… I just couldn't fucking do it. I didn't know what I was going to do, but I was leaning heavily toward doing my own thing and letting the label package me as a solo artist. I didn't feel great about that choice, either, but it was all I had at the moment.

Leigh said she'd stop by around five, and when I ended the call, I tossed the phone onto the desk and leaned back in the chair, commencing a stare-down with the contents of a manila folder that had arrived yesterday. It contained a single sheet of lined notebook paper littered with ballpoint scrawl, the frenetic penmanship unmistakable. The top of the paper was dated and time-stamped, 3:00 a.m. The night after the hookup with Ella that felt like eons ago now. The song, "Blue." Through the lens of verse and choruses that didn't make it into the clean copy Les had presented me with, his longing was evident. He'd passed the song off as being about an old girlfriend, and any telling clues had been swept clean in the final copy, but in the original it was clear who he was writing about. Looking at his scrawl made me ache in ways I didn't think I could. At the bottom, he'd attached a yellow sticky note: *It was real for me, and it always has been. Whatever else you doubt about me, please don't ever doubt that.*

It was amazing—scary, even—how a handwritten note like that could take all my anger and crush it in a fist of regret until all I was left with was a sad kind of emptiness.

I GAVE LEIGH A TENTATIVE SMILE AS I OPENED THE DOOR, BUT THE warmth of hers erased my hesitation as she leaned in for an embrace. It was good to see her again, and though I'd initially been upset, all things considered it had been one of the easier breakups in my life. Whether it was because we'd been friends long before dating, I wasn't sure, but I was glad there didn't appear to be any lingering animosity on her part.

"Well, you *look* good," she said as I greeted her and ushered her in.

I snorted and led her into the kitchen, where she eyed the pot on the stove skeptically. "Don't tell me you're cooking just for me."

"Technically I made myself dinner, and I'm inviting you to share it." I wasn't very domestic, but I knew how to cook. My mom had insisted that everyone needed to know how to make at least five things: spaghetti, meatloaf, pot roast, chicken and dumplings, and dressing. Tonight I'd gone for spaghetti.

"How generous." She grinned and slid onto one of the stools at the island, dropping her shoulder bag on the floor and removing a large, thick envelope that I eyed warily. I was starting to distrust envelopes. What came in them besides bills and reminders of my own mistakes?

"Some photos," she explained, when she noticed my cautious survey.

"I guessed that part. Of what?" I turned back to the stove and flipped the burner off, then stirred the sauce and let it sit while I pulled two bowls down from the cabinet.

I heard her fiddling with the envelope while I scooped noodles and sauce into the bowls, and when I turned around again, I froze. Spread over the island were dozens of photos of Les and me. I hadn't seen his face in weeks, had all but forced his name from my mind for just as long, so the sight of him multiplying across the countertop was a visual assault that stabbed into my lungs and left me breathless.

I brought the bowls with me to the island and set them down absently as I grumbled, "Could've used a little warning."

"That bad, huh?"

I didn't confirm her remark, just stirred my finger through some of the photos. Les and me backstage. The two of us onstage. Les making a stupid face. Me making a stupid face. Les scowling at the camera. Me scowling at something out of the frame. Probably Les. Me smiling at something out of the frame. Also probably Les.

I sighed.

"I've probably taken thousands of photos of you guys since I first saw you play at Jensen's. And after I talked to you at the cabin, God, I was still so upset." Out of the corner of my eye, I could see her nibbling at her lower lip, watching me shuffle through the photos. "But you're my friend, you know? Before we were anything else, we were friends, and it hurt that you didn't feel as strongly about me as I felt about you when we got together."

I started to interrupt to explain, to apologize again, but she shook her head, cutting me off. "That night I went back through all of my photos of you two. All of them. From that first show you guys did together at Jensen's to the one in Detroit two weeks before you guys went to Gatlinburg. And then it all made sense."

"What did?" I sounded blithely ignorant but couldn't ignore the prickle of knowing over my skin.

"See if you see it like I do." She dug through the photos, carefully sorting through and selecting them, then presented me with a stack. She put one elbow to the counter and her cheek in her hand, then nodded at me to go through them.

"Jensen's," she said of the first. Les and I stood on the tiny stage looking out at the audience with wild grins on our faces. Our posture mirrored each other. I flipped through a few more of the early shows and saw the shift in the photos she'd taken after we'd dropped the first album. More interaction between us, more shots where we were grinning at each other or watching each other. There was a friendliness and a sense of connection that came through. I drew in a deep breath when I got to a photo from the last show in Detroit that she'd been at. The intensity of Les's stare trained on me, that gaze I knew—the hungry, aching one.

Leigh pressed her lips together, arching her brows, like she'd caught me out on something and was waiting for me to fess up. When I didn't, she pressed, "It's so fucking evident Les is stupid over you that I can't believe I never gave it proper credit before." She shrugged lightly, somewhat ruefully as I dragged my eyes away from the picture and met hers. She stared at me evenly, then pushed her bowl aside and plucked another photo out of the pile, dropping it on the counter in front of me. It landed like an anvil around my heart. The picture was post-show, backstage. I couldn't tell where— the rooms mostly looked the same—but I knew it was on our last tour, probably close to the middle of it. In it, Leigh had captured me sprawled on a couch, hands behind my head, a lazy, goofy, satisfied smile on my face, my gaze on Les and clearly transfixed by him as he tried to step in front of the lens, his wide grin a blur of white.

"Whatever you two are or aren't, there's something there, and if you try to deny it, I'll call you a liar." She gave me a look. "I've photographed a lot of bands, Ev, and no one else, *no one else* that I've ever worked with comes close to the vibe between you two. I mean, it's glaringly obvious now. Maybe I just didn't want to see it because I wanted you, too, you know?"

I sank down onto the stool next to her, resting my elbows on the counter, my forehead to my fists. "Fuck, I don't know what to do. It's driving me crazy." I still felt the sting of betrayal, but I couldn't deny the component of me that missed Les intensely, just as I couldn't deny the part of me that worried about what he'd do next. It was a catch-22. "Just because there's a connection, though, doesn't mean it's healthy or... or viable in the long run."

"Yeah, I know, but if it's true you're going out solo... I don't know." She bit her lip, glancing down at the photos again, then back up at me, her voice softer this time. "I know you. You're miserable."

She did know me. And I knew her. She was stable and safe, creative and intelligent, more than a little attractive. So why couldn't I have felt for her what I felt for Les?

Sighing, she swept the photos aside and propped her chin on her fist. "I just hate the idea that you guys can't work out your differences."

"It's more complex than that." I drew in a breath and tried to explain it to her. I told her everything, beginning with how our tour had started falling apart after the thing with Ella, pausing when she winced for the third time. "Sorry, I can stop. I don't want to make you uncomfortable."

"No, it's not that." She waved her hand through the air vaguely. "I mean, yeah, it kind of is. It's just that... you know, I wish you'd been that into *me*."

"Believe me, me too."

The sad expression on her face made me grimace.

"Is it just because he's a guy that you have these hang-ups?"

"No! It's because it's fucking Les. Les, who can't keep it in his pants. Les, who never met a bottle of booze or a pill he didn't like. Les, who fucking told someone it was okay to sell my sex life. Pick your poison, because he's all of them." I realized I was gesturing violently and folded my arms over my chest tightly.

Leigh shifted on top of the stool, her expression shading thoughtful. "That girl could've sold that story anytime. She never needed permission from either of you. That she even asked is shockingly considerate, really. And kind of sad. She must really like you two."

I knew Leigh was right about Ella, but it didn't help. "That's not the point, though. The point is he didn't tell me either way. In fact, he actively hid it from me because he knew he'd fucked up."

Leigh inhaled, seeming to give up, and shook her head. "I think you should talk to him. He's out of rehab."

I knew that, but I wasn't sure how she did. She seemed to predict the question from the glance I turned in her direction. "I had coffee with him two days ago. He wanted to make amends."

"For what?" I picked up my still-full bowl and took it to the sink, my appetite gone, then lingered there with my back to the island so I didn't have to see those damn pictures up close anymore.

"I don't know, actually. He seemed to think that time he made a pass at me early on really pissed me off. It didn't, but I dunno... he said he had a long list and wanted to do it right."

I shook my head. "I haven't heard from him since his meltdown in Vegas." By design. I knew Byron had told him to leave me alone and let me approach him when and if I wanted to. I was undecided on that, too, though the longer I sat there with Leigh and those pictures, the more my resolve wavered and flickered inside me like a lightbulb on the fritz. I kept wondering how he was doing, *what* he was doing. Was he holed up in his house writing? Doing nothing? What did he plan to do next? Had he talked to MGD?

"He asked about you. How you've been. I told him I had no clue, because I didn't." She sniffed and fiddled with the ends of her hair.

"Sorry about that. I've basically blacked everyone out of my social life since I've been back." Except Rita and Byron. "How'd he look?" I tried to mask my interest with a bored expression, but the twist of her lips as she considered me said she wasn't buying it.

"Good. Healthy. Sad. All of those things, somehow. I could tell he was trying to follow the program, turn himself around. He said he's been doing a meeting a day. Told me about being in rehab. It was nice, really. A little awkward because I kept thinking of the two of you together, but nice."

AFTER LEIGH LEFT, I CLEANED UP THE KITCHEN, STUDIOUSLY avoiding the photos she'd left behind until I couldn't anymore. Then I sat down at the counter and flipped through them all again, one by one. Watching our rise and fall in stills caused a fresh, brutal pang of sadness to radiate through my chest. But when I picked up my phone and pulled up Les's contact information, I couldn't make myself press Send.

CHAPTER 39

Evan

I puttered around the kitchen the following day, making lunch and trying to stay out of Rita's way as she dusted and mopped. I sucked at the rocker lifestyle, all the way down to my hired hands; I kept wanting to take one of the rags on the counter and help Rita out the way I had my mom when I was a kid. When my phone rang, Rita shooed me away as she slid it over the counter toward me. "Make a business deal, sweetheart. I've got the dust bunnies covered." The ache that threatened to spread through me at the pet name turned into a groan as I glanced down at the screen. Blink. There was no love lost between us. At least on my end, but I answered anyway.

"What's up?"

"Hey, Porter, listen." He spoke fast, as if he was afraid I'd hang up. Probably a good instinct on his part, since I was glaring at the pantry as I threw a bag of bread back inside it. "I know you're not my biggest fan, and I wish I could fix that, but whatever, it's not why I'm calling. Les is doing a Facebook Live thing on his page, like now. He didn't tell anyone he was doing it, besides me, but uhhhh... I thought it might be something you'd want to see."

My stomach lurched into my throat, and I got off the phone with him as quickly as I could. What was Les up to now? My hackles rose at the same time I felt a stab of disappointment, recalling his social media frenzy when he'd been in Vegas. Had he fallen off the wagon already?

I tabbed over to Les's Facebook fan page on my phone and opened the video feed. The same fluttery surge that'd raced through me last night while I'd been looking at our old photos was exponentially multiplied by seeing him live. He looked, as Leigh had said, healthy and well rested. And sober. Goddammit, he looked *great*. He wore a plain white T-shirt, and his hair fell over his forehead in shower-damp tousles that he raked a hand through as he frowned at the screen. "Bear with me here, I'm not used to doing this. At all. Which is kind of surprising given the last tear I went on in Vegas. I don't remember shit about that, though."

Comments started pouring in, mostly exuberant greetings and hearts, a few bits of advice to tilt his laptop.

"Okay, how's that?" he asked, adjusting the screen. "Good? *Great*. So hello." He rubbed his palms together briskly, then ran them down his stubbled cheeks, seeming unsure what to say next. "I've got some things I need to get off my chest, probably against the advice of a publicist, but I'm done with publicists for a while. So you're getting just me. Unfiltered me. Except sober this time." Les panned his laptop around so we could see he was alone. I recognized the close-up black-and-white photographs of guitars on his living room wall. He'd picked those up on one of our stops in New Orleans because he'd thought the intricacy of detail was the coolest thing ever: *"Isn't it crazy that some human just came up with the wild idea of combining wood and strings to make some cool sounds, never having a clue it would become the obsession of a million jackasses like you and me, and that people would pay those jackasses for the pleasure of the sounds made with said wood and strings?"* I think he'd been stoned at the time. I might've been, too.

He pinched the bridge of his nose before continuing, "For viewers out there who aren't up-to-date, I'm fresh out of rehab after a colossal meltdown in Vegas, which I dearly wish I hadn't vomited out in painful detail on my Facebook page. Don't be like Les Graves, people. Just don't."

His self-conscious chuckle rang through the speaker, then he sighed. "But I'm leaving all of that up, because it's reality, and I've got an idea that Porter & Graves's fans have probably been feeling like they haven't gotten enough of that lately. I'm sorry for that, and the purpose of this video today is twofold: to clear the air about rumors and own up to my mistakes and take responsibility for them. Okay, technically, that's three things." He glanced down and chuckled at the comment feed where someone had typed "deny, deny, deny!" then responded, "We're way past plausible deniability now. No, fuck it, I'm gonna tell you my side straight.

"First thing I'll say is that I won't speak for Po—for Evan. I can't. I can only speak for myself, which is fine because really, all of this is my fault. Every single bit."

My next inhale got stuck in my chest. For a fleeting moment, I felt a prickle of fear that he might admit to cooking up the whole relationship thing with our publicist. I'd believed him when he said he hadn't in the parking lot. It didn't make sense. So I tamped down the insecurity and tried to relax my hand, which was gripping my phone so tightly my joints ached. Fuck, I missed him, and just seeing him onscreen brought the hollow ache of his absence from my life starkly to the fore.

"It's really complex and convoluted, so be patient," he continued, and started with the story of how he'd told Ella she could sell the tell-all of her night with us. "It would've been different if Ella had just decided to tell the story on her own, and she was definitely within her rights to. After all, she was a part of that night, but she was nice enough to give me a heads-up about it, and I should've told Evan about it, but I didn't. I invaded Evan's privacy thoughtlessly, without consulting him, and it was so fucking wrong it makes me sick to think about. And when I had an opportunity to come clean, I betrayed him again.

"Musician sexcapades aren't that big of a deal, I know, and if it had come out right after it happened, it probably would have been less of a deal, but it came out months later when Evan and I were really struggling in our friendship—and that's the other part that's my fault." Les's gaze had been focused off to one side as he spoke, but now he looked directly into the camera, the sincerity in his eyes gutting me. "Purely, one hundred percent my fault. I was being irresponsible, excusing my own behavior and doing stupid addict shit because I was struggling to cope with my own feelings for Evan. Feelings I didn't think I'd ever get a chance to express to him. Not if I wanted to remain part of the band. Because I was in love with him, and I have been for a long time."

My eyes went wide. I could literally feel it happen.

"Rita!" I called frantically, digging through bottles of cleaning agents and the photographs still lying over the counter for my car keys.

She popped her head into the kitchen.

"I need you to drive me to Les's."

I turned the screen of my phone toward her befuddled expression. "I'm watching him. I can't drive. Come on!"

She set down her broom and squinted at the live feed. "What's he up to?"

"He's... he's—" How could I explain to her that he was taking my carefully constructed yet shoddy wall of defense and dismantling it word by word? "Holy hell, woman, you're killing me, let's go." I exchanged the dustpan in her hands for my car keys and all but dragged her by the sleeve of her shirt out to my car, keeping my phone in my palm. Les lived in the Sylvan Park neighborhood which, in theory, was not that far from 12 South, where I lived. In theory.

Les rambled on as we got in the car, and I stared at the screen, transfixed and hardly breathing while my heart battered my chest.

"I didn't think Evan was open to it, so I buried it in other ways. Ways that affected our friendship and our music. And when the idea came about to capitalize on Ella's story by pretending to be in a relationship—a relationship I'd have pretty much given my left nut to have a shot at—I jumped on it, and I pressured Evan into it. At the very least, I thought maybe pretending would help get him out of my system and I could move on. It was a selfish choice and I

regret every second of it, because Evan never wanted to fool
anyone." He grimaced in apparent discomfort. "That's not who he
is, but he's also a loyal friend. Some of the stuff that happened
after that is personal and I'm not going to share it, but I do feel I
should own up to all those photos of us that have been in the
tabloids recently. Those were all prearranged, except our scuffle in
the parking lot. That was real and I deserved it, and I'm gonna try
to do better. I've been clean for thirty-two days now, and I've
learned enough to know I shouldn't make promises, but I'm trying
to do the right thing one day at a time, and this is how I'm starting
it."

We hit every light, and once we got on 440, traffic backed up
quickly and all I could do was regret not taking side streets. I struggled to stay still in the passenger seat, my entire body limned with
tension while Les kept talking.

"Turn it up, I can't hear him," Rita barked, glancing over her
shoulder before cutting into another lane.

"Shh!" I snapped back but clicked to turn the volume up.

Fucking hell. I glanced around at the standstill traffic, looking
for an alternative route. "Can we get off and take back roads? We'll
be here all fucking day."

Rita shrugged. "I can try." She cut down an access road and got
us off 440. We sped through side streets.

"*Good goddamn,*" Rita muttered, and I shushed her, catching
her smile as Les continued.

"So my last is my apology to you, the fans, the most important
part of our music. I'm so sorry for manipulating y'all, and I hope
you'll let me bear the blame and continue to support Evan in whatever he does, because he's the real deal, and without him, I'd still be
playing for loose change." He let out a long breath and collapsed
back in the chair, rubbing his fingers over his forehead as if drained.
"I'll be happy to answer any questions I can, so let 'em roll."

He went quiet for a handful of seconds, eyeing the bottom of the
screen, then straightened in the chair. "I don't know what's next for
me. Right now I'm focusing on my sobriety, and music's going to
take a back seat. There's a possibility we'll finish out the album, but

I'm not counting on it. And I'm okay with that. Considering what a shitty partner I've been, it's completely understandable."

Les had never been much for apologies, much less sincere ones, but the earnestness in his expression flowed off the screen and rolled through me, along with the overwhelming need to be there with him.

Onscreen, Les nodded and his eyes flitted down again before his brows pulled together in a frown. "Yeah, of course I still fucking love him. I wish I could've figured out a way to turn that off, because I'd have done it long ago, but I can't. Pretty much every song I've written over the last year has been about the bastard. I love him like fucking air, but I don't... that's just something I'll have to deal with. I have no expectations of Evan, and honestly, he's probably better off without me."

As soon as Rita pulled into his drive, I shot out of the car, phone still in my hand as I raced for the door. His voice pitched through my speakers as he chuckled at some other comment I'd missed, but the words hardly registered.

I banged on the door, and when he ignored it, started pounding.

Les glanced away from the camera. "Just a second, folks. Keep the questions coming, and I'll scroll back to get to them."

Even though I'd spent the past twenty minutes staring at his face, I wasn't prepared for how my pulse would kick into overdrive when he opened the door and I stood in front of him in person. He sucked in a deep breath, then let it out slowly, so slowly.

Myriad emotions passed over his face, and I could read every one of them: shock, elation, caution, hope, and the very last one, the one that did me in. Regret mingled with sadness.

The set of his mouth softened, his lips parting, and every thought in my head evaporated.

I launched at him and crashed my mouth against his. It wasn't the most romantic kiss in the books. It edged on violent and was messy because he was taken by surprise. He stumbled backward, and I had to flail at his shirt to keep him upright. But goddammit, there was an entire month's worth of pent-up emotion in it, and after a second, Les matched my fervor, his hands landing on my biceps and squeezing forcefully as he crushed me against him. I sank my fingers into the damp strands of his hair, inhaled the scent of his shampoo, and drowned myself in the taste of him. A quiet moan slipped from his lips, and he finally broke the kiss with a sudden tilt of his head.

"What are you doing?" Beneath my grip, a tremor ran through him, and his breath came harsh and hot against my cheek.

I swallowed a huge gulp of air and tried to collect myself. "I don't know." I released him to tug at the ends of my hair. "I didn't mean to do that. I'm kinda flying blind here. I guess I *shouldn't* have done that. You just opened the door and... shit, you occupy my every other thought. Do you know how annoying that is?"

"Um yeah. Trust me." Les canted his head to find my eyes and laughed softly. "So you think you could do it again? Because Jesus Christ, I missed this and didn't think I'd ever have it again."

I answered him with another scorching kiss, and he slid his hands around to my back, under my T-shirt, and behind my waistband to clutch a handful of my ass. I groaned at the friction of his hips against mine, and was ready to get him naked right there when he pulled away again, his eyes going wide in alarm. "Shit, the video!" He dropped his voice. "Do you think they can hear?"

I licked my lips, thinking fast, then brushed past him, heading for the laptop and dropping into his chair once I got there.

"What are you doing?" he hissed, shutting the front door and stalking after me.

I adjusted the camera and started speaking. "First of all, this isn't exactly how I'd planned on going about this, but here we are." A barrage of WTF's, heart signs, and boggle-eyes rolled up the feed. "And since Les has given you his account, I guess it's time for me to give you mine. Side note: we really suck at PR, and Les is right —this would definitely be against a publicist's advice, but I'm also tired of the facade. Everything Les said was true; he just ended the story early." I felt Les hovering anxiously behind me, but soldiered on, determined to set the record straight because I couldn't stand the idea of Les shouldering whatever fallout was to come on his own. "And I'm also done with image maintenance. I've always kept my private life private, not because I'm ashamed of it, but because it was mine and I thought, who cared? But I want to be transparent now for a few reasons." I glimpsed some of the comments and nodded. "I've never been open with my sexuality or sex life because again, I figured it was my own business, but I guess being in the public eye changes things, and I don't want anyone to feel ashamed about their sexuality or think *I'm* ashamed.

"The idea that I could be hurting someone by not being forth-coming doesn't sit well with me. I've been with both women and men, so yeah, I'd consider myself bi. But nothing prepared me for what would happen when Les and I embarked on the whole fake relationship thing and I discovered the feelings stirred up were very real for me.

"So when he said it was complex, he wasn't lying. It was and it still is, and I don't know what that means for our music, or even for us, but that's the whole story.

"I hope you'll understand that I'm gonna cut this short because I haven't seen or talked to Les in a fucking month, and I need to do that now." I reached for the mouse to shut down the feed, then paused and looked directly into the camera. "Last thing: Adam Slade, you can go fuck yourself."

I clicked to end the feed and swiveled around in the chair to face Les. He stood with one arm folded across his chest, a stricken expression on his face. He pressed the knuckles of one hand to the mouth I'd missed so much it almost hurt to look at, then dropped his hand and shook his head. "I can't believe you just told Adam Slade to go fuck himself. "

"I know. It was probably too much. But seriously, fuck that guy."

Les reached out to snap the top of his laptop closed. "Are you mad about the video? I wasn't sure what to do, but I was tired of going through other people. I figured direct was best."

"Nah, you're right. For the best. I'm tired of it, too."

He reached out, as if to touch me, then drew back, hesitant. "I missed you. So much."

The past five minutes had been pure adrenaline and reaction on my part, and now the reality of being in front of him slammed full force into me. I grabbed at the bottom of his T-shirt and pulled until he sank down on his knees in front of me, and then I leaned, pressing my forehead to his, closing my eyes, inhaling him. "Same."

"I'm so sorry, Ev."

I couldn't stand the sound of his voice cracking, or how his shoulders shook and curled inward. I slid from the chair onto the floor and put my arms around him. "I know. I'm sorry, too. I'm sorry for how I handled everything."

How often do you two disagree on something, whether music-related or not?

Evan: Constantly.

Les: Yeah, but how often do we agree, Porter?

Evan: Also constantly.

Les: Damn straight.

CHAPTER 40

A fter Evan sent Rita home, we sat at the kitchen table I'd probably only ever sat at twice, drinking coffee and talking about rehab, about sobriety, Evan's experience with Amanda Faulks, his dealings with the label. We talked for hours, until afternoon became night. We ate leftovers from my fridge for dinner, and I kept expecting Evan to get up at some point and leave, but he didn't. I hoped against hope that meant something, but after everything that had happened, I couldn't bank on it, and we still hadn't discussed what to do about our current album or the band in general. In spite of that explosive kiss at my front door, our future remained very much in limbo.

"Why'd you come here in the first place?" I finally asked once we'd migrated from the kitchen to sprawl on the sectional in the living room.

"I wasn't really thinking about it. It was gut reaction." Evan shifted against the cushions, his foot knocking against mine where they met at the vertex of the sofa's L shape and then settling there. A wiggle of my bare toes against his ankle drew a faint smile from him. "Leigh came over last night and had all these pictures of us, and it made me realize how much I missed you, and then when I saw you on the screen, I just—" He stopped and drew in a breath. "I just did it."

I folded my arms behind my head, propping myself up for a better view. I'd noticed in the kitchen that he was thinner. Not by much, but when you spent as much time staring at him as I had, even a few pounds registered. "I think you should still take that deal. It's huge. It's everything you always wanted. Financial security, all that." It hurt to say it, but I didn't want to be a liability for him anymore.

Evan sawed his teeth against his lower lip in consideration, so I kept going, just in case he was trying to be nice about it, which was totally something he'd do. "Really, you should go for it. I'm not just saying it and I'll secretly resent you later. I want you to do what you need to do."

"But maybe it's not what I want to do." His glance became a longer gaze, and damn, I'd missed having him look at me with that perfectly Evan expression—sincere, slightly troubled. "I don't want to make music without you, Les. I've tried and I can't make it feel right. We were meant to do it together, and the only way I wouldn't want to is if you thought it wasn't right for you anymore or if you thought it would threaten your sobriety."

"I want to, but..." I shook my head and sat up on the couch, pulling my knees in and resting my chin on my forearms. "I don't think I can go on tour for a while. I can handle the studio and playing shows here, but I don't want to mess up on the road, and I don't trust myself yet."

"Even with me there?"

"I don't want you to be my babysitter. It's not your job. I wouldn't be able to stand it. Just thinking about our last tour makes me want to crawl in a hole. How I treated you. The dumb shit I did. I need time. I need to take things slowly."

"Yeah, I get that." Evan nodded and drew in a breath. "Slow is good. We need time to think."

Admittedly, right then I wasn't thinking about much aside from how damn grateful I was just to have Evan in the same room as me again, and that we'd been able to talk, *really* talk like we used to.

Like friends. And in spite of that kiss he'd given me, if he just wanted to be friends, I promised myself I'd respect that no matter how much it hurt. Because I owed him that, and because I didn't want to hurt him again.

Silence stretched and finally, Evan pushed himself upright and glanced at the door. "I guess I should probably go home."

I clenched my lower lip between my teeth, then nodded, rising after him. "Sure. I can drop you off. Let me grab my keys."

I retrieved them from the kitchen, and when I returned, Evan was standing in front of the big black-and-white photographs on the wall. "I remember you buying these. That was a great show."

"Right after we found out we'd hit platinum for the second time." I smiled.

He studied the pictures a moment longer, then turned toward me, an odd expression on his face. "I mean, I should go home, yeah? That makes the most sense. There's a lot to think about and…"

"Yeah," I jumped in quickly. "I can touch base tomorrow."

I followed him to the door, and he'd pulled it open halfway when he paused, shut it again, and turned around, bumping into my chest.

"I don't want to leave," he said softly.

"You want to stay with me?" I held my breath. Because I didn't want him to leave. Not at all. Not ever.

"I mean, if that's okay?" His gaze searched mine, hesitant, as he feathered a light touch across my cheek, then my jaw that kindled a warm spark of hope and a rush of desire.

But God, the awkward politeness was going to kill me. "I want you to stay. Christ, Porter, I'm about to climb the walls wanting to touch you again." Sitting across the table and then across the couch from him all those hours made me physically ache, but I didn't want to push my precarious position when we still had so much ground to cover. I didn't know if it was the bald confession or because I'd called him Porter, but the tension that'd been hanging over us since that kiss broke and he grinned.

He was still grinning when I hauled him in by the waistband for a kiss, and we made our way back to my bedroom at the speed of slugs on a sidewalk in August, pausing to peel off our shirts, tripping over the top step of the stairs.

BY THE TIME WE GOT INTO THE BEDROOM, WE WERE BOTH PANTING and hard, grinding against each other. I yanked his pants the rest of the way off and backed up for a second, just to stare, just to feast my eyes on the delicious man in front of me that I could never seem to get enough of.

"You're looking at me like a cannibal right now." Evan arched a brow at me with an amused tug at one corner of his mouth, but I could tell he enjoyed every second of it.

I snickered. "Sorry, rehab only served vegetarian fare, so I've worked up a huge appetite for some—"

He smothered the rest with a kiss, then broke away in laughter. I slid his boxers down his hips and attacked his neck, kissing a line up his throat.

"Did I tell you I've started running again?" I licked his earlobe, then bit down.

He grunted and slid his hand over my ass, giving it a squeeze. "Mmm, that's sexy. Please do tell me all about your mile pace while you're getting me hard." His voice was laden with sarcasm, but when I reached down and squeezed his shaft in my fist, his breath hitched.

"Play nice, or I will. In monotonous detail."

He looped an arm around my waist, sliding his hand behind the waistband of my boxers and running his finger down the seam of my ass. "Is this considered playing nice?" he asked, feathering a light caress over my hole that made my legs go wobbly.

"I think that's considered playing dirty. Fortunately for you, I like that just as much. Now get inside me and light me the fuck up."

"Shit," he groaned, "I could listen to you talk like that all day." He pulled his hand free, wet his fingers in his mouth, and returned, roughly shoving my boxers down before he teased my hole and pushed the tip of one finger inside until I moaned.

"Will you settle for all night?"

I woke around three in the morning. The habitual waking
had come back in rehab. Sometimes I just lay in the bed; other times
I got up and wrote. The first night home after I'd gotten out of
rehab, I'd gone downstairs and played, but it only ended up making
me sad. Tonight I lay there watching the rise and fall of Evan's back
as he slept, then rolled over and stared out the window, thinking
about everything that had happened over the past couple of months.
My parents had flown in from Virginia to be with me for the first
week post-rehab, at their insistence, and though they meant well and
I understood their concern, we'd drifted apart after Evan and I had
hit it big with the first album, and I'd been glad when they left
again. I thought now maybe I should work on that, call them more,
something.

Evan draped his arm around my shoulder, spreading his fingers
over my chest, his body so warm against my back I couldn't help
the contented sigh that escaped me. I covered his hand with mine,
tracing the shape of his fingers and knuckles, the calluses from his
guitar strings.

"What're you thinking about?" he murmured into my neck.

I chuckled sleepily. "I don't even know where to start. Everything. The tour, the cabin, rehab, my parents. Every single moment
that's led to this one and how it feels so precarious and sweet at the
same time. How I want you to see that I'm taking sobriety seriously.
That I want it. That I want us—more than the music, even."

"I see it." Evan pressed his lips to my shoulder. "You wouldn't
have stuck it out in rehab otherwise, wouldn't have called Leigh or
reached out to those other people you were telling me about earlier.
Wouldn't have called your sponsor to check in tonight." Another
soft brush of his lips sent a shiver of pleasure running through me.
"I see it."

"I can't make any promises, though, you know that."

"I know." He got quiet after that, and I thought he was faltering, hesitating again, but after a moment, his lips resumed their soft trek along my shoulder and he rolled me onto my back, propping up on one arm to look down at me. "You keep acting like I never did anything wrong, but I did. I shut you out after Ella, and you didn't deserve it. At all. And I'm really sorry about that, because it changed us. So I don't want you thinking it was all your fault. I want to be better, too."

I closed my eyes when they began to blur and burn, and Evan cupped my chin, sweeping his thumb gently over my cheek until I opened them and focused on him again.

"There was that night at the cabin where you said I was wrong. I was. I want you and I need you, and they're the same thing for me, too. Maybe that's what's been wrong with the past and with my other relationships. I kept thinking about what I needed, what made logical sense, what I *should* want, what I *should* need. And I think you're the only person I've ever known who's both the one I want and the one I need." He dragged in a breath, bending to press a kiss to my chest where my heart beat wildly beneath, and when he spoke next, it was with his lips brushing against my bare skin. "I love you, Les, and I want you with or without the music."

Three words that hammered into my bones. My heart felt like it swelled and ballooned into the space around us, then went soaring up toward the ceiling, because I knew he meant it, that he'd never said those words in any other relationship. They were precious and small, and they were mine to keep.

Evan lifted his head, his lips hovering in front of mine as he said it again, then leaned a fraction of an inch forward to give me a kiss that was like our music. Thundering intensity and fragile complexity all at once. It was him and it was me in unison. A perfect harmony of us both.

CHAPTER 41

NINE MONTHS LATER

I was anxious like I hadn't been since our first show together when I'd been worried that somehow, despite our months of practicing together, Les and I would be out of sync or fall completely flat in front of a large audience.

I wiped sweat from my brow and tried to unstick my T-shirt from my back, then drained the rest of the bottled water Les had handed me earlier, my nerves popping and hissing inside me like live wires sparking.

"You all right there, sweetheart?" Les shot me a grin as he squeezed my shoulder, knowing the endearment would raise my hackles. I was certain he knew that I secretly liked his random pet names, but fuck if I was going to tell him. It was just a thing like many others between us. His other favorites: *darlin'*, *sweetie*, one time *sugar nuts*, which I guess was his take on *sugar tits*. That one had earned him a hard, impromptu fuck in the back of the tour bus. You know, as punishment.

What could I say? We had a weird relationship, but it worked for us. A lot of stupid moments of antagonism blended with some of the most intimate experiences I'd ever had with another human being. Most of the time, it was the simple things that got me, like when we'd be on the bus or just sitting around writing and Les would randomly plop down next to me, lie his head in my lap, and give me a cheesy grin until I rolled my eyes and pulled him up for a kiss.

"I'm fine," I said, tossing my empty water bottle at him, then picking up my guitar. When my hands started shaking, I clenched them into fists. Five minutes until showtime.

Les bent over to sweep up the empty water bottle, crackling the plastic a couple of times in my ear to both annoy and distract me, before he tossed it in a nearby receptacle. "Still want to go out for dinner after? I got us a reservation at Fusion."

I nodded absently. I couldn't even think about dinner right now, but Fusion had just opened and I'd mentioned wanting to go, so it was nice of him to remember. He did a lot of thoughtful stuff like that, and it was just one more thing that showed me I'd sold him too short in the past.

"Good." Les fiddled with the ends of his hair; it'd grown longer and unruly and thinking about how much he fucking loved when I pulled on it made me smile. He fiddled with his earpiece next. I guessed he was nervous, too. We were fresh off the tour for our fourth album, *Rise*—which we'd delayed for several months until Les felt confident enough in his sobriety—and playing our final show before a two-week break. We hadn't played the Ryman in ages, and it always felt like the shows mattered a little more when we were on home turf.

I bumped his shoulder with mine and gave him a smile that made him stop fiddling and grin back.

Les held true to his promise to put honest effort into staying sober. The first three months after he got out of rehab, he went to a meeting every day without fail. Now he went weekly. He'd worked the steps and made his amends, and I'd grown used to the random times he'd disappear to make a call to his sponsor, an old guy named Milt, who ended up becoming a friend to us both and frequently turned up at our house on the weekends. Yeah, *our* house. We'd moved in together two months ago after buying a spread outside of Belle Meade that needed a little TLC but had an amazing layout and an old barn we were in the process of converting into a home studio. Royalties off the fourth album helped a shit ton with that. Three songs off that album went to number one, including "Break Me," the song Les had busted out with at Grim's Gatlinburg, and we were currently working on a side project with Amanda Faulks that I thought was going to light up the charts. She and Les tangling their words together? It was a special kind of voodoo.

So with all of that going for us, there was nothing for me to be nervous about. Except the fact that I planned for this show to be the one where I asked Les to spend the rest of his life with me. Les liked being center stage; he liked a dog-and-pony show. I didn't and naturally would have planned something quieter and more private, but the idea of him being in one of his favorite places in the world when I proposed was too much to pass up. I loved the fucker, and there was no one else on earth who could get me so out of my element and make me enjoy it at the same time.

It had taken me forever to come up with the idea, and it was so fucking cheeseball that I knew he'd love it as much as he'd tease me eternally about it if I could manage to pull it off. Pulling it off was the tricky part, but I'd enlisted Mars's help.

Les dragged in a deep breath and slung the strap of his guitar around his neck as the lights dimmed. "I can't wait to sleep in our bed again," he muttered, and then his smile lit up as Mars gave us the go-ahead. Mars threw a wink my way in passing, which I knew meant he'd done his part. Now Les just had to cooperate with my attempt at psychological manipulation.

We walked out to an ovation of thundering applause, and I made our usual introductions while Les prowled around the edge of the stage as he was prone to. When we finally set up on the pair of stools in front of our mics and I played the opening notes of "Twist Me Up," our latest hit, Les ducked his head and caught my eye, speaking quietly to avoid being picked up by the mic. "Check out that chick's shirt on the front row. I should've worn mine."

I rolled my eyes but was ecstatic inside. One thing checked off the list. I glanced at the blonde wearing the "I will end you" T-shirt in the front row and gave her a wink. She beamed back. I didn't even know her name, but I imagined I would later, since Mars had given her and her boyfriend backstage passes for her role in my scheme.

We played through our first set with no difficulty, took a quick break, then returned for our second. The crowd was full of energy, standing up, singing along, and it went a long way toward easing my anxiety. Until we got to the portion where Les did his ask-the-audience bit.

He hopped off his stool, pacing back and forth, and the tempo of my pulse sped up as he searched the audience. Then he pointed at the blonde, grinning. "I kinda can't not pick you, because I have that same T-shirt."

The girl bounced and clapped her hands.

Les started his usual spiel. "So what do you want to hear? Anything in the world. Doesn't have to be ours. We may fuck it up royally, but we'll give it our best shot. And, by the way, speaking of fuckups, there's now a YouTube channel dedicated to all of our worst attempts at covers—thank you wayne17333. So you all can check those out if you want to hear Evan and me shattering our vocal chords with some Mariah Carey or me beatboxing a Barry White song. To whoever had the foresight to take a video of that night before Evan found me and tried to teach me right, thanks a lot. Really. I appreciate it."

The laughter died down, and Les stopped at the edge of the stage again, inclining his chin to the girl. "So what's it gonna be?"

I kept my eyes on the audience, afraid that if I looked down I'd see a puddle of sweat under me.

She licked her lips, shot me a quick glance, then cupped her hands around her mouth and called out, "Marry You?"

Les cackled. "Is that your boyfriend next to you?"

She nodded.

"Then I'm afraid I'll have to decline. He looks like he might be able to beat up my boyfriend, and I kinda need him, soooo... sorry."

She spoke again, and he leaned closer to hear. "Oh, right, of course! I knew that. Did I mention I have an ego?" He chuckled. "She meant the song. My bad. Okay. We can do that."

He wandered back in my direction, setting his mic back into the stand and glancing over at me. "Bruno Mars, yeah?"

I nodded, hoping I wasn't white as a sheet, then willed my hands not to tremble on my strings so I could start the damn song I'd been practicing for days.

"I've got this," I said into the mic, and started playing, afraid I was going to lose my nerve. Fortunately, Les jumped in a second later, adding in percussion by slapping the pick guard of his guitar as he played. We alternated verses back and forth, then the audience joined in and it ended up going over much better than I expected. I was still panicking inside, but when Les turned his back to me and sidled toward the end of the stage during the bridge, I hopped from my stool, loosened the strap of my guitar and let it hang at my side, then got down on one knee. I dug the ring box out of my back pocket, drenching it with my sweaty palms as I opened it, exposing the simple titanium band.

When I set it on top of my thigh, the roar of the audience climbed to fever pitch. Les waved a hand encouragingly and glanced back at me over his shoulder, like he wanted to check and make sure I was hearing what was happening.

Then he froze, amusement melting from his expression as he abruptly stopped playing.

The din from the audience died down, and everything went quiet. I swear I felt every single eyeball in the auditorium glued to me, but none so penetrating as the mind-blown stare Les fixed on me. I'd never felt so vulnerable in my life.

He took a single step in my direction before stopping short. "What are you doing right now, Porter?" he whispered.

"Hoping like hell you'll say yes?" It came out as a question. Fucking nerves.

"Holy shit, are you sure?" He ducked his head under the strap of his guitar and carried it at his side as he came slowly toward me, his features twisted with disbelief.

I nodded. "Sure enough to risk looking like a colossal idiot in front of a standing-room-only crowd, yeah."

Les set his guitar absently on his stool and reached down, picking up the box and taking my hand to pull me upright. Anticipation knotted every muscle in my body, and I was sure he could feel it as he laid his hands on my shoulders, his gaze fastening to mine. "Yes. Fuck yes. A hundred million times over and then some."

His mouth crushed mine, and I didn't care about the audience exploding in crashing applause and whoops, or the stage lights beating down on us, or the sweat running down my temples. I sank against him, kissing him back, dizzy with relief and joy.

When we finally detached, the roar of the audience hurtled toward the stage and lit me up from within. I took the box from Les and slid the ring on his finger, brushing my thumb over his knuckles when they trembled slightly.

I had no idea what we could possibly encore with that would top what had just happened, but I also had an idea it didn't matter much.

I WAS RIGHT. WHEN WE FINISHED THE SHOW AND TWO ADDITIONAL encores and finally escaped backstage with the audience still in frenzied applause, we were swarmed by back claps and congratulations. Byron pushed through the well-wishers and grinned, slinging his arms around us both. Mars rushed up, letting us know there was a group of reporters waiting for interviews. Les grabbed my hand and tugged me toward the green room. "Tell them they can all wait. I need, like, twenty minutes."

"Make it forty-five," I corrected, then slammed the door behind us.

Les pushed me into it, giving me another slow kiss that scorched me top to toe and had me hard in an instant. "I really underestimated you, Porter."

"Yeah? How's that?" I reached for his left hand, bringing it up to my lips, then kissing the tip of his ring finger before sucking on it and making him groan.

"You can still surprise the hell out of me."

"Just wait until we get home." Byron had helped me make sure the studio we were renovating was completed during the final leg of our tour, and I knew Les was going to be bowled over by the transformation I'd been secretly working on for weeks. I grinned and attacked his throat in nipping kisses, gratified when he went stockstill, then melted against the heat of my mouth, whispering, "I can't wait to marry you."

I felt exactly the same.

—The End—

Wondering why Dan Grim abruptly walked away from a lucrative music career to open a record store? And what's going on between him and motor-mouthed employee, Owen? Find out in Resonance.

THANK YOU & BONUS SCENE

There's a whole wide world of books out there. Thank you so much for choosing this one!

Readers are the heartbeat behind every book, and I'd be honored if you'd take a moment to leave a review of *Dedicated* on Amazon and Goodreads.

If you'd like a bit more Les & Evan, check out a free short & spicy Christmas-themed bonus scene here:
readerlinks.com/l/2314785/holidaybonus

ALSO AVAILABLE: WANT ME

Two roommates. One calculus exam. A whole lot of
extracurricular activity.

"Ever since my roommate Eric busted me taking care of some *personal business*, I can't get him off my mind. I've always identified as straight, but the way we veer off topic when we're studying has me rethinking everything."

smarturl.it/GetWantMe

"One of the best *dirty heroes I've ever read"* —**Goodreads review**

"Want Me has made me drool and dried up my mouth at the same time. My heart beat's been at high speed all through the book and I can't thank Neve Wilder enough for the steaming, touching and emotional experience she's offered me." —**Goodreads review**

"Wilder had my brows shooting up multiple times because hot DAMN, ya'll. The dynamic sizzles." —**Goodreads review**

NEED MORE NEVE?

Well, that's just lovely to hear! And you should definitely sign up for my newsletter at:

www.nevewilder.com/subscribe

As a thank you for subscribing, you'll receive a link to Ru and Quinn's story, Light Touch, a steamy novella-length prequel to the Rhythm of Love World, as well as other bonus scenes and shorts.

Please feel free to come hang out in my FB reader group, Wilder's Wild Ones.

MORE BY NEVE WILDER

Extracurricular Activities Series

High-heat new adult/college romance. Also available as audiobooks.

See the series here: readerlinks.com/l/2314784/easeries

Wages of Sin Series

High-heat contemporary romantic suspense co-written with Onley James.
Also available as audiobooks.

See the series here: readerlinks.com/l/2314788/wosseries

Rhythm of Love Series

Contemporary Romance set in the music industry. Also available as
audiobooks.

See the series here: readerlinks.com/l/2314786/rolseries

Bend (Novella), Rhythm 1.5

Nook Island Series

Contemporary romance

Sightlines (Novella), Nook 1.5

Ace's Wild Series

(multi author series)

Reunion (Novella)

ABOUT NEVE WILDER

Neve Wilder lives in the southern US, where the summers are hot and the winters are...sometimes cold.

She reads promiscuously, across multiple genres, but her favorite stories always contain an element of romance. Incidentally, this is also what she likes to write. Slow-burners with delicious tension? Yes. Whiplash-inducing page-turners, also yes. Down and dirty scorchers? Yes. And every flavor in between.

She believes David Bowie was the sexiest musician to ever live, and she's always game to nerd out on anything from music to writing.

And finally, she believes that love conquers all. Except the heat index in July. Nothing can conquer that bastard.

Join her for daily shenanigans in her FB group:
Wilder's Wild Ones

Website:
www.nevewilder.com

[f] facebook.com/nevewilderwrites

[O] instagram.com/nevewilder

[BB] bookbub.com/authors/neve-wilder

[a] amazon.com/author/nevewilder

Made in the USA
Columbia, SC
08 October 2024

43225791R00209